THE
ETERNAL
WONDER

THE
ETERNAL
WONDER

THE
ETERNAL
WONDER

a novel

PEARL S. BUCK

OPEN ROAD
INTEGRATED MEDIA
NEW YORK

This is a work of fiction. Names, characters, places, events, and incidents either are the product of the author's imagination or are used fictitiously. Any resemblance to actual persons, living or dead, businesses, companies, events, or locales is entirely coincidental.

Cover design by Jason Gabbert

978-1-4804-3970-2

Published in 2013 by Open Road Integrated Media, Inc.
345 Hudson Street
New York, NY 10014

Printed in the U.S.A.

FOREWORD

This novel written by my mother, Pearl S. Buck, was one she had been creating in the years before her death at age eighty in Danby, Vermont, on March 6, 1973. Her personal affairs during the final years of her life were chaotic: She had become involved with individuals who targeted her fortune, estranging her from her family, friends, staff, and publishers. She was virtually bankrupt. Her seven adopted children, of whom I am one, did not have access to her property, and the handwritten manuscript and a typed copy of *The Eternal Wonder* were taken by someone and disappeared for forty years.

After her death my siblings and I mounted an effort to recover what was left of her literary and personal estate, and after a number of years, we were ultimately successful. I became Pearl Buck's literary executor. However, before the family gained control of her estate, many items, such as her personal papers, letters, manuscripts, and property, vanished. The family was never informed of the existence of her last literary creation. In the years following her death the family recovered other items that had been taken. In 2007 the original manuscript of Pearl Buck's most famous novel, *The Good Earth*, was recovered. It had been stolen and hidden by a former secretary at some point in the mid-1960s.

In December 2012 I learned that a woman in Texas had purchased the contents of a Fort Worth public storage unit. The rent on the unit had not been paid up to that point, and under the law the storage company was permitted to auction off the contents. When the purchaser examined the unit she found, among other items, what appeared to be an original handwritten Pearl Buck novel of some three-hundred-plus pages, along with a typewritten copy. The woman wished to sell the manuscripts, and after a negotiation, the family acquired them.

We do not know who took the manuscript from Danby, Vermont; when it was taken; or how it ended up in a storage unit in Fort Worth, Texas.

MY MOTHER WAS BORN to Absalom and Caroline Sydenstricker in Hillsboro, West Virginia, on June 26, 1892. Her father was a Presbyterian missionary who, with his wife, Caroline, had first gone to China in 1880. They were granted a home leave every ten years and it was on the first, somewhat extended, leave that Pearl was born. In November 1892, the family returned to China. Pearl would return to the United States with her parents in August 1901 for a home leave lasting until August 1902; again for her college years, from 1910 to 1914; and once more from 1925 to 1926 to take a Master of Arts degree at Cornell University. She did not move permanently to the United States until 1934. Thus, for most of the first forty years of her life her home was in China.

She knew the land, the people, and the culture intimately. In 1917 she married John Lossing Buck, an agricultural missionary whose work took him and Pearl to remote parts of China. It was there that Pearl developed a deep awareness of the life of Chinese farmers, their families and their culture. This knowledge was evident in *The Good Earth*. In 1921 the Bucks moved to Nanjing where both taught at the university.

Pearl knew from childhood that she wanted to be a writer. As a young girl some of her early writing appeared in the *Shanghai Mercury*, an English-language newspaper. As a student at Randolph-Macon Woman's College she wrote stories and plays, won writing prizes, and was elected to Phi Beta Kappa.

In the late 1920s she wrote her first novel, *East Wind: West Wind*. She sent the book to a literary agent in New York City, who sent it to a number of publishers who rejected it, primarily because it was about China. Eventually, in 1929, the president of the John Day Company, Richard J. Walsh, accepted it, publishing it in 1930.

Walsh told her to keep writing. Her next book, published in 1932, was *The Good Earth*. This story was an instant bestseller and made her famous and financially comfortable. It also led to a romance with Richard Walsh, whom she married in 1935 after her divorce from Lossing Buck, and Walsh's divorce from his first wife, Ruby. The literary partnership of editor-publisher Walsh and writer Buck was to be an enormously productive and successful one. Until his death in 1960 Walsh edited and published all of Buck's books.

My adoptive parents, Pearl Buck and Richard Walsh, made their home in Bucks County, Pennsylvania. They also maintained an apartment in New York City, where the John Day Company was located. At the time of their marriage, Pearl had two children: Carol, her severely handicapped birth-child, and an adopted daughter, Janice. Walsh had three adult children from his first marriage who did not live with him.

With a new marriage and home, the Walshes decided to adopt more children. In early 1936 they adopted two baby boys, and fourteen months later an infant boy (me) and a girl. In the early 1950s they would adopt two adolescent girls. The family life was centered on what Pearl named Green Hills Farm, an estate of nearly five hundred acres that comprised a comfortably expanded former farmhouse for the family and several working farms that raised livestock and crops and were run by a manager and workers. At Green Hills Farm Pearl Buck would live and work from 1935 until she moved to Vermont for the last three years of her life.

In November 1938 Buck was awarded the Nobel Prize in Literature. Considered by many to be the highest accolade that a writer can receive, it was awarded for her body of work, which, up to that point, consisted of seven novels and two biographies, plus essays and articles. Many critics felt that Buck, at age forty-six, was too young, and that her work was not "literary" enough—too "readable" and "accessible."

Despite the critics, the prize confirmed in Buck's mind that she was an excellent writer, that the envious could be ignored, and that she would just sit down and do what she loved to do— write stories! When her life ended, her body of work consisted of forty-three novels, twenty-eight nonfiction books, 242 short stories, thirty-seven children's books, eighteen scripts for film and television, several stage and musical plays, 580 articles and essays, and thousands of letters.

I WAS A YEAR AND A HALF OLD when my mother won the Nobel Prize. I don't remember anything about the excitement my parents must have felt. The only souvenir I have of the event is a tattered postcard she sent me from Sweden after the prize ceremony.

Our home life at Green Hills Farm during the late 1930s and the 1940s was serene, private, and protected. The Japanese war, which had begun with the invasion of far-off Manchuria in September 1931—which was the precursor to Japan's all-out war against the Chinese and, eventually, the United States—did not impinge on the quiet of rural Pennsylvania. When our country went to war with Japan and Germany in December 1941 those battles were far away. We did have to quit our holiday house on Island Beach, New Jersey, when ships were torpedoed just off the coast and fuel oil from sunken tankers blackened the beaches.

Far from the bombs and battlefields, Pearl Buck was a fierce advocate for military and humanitarian aid for the people and armies of China. Though her country was locked in a life-or-death struggle with the armies of the Japanese empire, she wrote often in her articles of the need to understand that the common people of Japan had been led into a disaster by criminal leaders. Today, in the twenty-first century, the government and people of China honor Pearl Buck for her China relief work during World War II. At the same time her books that are set in Japan speak to the humanity and culture of that nation's decent people.

During my childhood the house was filled with books, as my father brought home the works of his other authors, and new books were sent to Pearl in hopes that she might write a promotional note in order to help a fellow writer's work. Fascinating men and women came to visit: Africans, Chinese, Europeans, and Indians. There were writers, intellectuals, diplomats, and the occasional politician. The visitors I remember best were the writer Lin Yutang, along with his wife and three beautiful daughters, and the famous watercolorist Chen Chi, who during his visits painted several pictures of our home. Frequent guests were the Indian ambassador to the United States, as well as Indian prime minister Nehru's sister Vijaya Lakshmi Pandit and her daughters. Our neighbors included Oscar Hammerstein, James Michener, David Burpee, and the colony of artists and writers in nearby New Hope, Pennsylvania.

In a wing of our home, attached to the main house by a passageway with French doors, were three offices. There was one each for my parents and one for their secretaries. My mother's office held her writing desk, a fireplace, and comfortable easy chairs, and it featured a large picture window that looked out over rose gardens and lily ponds and farm fields where our Guernsey cows grazed. There was a far view of a three-arched stone bridge that carried the public road.

In the quiet of rural Bucks County Pearl Buck wrote and wrote. After her trip to Sweden to receive the Nobel Prize in 1938 she did not travel outside the United States until the late 1950s. She ran her home and managed her staff and children with a firm hand. She did her creative writing for four hours every morning. In the afternoon she would answer fan mail and take care of business matters. She always had time to help her children with homework and piano lessons, and to exhort us to do our best work. Idleness was anathema.

Her years in China, which exposed her to the poverty of most of that nation's people in the late nineteenth and early twentieth centuries, instilled in her a belief that only through hard work could a person prosper.

ON JANUARY 4, 2013, the handwritten manuscript and typed copy of *The Eternal Wonder* were delivered to me. I opened the package from Texas. I looked at my mother's familiar handwriting and compared her narrative to the typewritten manuscript. There was no doubt that they were genuine. When I did my first read-through of the novel, I knew that it was her work, but could see that the book was in need of editing. It was apparent that someone, I don't know who, had made some changes when the handwritten document was typed. Whoever typed the original had misread some of the handwritten words, and my mother, writing with her usual speed, had made mistakes in timelines and transitions in various places. I felt that, had she lived longer, she would have changed parts and extended or altered the ending.

When Open Road Integrated Media, Pearl Buck's ebook publisher and the publisher of this work, presented me with the initial copyedit, I reviewed it, and together we tried to smooth out the manuscript's rough parts where we could, while changing as little as possible of the original work. My guiding principle was to try to stay true to what I know about my mother's writing and my father's editing.

As I read the book I was also amused to note a familiar device that my mother used in many of her books and stories. If she had an interesting experience or visited a special place, or met a fascinating person, she would toss the event, place, or person into one of her narratives. She would also use mundane details from her private life. At one point in this novel, Rann, the young man whose life we follow, is at home with his mother:

> He put the dog in the garage and then came back to the kitchen and sat down at the table while his mother cooked something.
>
> "Neither of us will be hungry," she said, "but I'll bake some gingerbread and make that special sweet sauce you like."

My mother was famous for her homemade gingerbread and a special sweet sauce, and we children always loved and looked forward to it.

At another point in the book the teenage Rann travels by ship to England. On board he meets a beautiful, widowed, aristocratic older woman. When they arrive in England she invites him to stay at her castle outside London. In 1959 my mother and I were guests at a castle north of London. It is this castle that she describes in the book.

I believe that it is important to bring this work to the public, despite its flaws. When I took the manuscript to Jane Friedman, CEO of Open Road Integrated Media, she agreed that the book should be published. Jane's team has worked extremely hard to ready it for release, and I am grateful to them all. I think my mother would be pleased.

But it is impossible to know just how Pearl Buck, had she lived, might have revised what is, as it stands, an imperfect work. She was a perfectionist and the work is far from perfect. She left no instructions as to how the novel should appear in its final form. Still, for her readers past and present this work presents a unique opportunity to really know her and to understand her feelings and beliefs. I lived in her house for almost twenty-five years. When I married and moved on, I was still in touch with her constantly until she died. So I was always aware of her broad interests outside of her life as a writer. She was a deeply committed advocate of women's rights, civil rights for minority populations, the rights of the handicapped, the rights of mixed-race children and adults, and religious tolerance. Indeed, she always stood for the less fortunate of the world. As you read the novel you will see that, to use the title of her translation of a classic Chinese story, she believed that "all men are brothers."

In a way, reading this story was like being at home again with my mother in her study, both of us at ease in chairs by the fire, while she shared her thoughts, knowledge, and opinions. The young genius who is the central character in this book could be considered an autobiographical figure, and the many characters who interact with and educate him speak as my mother would have spoken. Years after her death Pearl Buck still has a worldwide readership and her works continue to be translated into many languages. I think that in these pages Pearl Buck fans will find the kind of storytelling that they have always loved from my mother, and I hope they will experience some of the wonder that I did in reading it. Unless another hidden manuscript comes to light, this will stand as her final work.

Edgar Walsh
July 2013

THE
ETERNAL
WONDER

Life is the wonder with which
we are all infused. . . .

PART I

He lay sleeping in still waters. This was not to say that his world was always motionless. There were times when he was aware of motion, even violent motion, in his universe. The warm fluid that enfolded him could rock him to and fro, could even toss him about, so that instinctively he spread his arms wide, his hands flailing, his legs spreading in the sprinting fashion of a frog. Not that he knew anything about frogs—it was too soon for that. It was too soon for him to know. Instinct was as yet his only tool. He was quiescent most of the time, active only when responding to unexpected movements in the outer universe.

These responses, necessary, his instinct told him, to protect himself, became also pleasurable. His instinct extended into positive action. He no longer waited for outer stimulus. Instead he felt it in himself. He began to move his arms and legs; he turned over, at first by accident but then with purpose and a sense of accomplishment. He could move from side to side in this warm private sea, and as he grew larger he became aware of its limitations. Now and again hand

and foot struck a soft wall, but a definite wall beyond which he could not move. Back and forth, up and down, around and around, but not beyond—this was his limitation.

Instinct again worked in him to provide an impetus for more violent action. He was daily growing bigger and stronger, and as this became true his private sea grew smaller. Soon he would be too big for his environment. He felt this without knowing that he did. Moreover, he was impinged upon by dim, faraway sounds. Silence had been his surrounding, but now the two small appendages, one on either side of his head, seemed to contain echoes. These appendages had a purpose he could not understand because he could not think, and he could not think because he did not know anything. He could feel, however. He could receive a sensation. Sometimes he wanted to open his mouth to make a sound, but he did not know what a sound was, or even that he wanted to make it. He could not know anything—not yet. He did not even know that he could not know. Instinct was all he had. He was at the mercy of instinct because he knew nothing.

Instinct, nevertheless, guided him to a final awareness that he was too big for whatever it was that contained him. He felt uncomfortable, and this discomfort impelled him suddenly to rebel. Whatever he was in was too small for him and he wanted instinctively to be free of it. His instinct manifested itself in an increasing impatience. He flung out his arms and legs with such violence that one day the walls broke, and the waters rushed away, deserting him, leaving him helpless. At this moment, or thereabouts, for he still could not understand, since he did not know, he felt forces impelling him headfirst down an impassably narrow passage. He could never have made any progress except that he was wet and slimy.

Inch by inch, contortions of some sort compelled him onward, downward, in darkness. Not that he knew anything about darkness, since he could know nothing. But he felt himself impelled by forces, pushing him onward. Or was he merely being rejected because he had grown too big? Impossible to know!

He continued his journey, forcing himself through the narrow passage, forcing its walls to widen. A new sort of fluid gushed out, carrying him on his way until suddenly, with such suddenness indeed that he seemed expelled, he emerged into infinite space. He was seized, although he did not know it, but he was seized by the head, though gently, lifted up to a great height—by what, he did not know since he could not—and then found himself dangling by his feet, his head down, all this happening so quickly that he did not know how to respond. Then at that instant, he felt on the soles of his feet something sharp, a new sensation. Suddenly he knew something. He knew pain. He flung out his arms. He did not know what to do with pain. He wanted to return to where he had always been in those safe, warm waters, but he did not know how to return. Yet he did not want to go on. He felt stifled, he felt helpless, he felt utterly alone, but he did not know what to do.

While he hesitated, fearful without knowing what fear was and only conscious by instinct that he was in danger without knowing what danger was, he felt again the sharp dart of pain on his feet. Something grasped him by the ankles, someone shocked him, he did not know what, he did not know who, but he now knew pain. Suddenly instinct came to his rescue. He could not return, neither could he stay as he was. Therefore he must go on. He must escape pain by going on. He did not know how, but he knew he must go on. He willed to go on, and with this will instinct led him on. He opened his mouth and made a noise, a cry of protest against pain, but this protest was positive. He felt his lungs suddenly clear of liquid he no longer needed and he drew in air. He did not know it was air, but he felt it take the place of water and it was not static. Something inside instinctively impelled and expelled it, and while this went on suddenly he was crying. He did not know he was crying, but he heard his own voice for the first time, though he did not know it was his voice or what a voice was, but by instinct he liked crying and hearing.

And now he was righted, his head lifted, and he was cradled in something warm and soft. He felt oil rubbed over his body, though he did not know oil, and then he was washed, though he could only accept whatever was happening, since he did not know what anything was, but there was not pain, and he was warm and comfortable, though very tired without knowing it, and his eyes closed and he went to sleep, without even knowing what sleep was. Instinct was still all he had, but as yet instinct was enough.

FROM SLEEP HE WAS AWAKENED. He did not know the difference, for knowing was not yet part of his being. He was no longer in his private sea, but he was warm and enfolded. He was aware, too, of movement, though not his own. Simply he was moving through air instead of liquid and he was breathing steadily, though not knowing he did. Instinct impelled him to breathe. Instinct impelled him too to move his legs and arms in the air as once he had done in the private sea. Then suddenly, as everything happened to him suddenly now, he felt himself laid down on a surface neither soft nor hard. He felt himself held close against another warmth, and his mouth put to yet another warmth. Still not knowing, instinct stirred. He opened his mouth, he felt some small, warm softness pushed gently into his mouth, a sweetish liquid touched his tongue, instinctive pleasure seized his whole body, and he felt a necessity entirely new and unexpected. He began to suck, he began to swallow and was wholly engrossed in this new instinct. This was something he had never experienced, this pleasure in his whole being. As strongly as he had felt pain, he now felt pleasure. This was his first knowing, pain and pleasure. He did not know what they were, but he knew the difference between them, and that he hated pain and that he loved pleasure. This knowing was something more than instinct, although instinct had its part. He knew instinctively the feeling of pleasure and he knew instinctively the feel of pain. When he felt pain, instinctively he opened his mouth and cried aloud and even with anger. He learned that when he did this, what caused him pain stopped and this became knowledge.

WHAT HE DID NOT KNOW was that after a time when he felt pleasure, his lips parted and his mouth widened. Sometimes a different sort of noise came from him; he drew in his breath with delight. At the sight of certain Creatures this could happen, especially if they made noises to him and touched his cheeks or chin. He learned that when he showed his pleasure first, they responded with such noises and touches. This also became knowledge. Whatever he could do or cause himself, by his own wish and effort, became knowledge and by instinct he used his knowledge. Thus instinct led him to the knowledge of persons. At first he was aware only of himself, his own pleasure, his own pain. Then he began to associate certain persons with his pleasure or his pain. First of all persons thus associated was his mother. He knew her first only instinctively and by pleasure. He fed at her breasts and this was his primary pleasure. Sucking, he gazed instinctively into her face until its features became part of the process of pleasure. Instinctively, as he learned to smile when he felt pleasure, he first smiled at her.

Then one day he was shocked, even frightened, to discover that this pleasurable, pleasure-giving other could also inflict pain. He had been feeling an instinctive need for closing his jaws on something, for they were sore and feverish. When he had suckled enough to satisfy his hunger this day, he instinctively closed his jaws upon what was in his mouth. To his surprise she uttered a cry not unlike his own when he felt pain and at the same moment he again felt pain. It was on his cheek, a part of himself of which he had not yet been conscious. Instantly, by instinct, he burst into loud weeping, and he felt on his face something wet, like water. They were his first tears, and they were the result of a new sort of pain. It was not from his cheek, which was still stinging, but from a wound inside him which he could not define. It spread through his breast, an inner hurt. He suddenly felt alone and lost. This soft warm Creature who tended him day and night, who suckled him at her breasts and upon whom he was utterly dependent, had inflicted pain upon him! He had trusted her wholly, and now he could not trust her because she had hurt him! He felt separated, a being attached nowhere, and therefore lost. True, as he continued heartbroken, weeping, she gathered him into her arms, she rocked him to and fro, but he could not stop weeping. She thrust her nipple into his open mouth, offering him food again, the warm, sweet food that he always eagerly accepted, but he turned his head away and refused it. He cried until he no longer felt the inner pain and then he fell asleep.

WHEN HE WOKE FROM SLEEP, he was in his crib, lying on his right side. He turned on his back and then on his left side. With a desire new to him, he felt impelled to his right side and, still impelled, to turn onto his stomach. Then because his face was pressed against the bed, he was impelled to lift his head. Everything looked new and different, as though he had never been here before. He seemed to be gazing from a height. Moreover, he could turn his head to one side and another. He was constantly being surprised like this. Now he heard a loud cry and felt himself swept up into the arms of the Creature, she who could inflict such pain that he had wept himself to sleep. But this was pleasure he was feeling, a new sort of pleasure, having nothing to do with food. If he had felt inner pain, he was now pervaded by inner pleasure. He belonged to her again. He felt himself enfolded and attached again. She was making sounds, he felt her lips on his cheeks, in his neck. She called and another Creature came and stared at him. He looked from one to the other, feeling attached to them both. This was instinct again. He did not know them nor why he felt a part of them. But it was pleasurable. He felt his mouth move, his lips waver by instinct, he made a new sound and he heard cries of joy and surprise from the two others.

* * *

AFTER THIS HE FELT HIMSELF CHANGING almost daily. What seemed impossible to do, he felt impelled to do. It became entirely natural when he was in his crib to roll over onto his stomach and lift his head. Then he pushed himself up and his world grew bigger. He could see outside the crib. In a few days, how many he did not know, for he was still impelled by instinct, he found that he could also raise his body to his knees. On hands and knees he rocked back and forth, feeling motion throughout his body. It was pleasurable, and he did it again and again. After this, the days moved quickly. Instinct moved more and more swiftly to knowledge. Now it was a matter of habit to get on his hands and knees. He knew how to do it, and it was no longer enough. Instinct persuaded him to move forward, putting one hand in front of the other, his knees following, and then when he reached the limits of the crib, or the place the Creature put him by day, since he could go no farther, he grasped the wooden slats and pulled himself upward.

Now he was really at a height. At such a height everything, the whole world, looked different. He was no longer beneath. He was above. He was high above the world and he laughed with joy.

PRESSING HIS FACE BETWEEN THE SLATS, he saw the Creatures, those with whom he belonged, one or two, moving here and there. Instinct stirred in him, but it was also knowledge. He had many ways now of knowing. He watched with his eyes, he had seen without knowing at first, but now knowing came, when he continued to see—spoon, plate, cup—instead of breast, these, too, he knew were for feeding. He was learning to know. More time was spent now in learning than in instinctive movements. He was surrounded by things. Each of these had to be learned about, how it felt in his hands, or if it were too big to hold, then to touch. He liked to hold and to touch. He liked also to taste, which after all was only touching with his tongue. When he found this way of knowing, he put everything in his mouth or if it were too big, then to his mouth. That was how he found out about taste. Everything had a taste as well as a surface for touch. He began to know more and more, because it was instinct to learn and so to know.

HE BECAME ENTIRELY DEVOTED to the business of learning, and as part of this business it became necessary to move. He had found that if he put one hand in front of the other, one after the other, his knees followed. The narrow pen became too small to contain him. He felt impelled to get out, to go into the beyond and he cried, he shouted, using his voice to have his way until he was lifted out and into the beyond. Then on hands and knees he explored. When he reached a chair or table leg, his instinct to climb moved him to pull himself up to a greater height. At first he did not know what to do. He was on his feet, holding on to something with his hands, but what came next he did not know. True, he saw what other Creatures did, but he did not know how they did it. There was also the danger of falling. He had tried letting go with his hands and immediately he sat down so suddenly on the floor that he had felt it necessary to cry so that the Creature came and took him in her arms to comfort him. He did not know that nothing is permanent. Everything began with not knowing. He had to learn that he could try again and this began by instinct impelling him to continue to try.

The Creature helped him now. She held him by both hands and drew him to his feet. Then pulling him gently toward her, he found that by instinct one foot followed another and he moved. He could move! Never again would he be content to be contained in a space. He was a free Creature like the other Creatures. True, he still fell now and then, sometimes with pain, but he learned to push himself to his feet and start again.

This was new pleasure. He had no wish or will to go anywhere, to reach any goal but simply to keep on his feet and move. True, he was often attracted by some object to stop, to see, to feel, to touch, to taste, to learn by all such means what an object was and what its use. Once he knew, instinct moved him on to something new. Gradually he learned to balance himself so that he did not fall, or not so often.

MEANWHILE HE FOUND IT NECESSARY to make noises. His voice he had discovered almost immediately after he had emerged from the private sea, for instinctively he had cried from pain. Pain had taught him to make a noise of protest. Then he had learned laughter. He used both of these noises every day and often. But there were other noises of the voice. The Creatures used their voices constantly, sometimes for laughter, but also for other sounds. They used a certain noise for him, for example. It was the first special noise he learned, the first constant, the first word—his name, Randolph, Rannie. This word was most often used with a few others, again connected with pain or pleasure. They were two short words, "no" and "yes." No, Rannie—yes, Rannie—meant pain or pleasure. Words could not be learned by instinct. They could only be learned by experience. At first he had disregarded them. No meant nothing to him. But he soon found that, if he disregarded it, it was followed by pain, a sudden slap of his hand, or on his bottom. He learned then to pause when he heard the word "no," especially when it was followed by "Rannie," which meant him. He learned that everyone had a special word. He learned "Mama," he learned "Papa." They were the Creatures to whom he belonged and who belonged to him. They were the ones who said no and yes to him. They also said "come." He began to know by learning when to use "no" and "yes" himself. One day they said, "Come, Rannie, come, come." It happened that at this moment he did not want to come. He was busy with his own concerns. Instinctively he used the word he knew best.

"No," he said. "No—no—no."

Swiftly he found himself picked up by the tall one.

"Yes—yes—yes—," the tall one said.

This pleasant word was accompanied, to his surprise, by a sharp slap on his bottom. He began immediately to cry. He could cry easily, whenever he liked. Sometimes it helped, sometimes it did not. This time it did not.

"No, no crying," the tall one said.

He looked at the tall one's face and decided to stop crying. This was learning by knowing. One did not say "no" when a big one said "come" or "yes."

HIS REAL INTEREST, HOWEVER, was not in such incidental scraps of knowledge. His occupation, self-chosen, was investigation. He was obsessed by the desire to investigate, to open every box, to see if he could close it again after finding what, if anything, was in it, to open every door, to climb the stairs over and over again, to take out of closets the pots and pans, the tins, the boxes, to remove the books from the shelves, to open drawers, to unscrew jars and unstopper bottles. Once he had made a discovery, he saw no reason to replace anything as it had been. He had learned what he wanted to know, he was through with it. He enjoyed emptying drawers and unrolling tissue paper. He liked playing in water and turning it off and on in the bathroom. He saw no reason for his mother's outcries of horror, but when she said, "No—no, Rannie," he left whatever he was doing and continued his work elsewhere.

On his first birthday, which he did not understand, he was diverted by a single candle on the cake and upon learning how to blow it out, he demanded that it be lit again and again, so that he could try to understand what the light was. When the tall one lit the candle for the last time—"No more, Rannie—no, no, no,"— he decided to try another method of finding out what it was. He put his forefinger in the flame—and instantly withdrew it. He was too shocked to cry. Instead he inspected his forefinger, and looked inquiringly at his mother.

"Hot," she said.

"Hot," he repeated. Then, since he knew, he began to cry because hot was also hurt.

At this his mother took a bit of ice from her lemonade glass and held it to the now blistering forefinger.

"Cold," she said.

"Cold," he repeated.

Now he knew hot and cold. It was hard, this learning, but

exciting. When he ate the ice cream, he communicated his knowl-edge.

"Cold," he said.

He did not know why his two Creatures laughed and clapped their hands.

"Cold," they agreed. He had made them happy, he did not know why, but he was happy with himself and he laughed too.

HE KNEW NOTHING OF TIME but he was always conscious of his own body and its needs, and in this way he became conscious of time. Something in his belly, an emptiness that was almost pain but not quite, was such discomfort that it could only be stopped by food. This necessity divided the day into times. Darkness fell and he grew drowsy. His eyes closed and the mother Creature put him into warm water and warm, soft garments. He drank milk and ate comforting food and then in his bed he tried to play with a toy Creature but his eyes shut. The room was dark but when he opened his eyes again it was light. He got to his feet and shouted for his mother and she came in, all smiles, and lifted him out of the bed and he was washed and fed again and then he went about the business of his day, which still was to investigate everything over and over and pause upon what was new or, if he were alone, to investigate what she always said "no—no" about if she were in the room. Privately he felt no limits to this business of knowing. He had to know.

One day a new creature came into his knowing. The tall one brought it. It was small and soft, it had four legs, and it made a noise he had not heard before.

"Erh—erh!" the new creature said.

"Dog," the tall one explained.

But he was afraid of Dog and he drew back and put his hands behind his back.

"Erh—erh—erh," Dog said.

"See, Rannie's dog," the tall one said.

He took Rannie's hand in his and smoothed Dog.

"Dog," Rannie said, and was no longer afraid. This was new knowing. Dog had to be examined and his tail pulled. Why a tail?

"No—no," the mother said. "Don't hurt Dog."

"Hurt?" Rannie repeated, puzzled.

She pulled Rannie's ear sharply. "Hurt, no—no," she repeated. "See, like this—"

She smoothed dog gently, and Rannie, after watching, did the same. Suddenly Dog licked his hand. He drew back.

"Dog—no, no," he exclaimed.

The mother laughed. "He likes you—nice dog," she said.

DAY BY DAY HE WAS LEARNING new words. He did not know that it was unusual to learn words so early. He was only pleased that his parents laughed and clapped their hands often.

By the time he came to his second birthday he could even count. He knew that one following one and another and another and each had a name. He learned these names by accident one day with blocks. He put a block on the floor from a box full of blocks.

"One," his mother said.

He took out another and placed it beside the one. "Two," his mother said.

And so he proceeded until she had said "Ten." Here he went back again to one and repeated the names himself. His mother stared at him, then swept him into her arms in joy. When the father came home at dark, she put out the blocks again.

"Say them, Rannie," she told him.

He remembered the names easily, and the two looked at each other in gravity and astonishment.

"Isn't he—"

"It seems so—"

He said them over again very fast and laughing. "One—two—three—four—five—six—seven—eight—nine—ten!"

They did not laugh. They looked at each other. Then suddenly the father took some small round objects from his pocket.

"Pennies," he said.

"Pennies," Rannie repeated. He repeated everything they said to him, remembering afterward which word belonged to each object.

His father put down one penny on the carpet, where he knelt before Rannie.

"One penny," he said distinctly.

Rannie listened without repeating. It was obvious that this was one penny. His father put down another penny and looked at Rannie.

"Two," Rannie said.

And so on the game went until ten pennies finished it. They looked at each other, the parents.

"He does understand—he understands numbers," the father said, astonished.

"I told you," the mother retorted.

* * *

AFTER THIS, OF COURSE, everything had to be counted. Apples in a bowl, books on the shelves, plates in the cupboard. But what came beyond ten? He demanded this knowledge of his mother.

"Ten—ten—ten," he said impatiently. What came after ten?

"Eleven—twelve—thirteen—," his mother said.

He grasped the idea at once. Counting went on and on. There was no end to it. He counted everything and reached for the innumerable. He began to realize endlessness. Trees in the woods, for example, where they went for picnics—there was no use in counting them once he understood counting, so that it simply became more of the same.

Money, of course, was different from trees or daisies in a field. By the time he was three he knew that money must be given in exchange for what one wanted. He walked with his mother to the grocery store down the street and he saw her give pieces of metal or paper in return for bread and milk, meat and vegetables and fruit.

"What is?" he asked when he came home after the first time. He had found her change purse and, opening it, had laid in a row on the kitchen table the varieties of coins within.

She told him the name of each and he repeated each after her. He never forgot anything he once knew. He asked endless questions and he always remembered the answers. But he did more than remember. He understood the principle. Money was only money. It was nothing unless it was given in exchange for what was wanted. This was its value, this was its meaning.

His mother had looked at him strangely that day when he had repeated after her perfectly the names of the coins.

"You never forget anything, do you, Rannie?" she had said.

"No," he had replied. "I might need to remember, so I mustn't forget."

She often looked at him strangely, as though she were afraid of him.

"Why do you look at me hard, Mama?" he asked.

"I don't really know," she had replied honestly. "I think it is because I never saw a little boy like you."

He thought this over but without understanding it. Somehow it made him feel lonely, but he did not have time to think about it, because he wanted to learn to read.

"Books," he said to his father one day. "Why are books?"

His father was always reading books. He was a college professor. At night he read books and wrote down words on paper.

"You can learn anything from books," his father said.

It was a snowy day, a Saturday, when his father was at home reading books.

"I want to read too," he told his father.

"You'll learn when you start school," his father said.

"I want to learn now," he said. "I want to read all the books in the world."

His father laughed and put down the book he was reading. "Very well," he said. "Fetch me a piece of paper and a pencil and I will show you how to begin to read."

He ran to the kitchen, where his mother was cooking the dinner.

"Pencil and paper," he said briskly. "I am going to read."

His mother put down the big spoon with which she was stirring something in a pot on the stove. She went into the study, where his father was reading.

"You aren't going to teach that baby to read!" she exclaimed.

"He's no baby," his father retorted. "If you ask me, he never was a baby. He wants to read. Of course I'll teach him."

"I don't believe in forcing children," his mother said.

"I'm not forcing him—he's forcing me," his father said, laughing. "All right, Rannie—give me the paper and pencil."

He forgot his mother and she went away and left them. His father printed a line of marks on the paper.

"These are the bricks words are made of—twenty-six of them. They are called letters."

"All words?" he asked. "All those books full of words?"

"All words, all books—in English, that is," his father replied. "And each brick has a name of its own and a sound of its own. I'll tell you the names, first."

Whereupon his father repeated clearly and slowly the names of the letters. Three such repetitions and he knew the name of each letter. His father tested him by writing the letters out of order, but he knew them all.

"Good," his father said with surprised looks. "Very good. Now for what they say. Each has a sound."

For the next hour he listened closely to what each letter said in sound. "Now I can read," he exclaimed. "I can read because I understand."

"Not so fast," his father told him. "Letters can say several sounds if they are put together. But you've learned enough for one day."

"I can read because I know how reading is done," he insisted. "I know and so I can do it."

"All right," his father said. "Try for yourself, you can always ask."

And he went back to his own reading.

* * *

AFTER THIS SNOWY SATURDAY when he was three years old, he spent most of his time in learning how to read by himself. At first he had to ask many questions of his mother, running to find where she was in the house, making beds, sweeping floors and such things as occupied her from morning until night.

"What is this word?" he asked.

She was always patient. Whatever she was doing she stopped and looked where his small forefinger pointed.

"That long word? Oh, Rannie, you won't be using it for such a while—'intellectual.'"

"What does it mean?"

"It means liking to use your brain."

"What is brain?"

"It's your thinking machine—what you have in here."

She tapped his skull lightly with her gold-thimbled finger. She was sewing a button on his father's shirt.

"I have a brain in there?" he asked.

"You most certainly have—so that it almost scares me sometimes."

"Why does it scare you?"

"Oh, because—you're only a little boy not four years old yet."

"What does my brain look like, Mama?"

"Like everyone's, I guess—a wrinkly gray something."

"Then why does it scare you?"

"You do ask such questions—" She broke off.

"But I have to ask you, Mama. If I don't ask, I won't know."

"You could look in the dictionary."

"Where is it, Mama?"

She put down her sewing then and led him to the library and to a big book open on a small table and showed him how to find words.

"'Intellectual,' for example—it begins with an *i*, doesn't it, and here are all the *i* words but you have to see what the next letter is—*ia, ib, ic*—until you get to *in*—"

He listened and looked, absorbed and fascinated. This big book, then, was the source of all words! He had the key, he knew the principle!

"I won't ever need to ask you again, Mama. I know now, all by myself."

HE LIVED IN A SMALL TOWN, busy with people much older than he. It was a college town and his father taught every day except Saturday and Sunday. On Sunday in the morning he went to church with his parents. At first when he was small, for he did not consider himself small now that he was nearly four years old, his birthday less than a week away, he had been left in the basement in the church nursery. This had not lasted long. He had soon looked at all the picture books, had solved all the puzzles, and had successfully intimidated all the children by appearing much their senior. He was large for his age and he assumed the other children were babies. He was humiliated by being left with them, he thought their prattle absurd, and after two Sundays he asked to be allowed to sit upstairs in the church with the adults.

His father was doubtful and looked at his mother, questioning.

"Can he sit still, do you think?"

"I will sit still," he replied quickly.

"Let's give him a try. He doesn't like it downstairs," his mother said.

He did not really like it upstairs, either, but remembering his promise, he kept it. Inside his skull his brain busied itself by instinct. Not for a moment could it be idle. He pondered the words of the minister, ignoring sometimes their implication and considering instead their sound, their spelling, their meaning. His relentless memory imprisoned any word that was new and when he went home he consulted his constant companion, the dictionary. There were times when the dictionary failed him, nevertheless, and then he was compelled to resort to his mother, since it was intolerable not to know.

"Mama, what does 'virgin' mean?"

His mother looked up, surprised, from something she was stirring in a bowl on the kitchen table. She hesitated. "Why, I suppose it means not married."

"But Mama, Mary was married. She was married to Joseph. The minister said so."

"Oh, that—I suppose no one quite understands that. Jesus was born of what's called the Immaculate Conception."

He went away with two new words. Finding them far apart in the dictionary, he tried putting them together. They made no sense. He copied them in the capital letters, as yet his only way of writing, and returned to his mother in the kitchen. She had finished her stirring, she was washing bowl and spoon, and a delicious scent of baking cake pervaded the atmosphere. He showed her the printed words and made complaint.

"Mama, I still don't understand."

She shook her head. "I can't explain it to you, son. I don't really understand it myself."

"Then how can I know, Mama?"

"Ask your father tonight, son, when he comes home."

He folded the bit of paper and put it in his pocket. Before he could ask his father, however, he overheard, though by accident, a conversation between his parents. The kitchen window was open and he was in the backyard playing with his dog, or rather teaching him a new trick. Most of his play with his pet had to do with teaching him tricks and finding out what Brisk, the dog, could and could not learn. He had been laughing at Brisk's obedient efforts to walk on his hind legs when he heard his mother's protesting voice through the open window.

"George, you will have to explain things to Rannie. I can't do it."

"What things, Sue?"

"Well, he asked me what 'virgin' meant and what 'immaculate conception' means. Things like that!"

He heard his father's laughter. "I certainly can't explain an immaculate conception!"

"You'll have to try. You know he never forgets anything. And he is determined to know."

Thus reminded, he immediately left his dog and ran into the house to find his father with his question. His father was upstairs, getting into sweater and slacks. Spring was at hand and the garden had been ploughed.

"Virgin?" his father repeated. He hung up his professional suit in the closet and looked out the window.

"See the garden?" he asked.

Rannie came to his side. "Mr. Bates ploughed it this morning."

"Now we have to plant seeds in it," his father said. "But—"

He sat down and drew Rannie between his knees, his hands on the boy's shoulders. "Until we plant seeds there in that ploughed earth, we won't have a garden. Right?"

Rannie nodded, his eyes upon his father's keenly handsome face.

"So," his father went on, "it's virgin soil—virgin earth. All by itself it can't grow the things we want. Everything begins with a seed—fruits and vegetables, trees and weeds—even people."

"People?" Rannie asked, astonished. "Was I a seed?"

"No," his father said. "But a seed was your beginning. I planted the seed. That's why I am your father."

"What kind of seed?" he asked, astonished.

"My kind," his father said simply.

"But—but—where did you plant it?"

Questions rushed to his lips. He could not ask them fast enough.

"In your mother," his father said. "Until then she was a virgin."

"Immaculate conception?"

"I think so."

"Conception—"

His father interrupted. "Comes from the Latin word meaning an idea—an abstract idea—something that is at first just a thought. Then it becomes more—it's a concept—then a—"

"I was a concept?"

"In a way—yes. I saw your mother, I fell in love with her, I wanted her to be my wife and your mother. That was my idea, my concept. When you began, it was a conception."

"When Jesus—"

His father interrupted again. "Ah, we know he was born of love. That's why we call it the Immaculate Conception. It wasn't Joseph who planted that seed. He was getting rather old for seed-planting. Mary was young—still a virgin, perhaps. But someone who loved her planted the seed. We know that—someone very extraordinary, or there wouldn't have been the extraordinary child."

"Where did he plant it? Where did you—"

"Ah, that's the next question! Inside the mother person, the woman, there's a garden, a little enclosed spot, where the seed falls—and starts to grow. We call it the womb. It's the growing place for children."

"Do I have one?"

"No, you're a seed-planter, like me."

"How do we—"

"The instrument is the penis, and there's a passageway to the womb called the vagina. Look up both those words in the dictionary."

"Can I plant seed now?"

"No. You have to grow up first. You have to be a man."

"Can you do it whenever you like?"

"Yes—but I like to do it only when your mother is ready. After all, she has the work of growing the seed—taking care of it, and so on. The garden has to be made ready, remember."

"Can Brisk plant dog seed?"

"He can."

"And we'll have puppies? I'd like some puppies."

"We'll find a mother sort of dog."

"How will we know?"

"Well, she won't have a penis as Brisk does. A penis is a planter, you know."

"Does Mother—"

"No. I told you to look it up in the dictionary. Now, come out and help me hoe up the garden. That's your job just now."

He never ceased to think of the seed, nevertheless. Everything in the world, all that lived, began with a seed! But what made the seed? "In the Beginning," the minister intoned one Sunday morning in the church. "In the Beginning was the Word and the Word was God."

"Is God the same as the seed?" he asked his father on the way home.

"No," his father replied, "and don't ask me what God is, because I don't know. I doubt anyone knows, but everyone with any intelligence wonders, each in his own way. It seems as though there ought to be, or even must be, a beginning, but then again perhaps there wasn't. Perhaps we live in eternity."

"How you talk!" his mother said. "The boy can't understand."

"He understands," his father said.

The boy looked from one to the other of these, his parents, and he loved his father the better.

"I do understand," he said.

WHEN HE WAS SIX YEARS OLD, he started school. It was on a crisp autumn morning that the new life began. His mother had bought him a suit of clothes the week before, a dark blue suit, and his father had taken him to the barber for a haircut.

"Am I handsome?" he asked his mother as he stood in the doorway.

She laughed. "What a funny little boy you are!"

"Why do you say I am funny?" he inquired, wondering and even inclined to be hurt.

"Because you ask such questions," she retorted.

"As a matter of fact, you are quite handsome," his father said, "and you should be grateful, for it is an advantage to a man, as I have discovered."

His mother laughed even more. "O vanity—vanity, thy name is Man!"

"What is vanity—?" he began, but his mother gave him an affectionate push.

"Go ask your questions in school," she told him.

On the way to the school, which was only three blocks away in this quiet college town, so that he could walk, he pondered the gravity of the day.

I shall learn everything, he thought. They will teach me how to make engines. They will tell me why seeds grow. They will let me know what is God.

The peace of the morning pervaded him with joy and content. School was where he could learn everything. All his questions would be answered. He would have a teacher. When he reached the schoolyard, children were playing there, boys and girls of his own age. Some of them had mothers with them because it was their first day at school. His own mother had said, "Perhaps I had better come with you this first day, Rannie."

"Why?" he had asked.

His father had laughed. "Why indeed! He's right—and quite self-sufficient."

Now he did not pause in the schoolyard with the other children. Some of them he knew, but he had no playmates. He tired of them quickly when they came into his home yard and he preferred a book to games. Now and then his mother protested.

"Rannie, you ought to play with the other children."

"Why?" he asked.

"It would be fun," she said.

"I have fun by myself," he said. "Besides, what they think is fun isn't fun for me."

So now he walked straight into the schoolhouse and asked a man where the first-grade room was. The man looked at him, a gray-haired man—with a young face.

"You're Professor Colfax's son, aren't you?"

"Yes, sir," Rannie said.

"I've heard about you. I was a classmate of his once—before you were born. I'm Jonathan Parker, your principal. Come with me. I'll introduce you."

He put a hand on Rannie's shoulder and led him down the hall and around a corner and stopped at the first door to the right.

"Here we are. This is your room. Your teacher is Martha Downes—Miss Downes. She's a good teacher. Miss Downes, this is Randolph Colfax—Rannie for short."

"How do you do, Miss Downes?" Rannie said.

He looked into a lined, spectacled face, kind but unsmiling.

"I've been expecting you, Rannie," she said. They shook hands.

"Your seat is there by the window. Jackie Blaine is on one side of you, Ruthie Greene on the other. Do you know them?"

"Not yet," Rannie said.

The bell rang at this moment and children came tumbling into the halls. Most of the first graders had mothers with them, and some of the little girls cried when their mothers left them. Ruthie was one of these. He leaned toward her.

"Don't cry," he told her. "You'll have a good time learning things."

"I don't want to learn things," she sobbed. "I want to go home."

"I'll take you home after school," he told her. "Unless you came in a bus."

She wiped her eyes on the edge of her pink gingham skirt. "I didn't come in a bus. I walked here with my mother."

"Then I'll walk back with you," he promised.

On the whole, however, the day was disappointing. He learned nothing new, since he already knew how to read. He read through his first reader while Miss Downes was explaining letters and their sounds on the blackboard. He enjoyed the half hour of crayon work, for he devised a wheel-driven engine he had been thinking about to set in a dam he was building in the small brook that ran through the half-acre lot behind his home.

"What is that?" Miss Downes asked, examining it through the lower half of her spectacles.

"It's a water-powered engine," he replied. "I haven't finished it yet."

"What's the use of it?" she asked.

"It will keep the fish in the pool on the upper side. See, when they swim down, this wing will stop them."

"What if they swim up?" she asked.

"The wing will help them—like this."

She looked at him with shrewd, kind eyes. "You don't belong here," she told him.

"Where do I belong?" he asked.

"I don't know," she said almost sadly. "I doubt anyone will ever know."

HE PUT THIS REPLY into his mind as she passed on to the next desk, intending to ask his father what she meant, but the day ended in such turmoil that he never thought of it again. True to his promise, he waited for Ruthie and hand in hand the two of them walked up the street in the direction opposite that of his home. He heard some giggling among the other children but he paid no heed to it. Ruthie, however, seemed disturbed—indeed, almost angry.

"They're silly," she muttered.

"Then why do you care?" he asked.

"They think you're in love with me," she went on.

He considered this. "I don't know what that means."

"Because I'm a girl," she explained.

"You are a girl," he said. "That is, you are a girl if you don't have a penis. My father told me so."

"What's a penis?" she asked, her brown eyes large and innocent.

"It's what I have. I'll show—if you'd like to see it."

"I've never seen one," she said with interest.

They were walking in the shade of one of the huge old elms that lined the street. He paused and, putting down his books, he opened his fly and showed the small limp penis hanging beneath his stomach.

She was fascinated. "It's cute," she said, "so tiny! What do you use it for?"

"It's a planter," he told her, and was about to explain further when she surprised him by pulling up her short skirt.

"Want to see me?" she asked in all kindness.

"Yes," he said. "I haven't seen a girl."

She pulled down her small pants and he knelt in the grass, the better to examine the new sight.

He saw two soft pale lips, enclosing a pink opening that scarcely showed itself except for a rosy tip, smaller than the tip of Ruthie's little finger. It might have been a penis but it was absurdly small. Perhaps it was just for pretty, but it looked like the bud of a rose, a miniature rose such as his mother grew in her rose beds.

"Now I know," he exclaimed. He rose and, drawing up his zipper, he took his book bag, and they sauntered on, oblivious to the occasional passerby.

To his surprise, when they reached Ruthie's house, a modest two-story building on the edge of town, her mother was waiting at the gate. Her face was far from pleasant, although she was a pretty woman.

"Rannie Colfax," she said severely. "You are a bad, bad boy. Ruthie, go in the house and wait for me. Don't ever speak to Rannie again!"

He was shocked and amazed. "But I was only walking Ruthie home—she was afraid."

"Don't tell me what you were doing! *I* know—I've already been told by half the people in town. Go home at once. Your parents are waiting for you."

He turned and walked homeward in the same state of shock and amazement. What had he done?

* * *

RUTHIE'S MOTHER WAS RIGHT. His parents were waiting for him when he came to the door of the living room. His mother was in her rocking chair, knitting very fast on a red sweater she was making for him.

"You handle this," she said to his father.

She rose then and crossed the room to where he stood in the doorway, kissed his cheek and went away upstairs.

"Come here son," his father said.

He was sitting in the old leather armchair that had once belonged to his own father. How often he had been called to appear before him to answer stern, ministerial questions! The memory of his childish terror softened his heart now toward his own son.

Rannie drew near and stood waiting, his heart beating hard in his bosom. What had happened? What had he done?

"Push that hassock over here close to me, son, and let's get at the truth of all this," his father said. "Remember, it's you I shall believe. Whatever happened, I know you'll tell me the truth."

Rannie's heart calmed. He drew the crewelwork hassock close to his father's knees and sat down.

"I don't know what you mean, Papa, because nothing happened."

"Maybe it seemed nothing to you, son, but Ruthie's mother said you pulled up her skirts and—"

He was instantly relieved. "Oh that? Why, she'd never seen a penis, she didn't even know what it was, so I showed her mine. Then she said she'd show me, too, so she pulled up her skirt to show me. It's very different, Papa. You'd be surprised. It's sort of like a mouth, only it's not red, except for a tiny pink tip showing like the tip of your tongue. That's all there was."

"Did people pass by?"

"I didn't see them, Papa."

"Well, it seems they did see you and they told Ruthie's mother."

"Told her what?"

"That you were inspecting each other."

"But how else were we to know, Papa?"

His father frowned. "You're right, of course, Rannie. How else were you to know? I see absolutely nothing wrong in learning the truth about anything. The trouble is that most people don't agree with you and me. Now, I'm glad you've seen how Ruthie is shaped and if I were Ruthie's father—or mother—I'd be glad she had the opportunity to see how a boy is shaped. The sooner one knows the truth about anything and everything, the better for all concerned. But some people think there's sin in sex."

"What's sex, Papa?"

"It's another word for what I told you about—the seed-planting, you know, for a human child, which takes place between a man and woman. Ruthie's mother thought you and Ruthie were doing something like that, and since you're both only children, she thought it was wrong. I suppose in a way she was right, because there's time for everything and you haven't come to the time, nor has Ruthie."

"How will we know when we come to the time?"

"Your own body will tell you. For now, I'd be glad you know what you know about it, and go on to learn other things you don't know, of which there are plenty. The world is full of things you don't know. I'm going to buy an encyclopedia. It's better than a dictionary."

"Does it tell about everything?" Rannie inquired. In the possibility of such joy he forgot Ruthie and her mother.

"Just about everything," his father said, "and I smell something like cookies baking in the oven."

He rose and they walked to the kitchen, his hand on Rannie's shoulder. At the door he stopped.

"Just one thing—you did no wrong. If anyone says you did, or acts as if you did, send him—or her—to me."

"Yes, Papa," Rannie said.

But he paid little heed to what his father had said. The fragrance of cinnamon cookies made him ravenous and his mouth was watering.

THE NEXT DAY AT SCHOOL was another disappointing day, exactly as yesterday had been. Ruthie's seat had been changed to the other side of the room and a dark-haired boy, large for his age, named Mark, had been substituted. There was no importance to this, for he, Rannie, had forgotten about Ruthie. The disappointment lay in the fact, more and more obvious as the day went on, that he was not learning anything. He had already read through the first-grade reader, he had long past lost interest in crayon work, and the few books on a shelf were, he considered after he examined them, books for babies. The story Miss Downes read to the class was also for babies—something about bluebirds in the spring.

"Aren't you interested in this nice story, Rannie?" Miss Downes asked.

He had been drawing a geometric design of intertwined triangles while she read. He looked up from his paper, pencil in hand.

"No, Miss Downes," he said.

She looked at him hard for a few seconds, puzzled as he could see, and he felt it necessary to explain.

"I used to read stories like that when I first learned to read."

"When was that?" she asked.

"I can't remember when it was," he replied. But he put down the pencil, feeling it would be impolite to continue, and she went on with her reading.

At recess, to which he looked forward, he found himself isolated. Ruthie did not speak to him and he stood apart, watching the other children. He felt no shyness, only curiosity and interest. Squabbling took place over the swings, until a biggish boy, whose name was Chris, took leadership by appropriating the highest swing for himself. Then, noticing Rannie, he shouted.

"Want a turn?"

He had no desire for a swing, since he had one at home, but a vague desire for companionship made him nod his head. He took his turn and then, about to stand apart again, he found Chris at his side.

"Want to race to the gate—see who's first?"

"All right," he said courteously.

They raced, coming to the finish in a tie.

"You run real good," Chris said. "I can beat the rest of these babies. Say, I hear Ruthie showed herself to you!" Chris was from a higher grade than Rannie but it seemed that the news of his quest for knowing about girls was everywhere in the small school.

He stared blankly at Chris. "I don't understand what's so interesting about that."

"Oh, come on," Chris said.

He had no answer for this, for he had no interest in Ruthie now. Chris continued. "Know how kids get made?"

"Yes, my father told me," he said.

Chris stared at him. "Your old man told you?"

"Yes—my father," he said.

"Gosh, he must have a dirty mind," Chris said with contempt.

"I don't know what you mean," he said, surprised and inclined to anger.

The bell rang at that instant, and conversation was cut off. He went back to his seat, thoughtful and vaguely angry. He liked Chris, he liked his brusqueness, his force, even his roughness. In spite of a vague anger he decided to be friends with this boy, if he could. And he decided too that he would not tell his father what Chris had said.

IT WAS BECAUSE OF CHRIS that he did not complain to his parents about the stupidity of school. He raced off to school early every morning so that he and Chris could have half an hour of intense play before school began. Recess was the reward in the middle of the morning and they ate their lunches together. Unfortunately, Chris lived at the far end of town and his bus took them away from each other at the end of school, but this was compensated for, in Rannie's case, by the arrival of the encyclopedia, twenty-four volumes, all bound in dark blue with gold lettering. Immediately after he came home from school and after a sandwich and a glass of milk and a piece of pie or cake or some cookies in the kitchen with his mother, he read the encyclopedia, page after page, volume after volume. It was incredibly exciting, one subject after another, explained briefly but clearly, telling him things he had not known existed. He read until nightfall and his father came home. There were words he had to look up in the dictionary, of course, many of them, for his parents were relentless in their determination regarding the dictionary. He must find his own meanings.

"Never ask someone to do what you can do for yourself," his mother sermonized.

"I'll improve on that," his father said. "Never let anyone do something for you that you enjoy doing for yourself."

"Is that what you do?" she demanded.

"As far as life permits," he replied.

Rannie listened. The conversation between his parents interested him—indeed, fascinated him. It was always above his head, sometimes only slightly, but he had to stretch his mind. They never simplified themselves for him. Though they included him in everything they did, he was aware that somehow, somewhere, they were alone together, the two of them. On the subject of parents he and Chris disagreed totally.

"Parents are nuts," Chris said flatly.

"Mine aren't," Rannie said.

"Always hollerin' about somepin."

"Not mine!"

The disagreement was such that they became secretly curious about each other's parents. Thus, one Saturday, Chris accepted an invitation to inspect Rannie's parents by coming to skate on the frozen swimming pool in the backyard. Rannie had introduced Chris to his mother as she was making a weekend cake in the kitchen and he had been pleased to find that Chris was impressed by her blond good looks.

"She's pretty, all right," he agreed. "Where's your old man?"

Rannie had learned to understand Chris's language without using it. "He's in the study, writing a book. We don't bother him until he opens the door himself."

"Writing a book?" Chris asked incredulously.

"Yes—on the science of art."

"What's that?"

"It's what he's writing about."

"Sure—but what does it mean?"

"He believes that art is based on certain scientific principles."

"Oh, come on—what does that mean?"

"I don't know altogether—until he's finished the book and I can read it."

"You read books?"

"Of course. Don't you?"

"No. I hate readin'."

"Then how do you know anything?"

"How do you mean *know* anything? I ast somebody, if I want to know—like how do you go out west. I'm goin' to have a ranch out west when I grow up—say, ten, 'leven years from now. Come on—let's skate."

They skated and noon arrived before they thought it possible except that they were starving.

"Luncheon waits!" his mother sang out of the kitchen door.

So, their skates off and their ears scarlet with cold, they went into the dining room and found Rannie's father waiting behind his chair.

"Papa, this is Chris," Rannie said.

"Chris, I'm happy to meet you," his father said.

"You haven't washed, Rannie," his mother reminded him.

They went to the downstairs powder room, Rannie leading and Chris obviously impressed.

"Your ole man looks swell," Chris said. "Clean and all—like Sunday. Mine works in a garage—it's his garage. I'm gonna work there when I'm old enough. I work now in summer on the days I feel like it. But I'm gonna work every day when I'm sixteen and Pop'll pay me good money—he says so. He's okay if he isn't mad about somepin. Anyways, he don't drink. Ma's glad of that."

In spite of every effort on the part of his parents, however, Chris was completely silent during the meal, and immediately afterward declared that he must go home.

"I got chores to do," he explained abruptly.

THAT NIGHT HIS PARENTS CAME as near to a quarrel as he had ever heard. He was working on the water-powered engine, a project that had now progressed beyond the drawing he had finished in school. He had worked on it only intermittently in school, for he had learned even in his brief experience with himself that there were periods when he must allow his brain to rest by putting it to other matters. If he allowed it to puzzle too long over an invention or task, then there would come a moment when it simply refused to clarify a difficulty that must of course be clarified. Every puzzlement must be clarified. What he was working on now were the angles of the paddles or wings of the wheel. Each must be slightly different from the other, yet exactly in the right relationship to every other. It was in this moment of delicate adjustment that he heard his father's voice infused with unwonted irritation.

"But Susan, the boy is learning nothing in this school!"

His mother replied with equal vigor. "He's learning how to live with people of his own age!"

"Susan, you don't realize our responsibility for a brain like his!"

"I don't want him to grow up lonely!" Her voice broke, as though she were trying not to cry.

"But he will always be lonely—you must accept the fact!"

"On certain levels I do accept it, but not on every level. He must be able to live with other people, enjoying other people even if they can't be on his level. He must have some relief from himself."

"He can never have relief from himself. A few hours—no, not even that. In fact, he will never be as lonely as he will be with other people."

"Oh, why do you say that? You break my heart."

"Well, it stands to reason—it's when he is with other people that he will feel his difference most keenly."

"Darling, what shall we do?"

"Teach him to accept himself. He's a loner. We know it. He must know it—and learn that he has joys and resources that ordinary people can never know. He'll know wonder as long as he lives—think what endless joy that will be! Always the reaching mind, always the searching curiosity! Don't feel sorry for our son, Susan, my love. Rejoice, that unto us such a son is born! Our responsibility is to see that he fulfills himself, that he is not wasted. He must be allowed to proceed at his own top speed. No, Susan, I insist—we have to find the right school, the right teachers, even if we have to make it. Miss Downes knows it, bless her. She's miserable at not being able to devote herself to him. That's why she told you he should be in the sixth or seventh grade. I say he shouldn't be in any grade but his own. He must go at his own speed. It's our responsibility to see that he has his freedom."

THE NEXT AUTUMN HE FOUND HIMSELF in a new school in the same town, a small new school whose principal and teacher was his own father. There were other pupils, three girls and four boys. He did not know any of them. Five of them came from neighboring towns, two boys were from his own town, their fathers professors in science. The schoolroom was a large attic above the college gymnasium. The four walls were filled with shelves of books, except for the dormer windows. The building was so high that these windows looked out on treetops, and he had the feeling of being on a mountain. There was no schedule of studies. Sometime during the day his father introduced a subject, mathematics or science or literature. He read to them, up to a point, and then, posing a problem, he left it to them to solve. They could search among the books unguided or ask for guidance if they liked. Almost always the boys searched unguided. Almost always the girls asked for guidance.

"Not because the girls are inferior," his father told his mother one evening. "It is only because they think they are inferior."

"Or are afraid they are," his mother said.

"Same thing?"

"Not at all—if they're only afraid, they still have hope."

No one mentioned grades, no one spoke of marks. He himself grew interested in Latin because of his absorption with words, and was soon reading Virgil with relish. One language led to another and then his father introduced new teachers, a French woman, an aging Italian singer whose voice had cracked, the Spanish professor who was the head of the foreign language department in the college.

His father drew upon the college faculty for all their teachers. New pupils came from other parts of the country, until they reached the limit of twenty.

His father seemed to exert no pressure upon his pupils, but if a pupil lagged in curiosity or concentration he paid particular heed to that one for a matter of weeks until curiosity awakened again. If it did not, the pupil was returned to where he came from.

"Why did you send Brad back to New York, Father?"

"Talent isn't enough, brains aren't enough," his father replied. "There has to be the hunger and thirst to know that involves energy and perseverance. I try to rouse the desire to know. If I fail, then I send the child home to his parents."

"You're experimenting with these children," his mother observed somewhat coldly.

"It's an experiment," his father agreed. "But I am not making it. I am only discovering what is there—or not there. I am sorting."

HE WAS TWELVE when he was ready for college entrance examinations and he passed them with ease.

"Now," his father said, "you are ready to see the world for yourself. I've been saving for years for this day. Your mother, you, and I are going on a long, long journey. We may be gone for several years. Then, perhaps at sixteen, you'll go to college. I don't know. You may not want to go."

Alas, the long, long journey with his father and mother was never to take place. Instead his father took an entirely different journey with them—a lonely journey into death. It began so slowly that none of them noticed its beginning.

"You are working too hard," his mother said to his father one day in June. They were to go abroad in July.

"I'll rest a week or two after school closes," his father replied.

He remembered his father always as tall and thin, and he had scarcely noticed his suddenly excessive thinness. Now he looked at his father. As usually they did after their evening meal, they sat on the cool side porch, facing the lawn enclosed by a hedge high enough to shield them from the street. His father lay outstretched on a long chair. Nothing more was said. They sat listening to the music from the stereo in the living room. But he was to remember that evening forever, because, after his mother had spoken, he examined his father's face as he leaned back in his chair, the eyes closed, the lips pale, the cheeks hollowed. He observed a certain fragility that had not been a part of his father's natural appearance. That night he went to bed anxious, and he drew his mother aside. "Is my father sick?" he asked.

"He's going to the hospital the day after school closes and have a thorough checkup," his mother said, and she pursed her lips together firmly.

He hesitated, noticing everything without knowing, as he always did, the shape of his mother's lips, the upper one bowed, the lower full, a beautiful mouth. And at the same moment the environment impressed itself upon his senses, the open windows and the triangled leaves of the sycamore trees stirring in the breeze, the picture upon the wall over the mantelpiece of soft green hills, a winding country road, a stone wall, a house and barn, and over it all the mistiness of early spring. SPRING AT WOODSTOCK, the top of the frame read. Woodstock, Vermont, was his mother's hometown, and the picture, she always said, kept her from being homesick here in Ohio. But there seemed nothing more to say, and he went on his way to his room and bed.

All during the long summer he lived a double life, his own and his father's. His own was troublesome enough, for at twelve he was large for his age and he seemed strange to himself, his feelings strange and new, his body changing, growing so fast that clothes he wore easily enough one day were too small for him a month later. His emotions quickened, whether because he knew now that his father was dying, or because his body was taking on a life of its own, his muscles strengthening, his whole being impatient for what he could not define, his penis enlarging and making its own demands on him as though it were some sort of separate being with a life separate from himself, a querulous creature whose demands he did not know how to satisfy.

His father's weakening hold on life made him unwilling, almost ashamed, to inquire why his own life was burgeoning, and his mother, he reasoned, would not be able to understand. It was then that he thought of Chris, that early friend whom he had scarcely seen in the intervening years. Not since he had stopped going to public school had he seen Chris, except occasionally on the street. He had learned that Chris had dropped out of school and was working at his father's gas station at South End.

South End was the opposite side of town and there was nothing to bring them together. He knew now that he and Chris belonged to different worlds, as far apart as different planets, even. He knew this and yet the knowledge made him desperate with loneliness.

The knowledge, also, that his father was dying added even more to his loneliness.

Inside his father's gaunt frame there grew a cancer, a creature insensate and mindless, yet with a life of its own. It fed upon his father's flesh and bones, it sucked his father's life away, it spread its crablike tentacles farther and farther into his father's frame until his father was the appendage and the thing the creature. His father became an image of pain, drowsy with drugs, drawing one slow breath after another until each seemed it must be the last.

And all this time the summer went on its luxuriant way, the corn growing tall, the wheat ripe, the hay cut.

"Two months—maybe," the doctor said.

Two months—an endless time to endure, yet too swift, and his father was already out of his reach. A faint smile when he came into his father's room, the skeleton hand reaching and clinging for a moment and then loosening, the eyes half-closed and glazed with pain, and this was all he knew now of his father. He was wildly restless, angry, rebellious, and there were times when he wept, alone and helpless.

ON A SUNDAY AFTERNOON the house grew intolerable. His mother was relieving the nurse they had now to employ and the house was empty. He could not read in the tensity of waiting and yet waiting with unutterable dread for his father's last fluttering breath. One month of the two had passed and this last month was eternity. Everything was changed. His mother was far away, wrapped in her own stern solitude of sorrow. All the people they knew—his parents' friends, his schoolmates, everyone—were infinitely far away. He needed to see someone who knew nothing of what he was suffering, who would not ask him how his father was. He needed youth and health and life and in impetuous desperation he set forth to find it. He set out to find Chris.

"THAT AIN'T YOU, IS IT?" Chris shouted. He had grown into a burly youth, red-faced, loud-voiced, his full mouth pouting, his blond hair crew-cut. He wore soiled green coveralls and his nails were black.

"I'm Rannie Colfax, if that's who you mean."

He put out his hand but Chris drew back.

"I'm all black grease," he said. "Say, what you doin' with yourself these days?"

"We were going on a long tour around the world but my father was taken ill—cancer. He's—very ill."

"Too bad—too bad," Chris said.

A customer stooped and, putting his head out the window, he bawled, "Fill her up—high-test—"

"What you doin' tonight?" Chris asked from the gasoline tank.

"Nothing—I just thought I'd look you up."

"Me and little ole Ruthie," Chris said, snickering.

To his surprise, Rannie felt a strange stir in his groin. "How is she?"

"Pretty," Chris said. "Too pretty for her own good—or mine. I might marry her one of these days, if she can ever be pinned down."

"But Chris, how old are you?" Rannie asked in astonishment.

"Fifteen—sixteen—somepin like that. My ma's never sure just what year it was she borned me."

"But Ruthie—"

"She's thirteen, but she's all dolled up to look sixteen. She's rare, she is. Lots of fellers—but she likes me best, she says—acts it too. I make good money here with my dad—ornery old cuss!"

"I'd better be home tonight," Rannie said. "I don't like to leave my mother alone just now."

"No, well, you're right at that, I guess. Gee, I'm sorry about your old man. But come again, will ya, Rannie?"

"Yes, thank you, Chris. It's good to see you."

"RANNIE!" HIS MOTHER WAS SHAKING him awake. "The doctor is here. Your father is—dying."

He leaped out of bed, instantly awake, and put his arm about her. She leaned against him for a few seconds and then drew him with her.

"We mustn't waste a minute," she said.

He followed her into the room where his father lay, stretched straight upon the wide old four-poster bed. The doctor sat beside him, his fingers on the dying man's wrist.

"He has lost consciousness, I think," the doctor said.

A whisper came from his father's stiff lips—

"No—I am still—here."

With effort he lifted his eyelids, searching.

"Rannie—"

"I'm here, Father."

"Susan—love—"

"I'm here, darling."

"Give our son—freedom."

"I know."

A silence came, so long that those watching thought it was forever. But no, his father had not finished with life.

"Rannie—"

"Yes, Father."

"Never give up—wonder."

"I never will, Father. You've taught me."

"Wonder," his father whispered, gasping for breath. "It's the beginning of—of—all—knowledge."

His voice stopped. A slight shiver shook his skeleton frame. Now they knew he was gone.

"Father!" Rannie cried, and seized his father's clasped hands in his own.

"It's over," the doctor said, and, stooping, he closed the glazing eyes. Then he turned to Rannie. "See to your mother, my boy. Take her away."

"I don't want to be taken away," his mother said. "Thank you, Doctor. Rannie and I will just stay here with him for a while."

"As you like," the doctor said. "I'll report the death and send someone to discuss details with you."

He shook hands with them gravely, kindly, and left them. They stood side-by-side, together and yet forever separate, as they looked down on the quiet figure of the man they both loved so well, yet each so differently. Memories, too, were altogether different, and so was the future each faced. What, Rannie was thinking, shall I do without him? Who will tell me the truth about everything or where to go to find the truth? Who will help me to know what I am and what I ought to be?

What his mother was thinking he did not know, because he did not yet know what love between man and woman was, although wonder was beginning. He could not wonder now for he wanted only to see his father in his memory as alive and strong. Instead here lay this still, inert figure of a man, a mere shadow of the man he had known and looked to for nearly everything for all of his life.

He turned to his mother, seeking comfort, thinking at this moment only of himself.

"Oh no," he sobbed. "No—no—no!"

His mother said nothing. She put her arms about him, and after a moment she spoke.

"Come," she said. "We can do no more for him now—except live as he wanted us to live."

And she led him away.

LIFE BEGAN AGAIN SOMEHOW. The few days before the funeral were a dull maze of grief, the funeral was an hour of incredible agony.

"Dust to dust—," the minister intoned at last, and he heard the dull thud of clods falling upon the coffin. He and his mother stood hand-in-hand, transfixed in horror, until someone, the minister or a neighbor, someone, led them away. Someone said, "This at least you need not endure."

And they left the others and were driven back to the house, which no longer seemed a home but only a house that happened to be theirs.

Someone said, "Tell me, would you rather have us stay with you or would you rather be alone?"

"Thank you—we'd rather be alone," his mother said. They were left then, alone in the house. The foolish dog leaped and jumped about them joyously, and neither of them could bear it.

"Put the dog in the garage," his mother said.

He put the dog in the garage and then came back to the kitchen and sat down at the table while his mother cooked something.

"Neither of us will be hungry," she said, "but I'll bake some gingerbread and make that special sweet sauce you like."

"Don't bother, please, Mother," he said.

"I'm better doing something," she said.

He sat in silence then, watching her and wishing he did not think of his father lying white and still under the newly piled earth. He tried indeed most earnestly to remember his father as he had been when he was well, the autumn days when they had tramped in the woods, the winter days when his father had taught him how to ski, the summer days when he had taught him how to swim. It seemed to him now that everything he had learned his father had taught him. Who would teach him now?

"It is terrible—terrible—terrible—"

The words burst from him and his mother stopped her stirring in the big yellow bowl and looked at him, spoon in hand.

"What are you thinking, son?" she asked gently.

"He's lying there all alone—in the ground—in the *ground*, Mother! There ought to be a better way."

"Yet I couldn't bear to think of his body—his beautiful, beautiful body—burned to ashes," she cried passionately. "A handful of ashes—no, I couldn't bear it. There'd be nothing left.

As it is—he's decently clothed, he's in a sort of bed—alone, of course."

Suddenly she began to weep in great, heaving sobs. She dropped the spoon into the bowl and covered her face with her hands. He leaped to her side and put his arms about her. He was as tall as her now, and suddenly he felt her small and in need of help and protection. But he did not tell her to stop crying. Somehow he knew better than that. He could no more take his father's place with her than she could take his father's place with him. They had to continue as they were, mother and son, sharing as much of life as they could.

As though she felt what he was thinking she suddenly stopped weeping. She lifted her head from his shoulder and pushed him gently aside, wiping her eyes with her apron.

"I must finish the gingerbread," she said.

He left her then and went upstairs to his own room and, drawing the armchair to the window, he sat watching the dusk change to darkness. He was not thinking, he was only feeling— feeling his loneliness, feeling his mother's loneliness, feeling the emptiness of the house, the emptiness of his world. He did not turn on the light but sat in darkness until his mother's voice called up the stairs.

"The gingerbread is just perfect, Rannie!"

Her voice sounded natural, and almost gay. He went downstairs then and into the brightly lighted kitchen.

"I've also made Irish stew," she said, "and a tossed salad. The gingerbread is for dessert."

She had set the table for their evening meal in the kitchen and this she had never done before. Until now they had always eaten dinner in the dining room. He could not imagine his father eating this meal in the kitchen. Now he sat down, glad that his mother had put these two places here, so differently from their usual meal. Suddenly he was very hungry and later was ashamed of himself that he ate every bit of the Irish stew and salad she put before him and still ate two huge helpings of the hot gingerbread and its sweet, spiced sauce. Afterward he felt full and sleepy and they went early to bed.

IN THE MORNING SHE SET the table again in the kitchen. He had not slept well, waking fitfully and often to think of his father lying alone on the hill. His imagination, always too quick to summon reality, brought to life before him the picture of his father's body lying in the grave. He saw, again, every detail of the dead thing once his father but now no more. He saw the closed eyes, the sternly set mouth, and even the pale folded hands. The hands were the most dead. His father had beautiful hands, strong and well shaped, active hands, working, gesturing, always expressive. The stillness of his father's hands he could not forget.

"Would you like scrambled eggs, Rannie?" his mother asked.

She was calm this morning. But he could tell by her eyes that she had wept in the night, unsleeping.

"Thank you, Mother," he said, and again was ashamed that he could be so hungry in the midst of sorrow.

His mother scrambled eggs and made bacon and set them before him. Then she went to the window and fetched a pot containing an amaryllis bulb. A handful of sturdy green leaves surrounded a thick stem that bore two open flowers, still in bud but almost ready to open. She set the pot on the table.

"Those two flowers opened yesterday," she said. "I wonder if the third one will open today. Three is the perfect number for amaryllis, I always think."

She spoke conversationally, almost as though he were a stranger, or only a neighbor, a visitor, but he understood that she was trying to begin life again, that she was determined not to weep again, at least in his presence, and he tried to help her.

"The bud looks as though it were ready to open now," he said.

He ate his breakfast slowly. His mother drank coffee and buttered a thin slice of toast.

"Won't you eat an egg, Mother?" he asked, suddenly anxious. She was all he had now. Their relatives were all far away and he did not know them except by hearsay.

"I will eat when I can," his mother said. "It will take time to get back to myself. Today I must get his clothes packed into boxes to send to the Salvation Army."

"Shall I help you?" he asked.

"No, dear," she said. "I think I want to do it alone. He wanted you to have all his books, of course. But you should use the study now as your own. Feel free to change it as you like."

He knew it was not easy for her to speak these words, but she was trying to do what his father wished—to give him freedom. But freedom for what?

Suddenly he noticed the amaryllis bud. It was already half-open! While they had been talking, between long silences, the bud had become almost a flower, though not quite full-blown. He pointed it out to his mother. She laughed, for a moment forgetting.

"Why, so it has," she exclaimed. "I never knew an amaryllis

bud could open so quickly. But then I've never sat in front of one just as I am sitting here now."

She gazed, half-dreaming, at the flower. "It's symbolic, some-how—the opening of a new flower at this moment when we're so sad. It means something—I don't quite know what—but as though your father were saying something to us. It's comforting somehow."

She looked at him wistfully. "Oh, Rannie, I do hope I'll be the sort of mother you need! I've always left you to your father since you were a baby, that is . . . because he's . . . he was so much wiser than I, and he knew you were no ordinary child. I hope . . . I hope I'll be able to . . . not of course take his place—that I could never, never do—but fulfill my own place as perhaps I haven't, because perhaps I haven't felt it necessary, but you must help me. You must tell me if there is anything I should be doing that I'm not doing, for it won't be lack of willingness, darling, but just that I don't know enough."

He met her pleading look with a tenderness he had never felt before. All his deepest love he had given to his father, but now he saw her separately, a childlike creature and yet a woman, of whose flesh he had been born and to whom in a way, too, he belonged.

"There is something you can do for me, Mother," he said.

"And that is?" his mother asked.

"I'd like to know everything about my father—everything— everything. I realized now that when we were together we always talked about me—or something *I* was thinking about. I was selfish."

"No, you weren't selfish," she said quickly. "He was simply— overcome with joy that he had a mind like yours to teach, to work with. He—he was—a born teacher and he revered a fine brain. He used to speak of your—your brain—as a treasure."

"But I want to know *him* now," he said.

She looked at him with a wondering love. "How could you know? . . ." she murmured.

"Know what, Mother?"

"That what you have just said comforts me as nothing else could! I'd never have thought of it myself—that I, *I* could keep him alive for you! I'll do my best—I'll remember everything. I can't all at once, you know, Rannie—but as one thing and another happens in our lives, I'll remember."

And in comforting her he himself was comforted. They had a way now to live, a purpose in their life together as mother and son. They would keep his father alive.

IT WAS NOW EVENING and they sat in the study. She had decided that the study was the room where it would be best for them to talk. It would bring his father nearer, she said. Nothing in the room was changed. On the desk his manuscript lay half-finished in his father's fine, close handwriting. Someday, his mother said, he, the son, would finish it. His father had allowed it and he had been reading it slowly, carefully, understanding and not under-standing the philosophy it proclaimed, and yet fascinated by it. Every scientist an artist? Every artist a scientist? What was the secret they held in common?

"Light the fire, son," his mother said. "There's snow in the air."

He stooped to set the lighter ablaze beneath the logs, as he had so often seen his father do. The logs were dry and the flames roared up the chimney.

"Sit in his chair, son," his mother said on this, the first of their evenings. "I like to see you sitting there."

He settled himself in his father's chair. He liked sitting there, his body settling into the hollows his father's body had shaped during the years.

"I met your father in college," his mother began. "I thought he was the handsomest man I'd ever seen. He wasn't the sports type, not the football hero and all that, though he played a sharp game of tennis. When he found I was the champion tennis player, he challenged me promptly. I beat him—"

She paused to laugh, her eyes suddenly sparkling. "I don't think he liked that too well. And I told myself I was a fool and probably he'd never want to see me again. But I was wrong. He told me afterwards, when we'd got to know each other quite well, that he liked me for doing my best against him. He thought he was pretty good, and he confessed to being mortified at being beaten by a girl, but he'd have thought the less of me if I'd done any pretending. That was one thing he was always firm about. 'I want the truth from you, Susan.' I can hear him say it now."

She paused, a half smile on her face, and looked across to him, sitting there in his father's chair. "I got the habit of truth, son—and I'll never tell you anything but the truth. Let's make it a bargain—truth between us for your father's sake."

"It's a bargain," he said.

She was silent for minutes, thinking. Then she began again, "I don't want to go too fast. I want to make it last a long time. There'll be evenings, too, when you want to do things. Evenings when we'll have to decide what we should do. What do you want to do, son? I don't think we ought to take the tour—we'll need the money for your college education, even though they will give you your tuition as a scholarship for your father's sake."

"I'll go to college," he said. "I can start at the beginning of the term in the New Year."

"But you're not thirteen yet—and all those older pupils—what will they do to you?"

"Nothing, Mother. I'll be too busy."

"But you'll miss all the fun of being your age."

"I'll have other things," he said briefly, but he did not know what things, so he urged her to go on with her story. "Go on, Mother."

"We soon fell in love," she went on shyly. "In those days love was something important—not like today. But he said we wouldn't be married until after his graduation. I was only a sophomore, but I didn't want to go on. I only wanted to be with him. So in June we were married. It was a lovely wedding, I was the only child in my family, and they all wanted me to have the prettiest possible wedding. Besides, they liked your father. That's one thing I didn't like about coming to Ohio, Rannie, after your father got his doctorate. It brought us far away—so that you haven't known my family. And since your father's parents were dead and he was an only child, there's been only the two of us to be your family."

"I haven't missed anything," he said.

She was silent a long time now, her eyes fixed on the fire, dreaming, remembering, half-smiling. He sat silent, waiting, inwardly restless, and yet not wanting to break into her thoughts.

It was to be true of all these evenings. She relived her life, dreaming, remembering, half-smiling while he sat waiting, inwardly restless. Suddenly she would look at the clock, astonished at the time.

"Oh, it's late," she would exclaim, and the evening was ended.

Each evening he sat there submissively, his eyes fixed on the fire, and as his mother's voice flowed on, broken now and again by laughter or a long sigh of remembrance, he enjoyed in himself the ability to see what she was saying. That is, as she finished describing an incident now long past, he saw it all as clearly as though taking place before him. He was aware of this ability, for as he read a book, whatever it was—and this had been always true ever since he could remember, or so it seemed to him—he saw what he read, and not the words or the pages on which they were printed. The ability had been of special value to him in school, always, and especially in mathematics, for when a problem was presented by his teacher or the textbook, he saw not the figures but the situation they presented and the relationship to the whole, so that he was ready with the answer immediately. Sciences, too, had been made very easy for him by this ability to visualize simultaneously as he read or listened.

So now he saw his father as his mother told of her life with him as a young man. It was actual seeing. He had this ability that he supposed everyone had, until he discovered later on in his life that it was unique, and that he could actually see, in shape and solidity, a person or an object of which he was thinking. As his mother described his father, he saw the tall young man, fair-skinned, fair-haired, quick to laugh but always ready to listen and to wonder. He had never told anyone of this visual ability, but now he told his mother.

"I see my father as he was, before I was born."

His mother stopped and gazed at him, questioning.

"He walks very fast, doesn't he? Almost running? He's very thin but strong. And he had a little clipped mustache, hadn't he?"

"How did you know?" his mother cried. "He did have a mustache when we first met, and I didn't like it, and he shaved it off and never let it grow again."

"I don't know how I know, I don't know how I see, but I know so well that I see."

His mother looked at him wistfully and in awe, and she waited.

"Sometimes," he went on almost unwillingly, "I think it is not good."

"For example?" she inquired when he paused.

"Well, in school, for example, especially in math, the teachers thought I was cheating when we were doing mental arithmetic. But I could see. I wasn't cheating."

"Of course not," his mother said.

He did not notice it then, and it was not until years later that he thought of it, but from this time on his mother told him no more of his father. She devoted herself to him, usually in a silence that was almost awe. She paid heed to his food, preparing him the most nourishing meals she could devise, and was anxious that he had sufficient sleep. But he forgot her. His mind was crowded with visions of creations. His thoughts were always of creations. But he ate voraciously, for his body was beginning to grow very fast. Until now he had been a boy of medium height. Suddenly, or so it seemed to him, he was nearly six feet tall, though he was not yet thirteen. He was so tall that it seemed to him he got in his own way. There was one advantage to this extreme height. It made him less conspicuous at the college. His face was still a boy's face, but his bones were gangling, and he was as lean as a big bird, and still he held his head high.

* * *

HIS PROBLEM WAS THE ETERNAL question: What should he be? Inventor, scientist, artist—the energy he felt surging through him, an energy far more than physical and yet pervading the restlessness of his body, was a burden to him until he could find the path for its release. He felt restrained and repressed. He sat in his college classes, holding himself in, forbidding himself the luxury of impatience with the slowness, the meticulousness of his teachers.

"Oh, get on," he muttered under his breath, his teeth clenched, "get on—get on."

He envisioned what they meant before they had finished a point. His imagination obsessed him. The very atmosphere was floating with ideas. He had so many ideas in the course of a day that he bewildered himself. How could he bring them into focus? What was this imagination of his, continually busy with creation but uncontrolled and perhaps uncontrollable? At least, he did not yet know how to control it and could not know until his will directed and compelled him to control his imagination.

So far as he could discover, none of his classmates suffered as he did. He had no friends, for mere friendliness, and he was by instinct eagerly friendly, did not mean friendship. He felt, at times, that he was in a desert alone, a desert of his own making merely because he was as he was. He had long ago outgrown his mother and he had almost ceased to think of his father. He was totally absorbed in the problem of himself and what direction he should give himself. He lived in absolute loneliness for most of his time at college.

One day in his third year, a chance remark of his professor in psychology class caught his attention.

"Most people," the professor said, "are merely adaptive. They learn as animals learn—a chimpanzee rides a bicycle, a mouse follows a maze. But now and then a man is born who is more than adaptive. He is creative. He may be a problem to himself, but he solves his problems through his imagination. Once his problems are solved, his mind is free to create. And the more he creates, the more free he is."

A sudden light broke across Rannie's mind. He sought out the professor after the class, lingering until every other student had left the classroom.

"I'd like to talk with you," he told the professor.

"I've been waiting for you to say that," the professor said.

"I SHAN'T BE HOME this evening," he told his mother. "I have an appointment with Dr. Sharpe. He's expecting me. I may be late—it depends."

"Depends on what?" his mother asked.

She had a quiet, penetrative way of asking questions. He looked at her, thinking not of her but of her question.

"I don't know yet," he said. "I don't know how the talk will go. If I don't learn anything from it, I'll be home early. If I do, I'll be late."

He ate his evening meal in the silence of abstraction. They had continued to eat their meals in the kitchen. While his father lived this meal had been the one formal occasion of the day, always set in the dining room. Breakfast was a brief pause at the kitchen table, luncheon a random sandwich, but his father liked the grace of dining at night with a change of garments, a table set with silver and china and a bowl of flowers. The dining room had never seemed too large for the three of them, but alone with his mother it was too large, too empty.

"I don't know Dr. Sharpe very well," his mother was saying.

"Neither do I, really," he replied. "It's good to have someone young with fresh ideas. I've known the other professors all my life, it seems. They're all right, of course, but—"

His mind took over again and he fell silent. His mother prodded him.

"But what?"

"But what?" he repeated. "Only that I like having something new. Especially if it's something I am already thinking about."

"And that is? . . ."

He glanced at his mother's questioning face and smiled, half shyly, "I don't know—creativity, I suppose!"

Half an hour later he was in Donald Sharpe's small living room. They were alone, for Sharpe was a bachelor and kept his own house, except for a cleaning woman once a week. It was a charming room, decorated with taste and design. Two French paintings, in the style of the Old Masters, hung on facing walls, and on a third, opposite the chimney piece, was a Japanese scroll. An easy chair covered in old gold velvet was on each side of the fireplace. The autumn was late autumn, the evenings were chill, and a wood fire scented the room.

He felt at ease and somehow comforted in this room as he had not been comforted since his father died. The gold velvet chair fitted his lanky body, and he liked its luxurious softness. Donald Sharpe sat opposite him, and on the small table beside him was a tall-stemmed wineglass.

"You're still quite young, Rannie," he had said, "but this is such a gentle drink that I don't think it will count."

So saying, he had poured a glass of wine for his visitor and Rannie had tasted it and set it down on the table beside his chair.

"You don't like it?" Sharpe asked.

"Not really," he replied honestly.

"It's an acquired taste, I suppose," Sharpe said.

That was how the evening began. Now it had progressed to solid talk, interspersed with long moments of working silence.

He was a handsome man in a dark way, almost too handsome, not tall, and with a feminine lightness of bone structure. His eyes were his most notable feature, large and dark under clearly marked brows, their gaze penetrative, bold, or stealthy by turns. He continued to speak.

"Of course imagination is the beginning of creation. Without imagination there can be no creation. But I'm not sure that explains art. Perhaps art is the crystallization of emotion. One has to feel an overflow. I write poetry, for example. But days and months go by—sometimes a year or even longer—when I write nothing, not a line, because I've felt nothing deeply enough to crystallize. There has to be a concentration of emotion before I can crystallize it into a poem. I feel a relief, actual relief, emotionally, when I've written the poem. I *have* it, I have something in my hand as solid as a gem."

His voice was beautiful, a baritone flexible and melodious. He leaned forward suddenly and with a total change of manner he put forward a question.

"What is your name—I mean, what do they call you at home?"

"My name is Randolph—Rannie for short."

"Ah, but I always choose a special name for someone I like very much—as I do you. I shall call you Rann—two *n*'s."

"If you wish—"

"But do *you* wish?"

"Rann—yes, I like it. I'm too big for diminutives."

"Much too big! Where were we? Emotion! It's still not at all clear to me, however, why we feel compelled to create art. I suppose it began in an awareness of beauty—dim, at first, perhaps merely surprise at a sudden sight of a flower or a bird. But the *ability* must have been there—the ability to perceive—which must have meant a step in intelligence, an awakening, a wonder."

He listened to Sharpe's voice in the same way he listened to music, half sensuously, and only now and again venturing to speak.

"But when did science begin?" he asked.

"Ah, very late," Sharpe replied. "Natural man, the uneducated mind, poetized in myth and dream before he analyzed, I suppose, contradictorily enough, science began with religion. Priests had to learn time-telling and so they had to match the seasons and the stars—accuracy, in a word, which is the basis of science—and this led to factual truth. Galileo laid the foundation of modern science, of course, experimentally speaking, using bodies in motion and measuring and observing until he affirmed a theory—*the* theory—that the sun was the center of the universe, for which he died in banishment. Later, Isaac Newton put this same theory into mathematics! Yes, science is creativity as much as art is—the two go together—*must* go together, for each is basic and indispensable to human progress."

Hours passed while he listened, now and then asking a question, but all the while yielding to the fascination of the man. The clock on the mantelpiece striking midnight startled him.

"Oh, I must go home—I still have a theme to finish for your class tomorrow, sir!"

Sharpe smiled. "I'll give you an extra day. You've given me a pleasant evening. It's not often that I have a listener who knows what I am talking about."

"You've clarified my own wondering and thinking, sir."

"Good! You must come again. A teacher keeps searching for the ideal pupil."

"Thank you, sir. The search is mutual."

They clasped hands, and Sharpe's hand strangely felt hot and soft. It surprised him and he withdrew his own hand quickly.

When he reached home, his mother was sitting up for him in the kitchen.

"Oh, Rannie, I was wondering—"

"I've had a wonderful evening. I've learned a lot. And—Mother!" He paused.

"Yes, Rannie?"

"I wish you wouldn't call me Rannie anymore."

"No? Then what? Randolph?"

"Just Rann—with two *n*'s."

"Very well—if you wish. I'll try to remember."

"Thanks, Mother."

She looked at him strangely, nevertheless, as though she were pondering a question. But he put off questions.

"Good night, Mother," he said, and was gone.

He was sleepless. Donald Sharpe had awakened his whole being. The question now focusing itself in his mind was himself. What was he, artist or scientist? He felt the impulse, the urge, the necessity to create somehow compelling him—but to what?

How could he know what to do when he did not know himself or who he was? How was this to be discovered? He felt a mighty impatience with going to school. What was the use of learning about the past, and of studying what other people had done? Yet was it not helpful to know what they had done? Galileo, for example, had been everything—musician, painter, scientist. But had he learned all this in school or had he learned by himself and for himself?

He was kept awake by his own questions. Around him the house was dark and silent. Downstairs in the dining room the old grandfather clock, which had belonged to his Dutch great-grandfather on his mother's side, twanged out the early morning hours, one and two and finally three. The moon sank below the horizon before dawn brought him to sleep. It was a troubled sleep, broken by confused dreams. But the confusion was dominated by the recurrent appearance of Donald Sharpe.

When he woke in the morning, the sun was streaming through the eastern window of his room. He woke in a strange and quiet peace, altogether different from the turmoil of the night. This peace, as he lay enjoying it, savoring its rest, centered about Donald Sharpe. He relived again the hours that had passed so quickly the night before. Not since his father's death had he enjoyed anything as much as the evening. Indeed, perhaps he had never had such enjoyment before; the stretching of his mind to meet Sharpe's had been stimulated by the charm of the man, his youth, his maturity, even his physical beauty stirred the very soul, an attraction beyond any person he had ever known. And this attraction was to a living person, someone who might become, perhaps already was, his friend. He had never had a real friend. Boys of his own age might be partners in sports and casual occupations, but he had met none with whom he could talk on terms of equality. Now he had a friend!

The certainty ran through his blood, an elixir of joy. He sprang out of bed and rushed to meet the day, a shower, clean clothes, an enormous breakfast. He had not been hungry for days. Now he could scarcely wait to get to his breakfast. His first class of the morning was with Donald Sharpe.

"YOU MUST PAY HEED to your conscious mind," Donald Sharpe said.

He stood before his class, a hundred or more students sitting before him, rising tier upon tier until the last row under the ceiling. He spoke to them all, but Rann, seated in the middle seat of the first row, met his warm, half-caressing gaze.

"Feed it and then heed it," Sharpe said, smiling. "The subconscious mind is different. Feed it by not heeding it. Let the subconscious mind be as free as a hummingbird in a flower garden. Did you ever watch a hummingbird? No? Next time watch! A hummingbird is the swingiest of birds. It darts here, there, everywhere, tasting this flower and that, trying one garden and another. So with your mind! Let it be free. Read anything, everything, go everywhere, anywhere, know something about everything and all you can about as many things, as many people, as many worlds, as you can. Then when you pose a problem, heed your subconscious mind. Wait for it to draw out of its stores the information you need, upon which you can base your decision. Sometimes the information you need will express itself in a dream while you sleep, or even in a daydream. I believe in daydreaming. Don't let your parents—and teachers—tell you that daydreaming is idleness. No, no—it gives the subconscious mind a chance to speak. Newton pondered gravity in many daydreams until one day a falling apple triggered his subconscious mind and told him that gravity was an interplanetary force. Two brothers—the Montgolfiers—were daydreaming before a fire they had lit on a chilly evening and they noticed that the hot air carried bits of paper up the chimney— why not a balloon of hot air to carry a man into the sky?

"And not only scientists, but artists use the subconscious mind. Coleridge dreamed his poem *Kubla Khan* before he wrote it, which he did the moment he woke—and forgot when a friend interrupted him, alas! Our modern artists, some of them, use the subconscious mind before it is directed into its crystal form—example: James Joyce in literature, Dalí in art—interesting, but perhaps too literal to convey meaning. The subconscious mind has to be pressured by need, by demand, before it will focus and produce the necessary information in organized form. This is the method of art."

Rann raised his hand and Sharpe nodded.

"Doesn't a scientist have to imagine, or dream, as much as an artist does—perhaps more? Because he knows so definitely what he wants to achieve."

"He knows," Sharpe said, "and therefore his search among his dream materials is directed. But sometimes it is not. Sometimes his focus comes out of wonder. Wonder—then ask why! That's a technique too—though a technician is not a pure scientist. Yes, I'd say a real artist and a pure scientist are related. Matter of fact, most top scientists are also musicians, painters, and so forth, as you will discover when you come to know them."

"Can artists be scientists?" Rann asked.

Question and answer sped between them like lightning and thunder.

"Yes," Sharpe said firmly. "Not basically in dream stuff, but artist imagination lays hold on any effect as material. Electronic sound produces a new kind of music, new color formations affect painters. The artist receives the new material, makes it his own, and through it expresses his reactions, his feelings."

"I see a difference between scientists and artists," Rann declared.

"Tell me," Sharpe commanded.

"Scientists invent, discover, prove. Artists express. They don't have to prove. If they are successful—"

"That is, if they communicate—," Sharpe interpolated.

"Yes," Rann said.

"Right," Sharpe replied. "You and I must talk about this further. Stay after class a moment." He glanced at his wristwatch. "Class dismissed."

To Rann, lingering at his desk, he said almost abruptly, "I have a committee meeting tonight. Come over tomorrow night about eight. If you have your theme finished, bring it to me."

"Yes, Dr. Sharpe," Rann said.

For a reason he could not explain he felt almost rebuffed, and he went away puzzled to the point, almost, of wound.

"YOU'RE NOT EATING," his mother said.

"I'm not hungry," he said.

She looked at him, surprised. "I've never known you not to be hungry. Do you feel sick?"

"No," he said.

"Has something happened today?"

"I went to my classes as usual, but I have a theme to write tonight. I keep thinking about it."

"What's it about?"

Her persistence drove him near to anger. "I don't know yet."

"What class is it for?"

"Psychology II."

"That's Dr. Sharpe."

"Yes."

She reflected briefly. "There's something about that man I don't like."

"Perhaps you don't know him well enough."

"He wasn't a special friend of your father's."

"Were they *not* friends?"

"I don't remember that I ever heard him speak of Donald Sharpe."

"They weren't in the same department."

"That's another thing. It would have pleased your father if you'd chosen his department—English."

"Father always wanted me to choose for myself."

He tried to keep irritation out of his voice, for he loved his mother in the depths of his being. On the surface of his life, his daily life in this house that he had shared with her as long ago as he could remember, she was beginning to irritate him in ways that made him ashamed and puzzled. He had always loved her wholeheartedly and simply with childhood love. Now his love was tinged with a sense of repulsion that was almost physical. He did not like to know that he had been formed in her womb, from whence he had emerged red with her blood. Especially he hated to hear her advocate breast-feeding when she spoke with young faculty wives in pregnancy.

"I nursed my baby," she would declare.

It sickened him to think of himself ever as a baby sucking at her full breasts, and that she was in fact a very pretty woman, her smooth fair hair scarcely gray, and blue eyes gentle, and her features finely cut, the mouth especially soft and tender. Her very prettiness added to his conflict about her. It seemed unnecessary, even unwise, for a mother to be so pretty that other people remarked on it, and since his father's death, especially, that men liked to talk with her, young or old they liked her, and this roused in him a cold sort of jealousy, for his father's sake.

In his instant and unavoidable imagination he saw the process of himself feeding at her breast, and tried not to see it. It had become disgusting to him. He wished that he could have been born in some other way and independently, out of the air, or chemically in a laboratory. As yet he was not attracted to women, and he avoided the memory of Ruthie's rosy organs, though sometimes, to his surprise, he dreamed of her, although he had not seen her for years, nor Chris, either.

Such facts he put away as he sat at his desk in his own room before his typewriter. His subject, which he wrote in careful capitals, was INVENTORS AND POETS.

"The dreams of poets," he began, "led to the inventions of scientists. A poet imagines himself in the body of a bird. What is it like to fly above the treetops, what is it like to soar in the sky? If he is only a poet, then he only dreams. But if he longs to make his dream come true, he imagines himself flying somehow just as he is, a man without wings. Yet wings, it is obvious, he must have if he is ever to fly and so he must manufacture wings. He must make a machine which will lift him from the earth. He dreams again but now of such a machine, and with his hands, guided by his dream, he tries until he succeeds in making an airplane. It may not be the same man who finishes the making of the machine. Many men worked on aircraft before one was successful, and the dream itself was as old as Icarus. But the dream came first. Dreamer and inventor both are necessary. They are the creators, the one of the dream, the other of its concrete and final form."

The thoughts poured into his brain, and his fingers flew to put them down. When the pages were finished—twenty pages, more than he had ever written before—it was midnight. He heard his mother pause at the door, but she did not open the door or even call. She merely paused; he thought he heard her sigh and then she went away. He was growing beyond her direction and she knew it. But then, so did he, and thinking about it as he made ready for bed, he became aware that he might feel lonely, thus separating himself from her as inevitably he must if he were to grow to be himself, except that he had a friend, a guiding friend, a man, Donald Sharpe. Tomorrow he would see him again. He would get up early and correct his theme and without copying it over, he would hand it in. And Donald Sharpe, his friend, his teacher, would say, "Come around this evening, and we'll talk about it."

He went to bed and was sleepless in a certain excitement.

"I SHAN'T CRITICIZE THIS, RANN," Sharpe said, ruffling the sheets of closely written paper.

"I want you to criticize," Rann said.

He was aware of Sharpe's powerful charm, resisted it and then succumbed to it. It was a combination he felt helpless to resist, an aura of the spirit, a scintillating intelligence shining through the dark eyes, a physical presence of attraction. He felt a strange new longing to touch Sharpe's hands, almost too perfectly shaped for a man's hands, the skin fine grained and smooth like the skin on his face, the bone structure sculptured and delicate in spite of size.

Sharpe glanced at him over the pages and flushed as his eyes met the boy's fascinated gaze. He put the papers on the small table beside his chair.

"What are you thinking, Rann?" he asked softly.

"I am thinking about you, sir," Rann said. He spoke in a daze of feeling that he could not comprehend.

"What about me?" Sharpe asked in the same gentle voice.

"You aren't like anyone I've ever known—and yet I don't really know you."

"No," Sharpe said. "You don't really know me."

He rose and came to Rann. He put his right hand under Rann's chin and tilted his face upward. Their eyes met in a long and silent gaze.

"I wonder," Sharpe said slowly. "I wonder if we are going to be friends."

"I hope so," Rann said.

"Do you know what I mean?" Sharpe asked.

"Not quite," Rann said.

"Have you ever had—a—friend?"

"I don't know," Rann said. "School friends maybe—"

"A girlfriend?"

"No."

Sharpe let his hand drop abruptly. He walked over to the long French window closed against a light rain that was changing to drifting snowflakes. He stood looking out across the darkening campus, and Rann, watching him, saw his hands clench behind his back. He did not speak, half-afraid to break Sharpe's silence. Then suddenly Sharpe turned and went back to his chair. His face was pale and set, his lips pressed together and his eyes averted from Rann. He took up the sheets he had laid on the table, and put them together.

"I don't want to criticize this yet," he said in his usual voice. "You have an excellent idea here—the relation between the creation of science and art—but you've dashed it off. I want you to take it back, think it through, and rewrite it. Yes, it's already well done, but you can carry it much further—complete it. Then when you've finished the creative work, we'll criticize it together, you and I. If it's as good as I think it will be, we might even get it published in a magazine where I publish some of my own stuff."

"Wouldn't it help me to hear your preliminary criticism, sir?"

"No. There must be no criticism during the creative process— not even self-criticism, Rann. Creation and criticism are antithetical and cannot be carried on at the same time. Remember that. You're a creator, Rann. Of that I now have no doubt. I envy you. Leave criticism to me. I'm a critic by nature, and a damn good teacher as a result."

He smiled and handed the sheets back to Rann. Then he stood up.

"Your mother will be wondering where the hell you are. I am responsible for delivering you safely into her hands. It's midnight. How the hours fly when one is—interested!"

He followed Rann to the door of the hall. There he paused, his hand on the knob. Still a few inches shorter, Rann, the boy, looked up and met the dark and tragic eyes of the man. Yes, tragic was the word. Sharpe's eyes were filled with sadness, though his lips smiled as he looked down upon the young and wondering face. Suddenly leaning forward, he kissed Rann's cheek.

"Good night—good night," he said, his voice a whisper. "Good night, my dear!"

"DID HE LIKE YOUR THEME?" his mother asked. She did not usually wait for him to come home because she knew he did not like it. It made him uneasy, or at least less free if he thought of her sitting there by the fire in the living room, waiting for him. But tonight she was there.

"It's only in rough form," he said. "I have to do some more thinking on it."

"What's it about?" she asked.

"I can't explain," he said shortly, and then, in apology, "I'm tired—we had a real session."

She rose. "You'd better go straight to bed. Good night, son."

"Good night," he said, and then, hesitating, he kissed her cheek as usual.

Each night he kissed her cheek with increasing reluctance, a childhood habit he wished he could break without hurting her. While his father lived, he had kissed them both, but now he wanted to be done with it. He went to his own room in confusion with himself. He did not want to kiss his mother, but he still felt on his own cheek the touch of the man's lips—Donald

Sharpe, his teacher and, he had taken for granted, his friend. The kiss remained there, at once repulsive and exciting. What did it mean? He knew that in some countries, in France, for example, men kissed men and it was merely a greeting. But this was not France. And he had never seen a man kiss a man. He, of course, was not yet fully a man, but he was fifteen, he was growing tall and he had to shave once in a while. He could not accept the kiss as casual. It was too unusual. He felt half-shy, half-pleased, but puzzled. Of course he knew things, his father had talked to him, but he had scarcely listened—he'd been interested at the moment in some project he had begun with turtles' eggs. He had found the eggs one Sunday when he and his father had walked, as they usually did on Sundays, outside the town in the fields. It had been spring and they had stopped at a pond and he brought the eggs home and hatched them in the garage, three of them at least, but the turtles had died.

He bathed now as usual before he went to bed and, lying full-length in the lusciously hot water, he surveyed his changing body with a new interest that he could not understand. It was the same body he washed every night, but tonight he was different. He felt a new life in his body, a sensitivity, an awareness, not yet an emotion but an awareness. Did the kiss mean some sort of love? Could this be possible? A sign of friendship, perhaps? But did men kiss when they were friends? In college he had no friends, since he was always so much younger than the others.

However his mind wandered, it kept returning to Donald Sharpe. He saw himself sitting in that library facing the man he so admired. He saw Sharpe's face, handsome in a delicate, vivid fashion; he heard the melodious voice, the rapid brilliant speech.

Then he saw himself at the door and felt again not only on his cheek but throughout his whole body the touch of Sharpe's lips. Alarmed, enticed, and half-ashamed, he got himself out of the tub abruptly and dried himself with quick, harsh rubbing of the big towel. In bed, his pajamas buttoned and the string fastened about his waist, he turned on the bedside light and took up the book he was reading, *Prodigal Genius: The Life of Nikola Tesla*, by John J. O'Neill. The powerful figure of Tesla absorbed him until he slept.

The next morning he felt a new impetus to rewrite his theme and make it as perfect as possible. His professor felt something special toward him, and he longed for Sharpe's praise and further criticism.

"TESLA," SHARPE SAID, "was of course the real genius—not Edison, although Edison was the better businessman and was clever at publicity. But Tesla was the creator at the most authentic pitch. He was a finely educated man, and Edison was not. Tesla had a profound knowledge of the past. It was at his service. When he established his own laboratory—it took him a while to realize he must have control of his own work—the whole world was astounded at all that poured out of it, the amazing inventions, the absolute proof that his complete alternating-current system had immense advantage over Edison's direct-current system. There's never been anything like it in importance—at least in the field of electrical engineering. Edison's system could only serve an area about a mile in diameter, while Tesla's system could transmit for hundreds of miles. . . . Are you listening to me, Rann?"

"Yes, sir," he said, but he was not. He was watching the mobile, handsome face opposite him. The fire burned between them, he on one side of the fireplace and Sharpe on the other. Outside, an early snowstorm wrapped the house in silence. There was no wind. The snow fell thickly, silently.

"The real problem," Sharpe continued, "was to find a man whose mind was large enough to comprehend and put to use the discoveries and inventions of a genius as great as Tesla's. Westinghouse was that man."

He put down the sheets of Rann's thesis. "It's a strange truth," he said, musing, "that every genius has to find his complement, the man who understands and can put to use what the creator creates. We don't seem to find creativity and its practical application in the same person."

He looked, half-smiling, at Rann's eager, listening face.

"What a beautiful boy you are," he said softly. The sheets slipped from his hands to the floor. "I wonder what we are to be to each other, you and I! Do you ever dream of love, Rann?"

Rann shook his head, entranced, shy, suddenly almost afraid—but of what?

Sharpe stooped and collected the sheets. He put them neatly together and placed them on the table beside his chair. Then he went to the wide window at the far end of his study and looked out. A streetlamp shone dimly through the all-but-impenetrable snow. He drew down the shade. "You had better spend the night with me," he said, returning to his chair. "Your mother will worry about your walking so far in this storm. So shall I. You may have my guest room. That's where my younger brother stays when he comes to visit me."

"I'll have to telephone my mother," Rann said.

"Of course. There's the telephone, on my desk. Tell her my Filipino houseman will give us a good dinner."

He took up the sheets and glanced over them one by one, seeming not to hear the conversation.

"He's invited me to stay because of the storm. But will you be all right, Mother?"

"Oh yes," his mother said, almost gaily. "Mary Crookes is here. She came in an hour ago—she was shopping and simply couldn't get home through the storm. She was just breathless when she reached our house. I'd asked her to stay, anyway. It's really not safe to be out alone in such a storm. The wind is beginning to blow a gale. I'll feel safe about you if you're with Dr. Sharpe. Good night, darling—see you tomorrow."

Rann hung up the receiver. "By chance she has a friend with her—someone who lives on the edge of town and came in to shop and got caught in the snowstorm."

"Splendid," Sharpe said absently as though he did not hear. "I've been looking over this paper again. You've done a brilliant job—really exciting. Ah, I hope I can be useful to you! I'm so sure you've a rare quality, Rann—I can't tell exactly what direction it will take. I don't know your center of interest. That's what makes a creator—to have an eternal, unchanging interest in something and the capacity for dedication to it—a life interest, something you know you were born to do."

"I want to know everything first," Rann said.

He caught Sharpe's look, a look yearning and strange, half-shy and half-bold.

"There is so much I don't know," Rann continued.

"There's so much I don't know about *you*," Sharpe retorted. He turned away and seemed absorbed in straightening the pages he held in both hands. "For example—your father is dead. Your mother is a shy woman. How are you to know anything about—let's say—sex? You're in for a great deal of temptation, my boy—women being what they are today—anything goes when they see a handsome young man. I wonder if you know how to protect yourself. It would be so disastrous to your development if you should imagine yourself in love with some girl—or woman, even, for it's more likely that a brilliant young mind is drawn to an older woman—well, the disaster would be the same. And you're so *vulnerable*, dear, with your extraordinary imagination! If I can save you from something like that, merely by being your friend—"

"I don't know any girls," Rann said bluntly. "As for older women—" He shook his head. This discussion was distasteful to him.

Sharpe laughed. "Well, just let me know when and if, and I'll come to your rescue!"

HE WENT TO BED THAT NIGHT with a warm sense of comfort and of mental and spiritual stimulation. Not since his father's death had he spent such an evening. Perhaps never had he spent such an evening, for Sharpe had a sense of humor that even his father had lacked. Moreover, Sharpe had traveled in many parts of the world, in remote parts of India and China, in Thailand and Indonesia, and he had tales to tell of experiences amusing or perilous. He had spoken again and again of love.

"Those ancient people understand the arts of love as we will not in a thousand years. We are a very crude people, dear boy. Perhaps 'simple' would be a kinder word. As for sex, we have only a primitive notion of its full expression as a means of communication between two persons. Boy plus girl equals sex—that's about as far as we go. We know nothing of the subtle interplay between two minds, two personalities, the art of physical approach and caress between two persons, whatever their sex. Sex itself is nothing—the lowest animals practice it. It is ennobled only by those who understand it as the Asians do—sex refined by centuries of experience, by poets and artists."

When they parted for the night he had withdrawn somewhat shyly, lest Sharpe kiss his cheek again. But Sharpe had not done so. He had merely put out his right hand.

"Good night, dear boy. Sleep well in that vast old bed that belonged to my great-grandfather in Boston. By the bye, you'll find the bath salts in your bath very refreshing. I put a bottle there for you. I use them myself—something I discovered in Paris last year. Dream sweetly, dear boy. Breakfast is at eight—just right for our nine o'clock class—if we can stagger through the snow in the quadrangle!"

He had tried the bath salts in his hot tub almost with embarrassment, unaccustomed to the heretofore feminine aspects of such pleasures, and had been surprised at the strong bittersweet fragrance that made him feel clean and stimulated. The soap, too, was unfamiliar, an English soap, generous with foam so that he soaped even his hair. When he was saturated with the hot fragrant bath he rubbed himself dry with an enormous brown towel and put on, somewhat hesitatingly, the white silk pajamas laid out on the bed. The silk against his skin, the smoothness of linen sheets when he drew the soft, light blankets over him, surrounded him with a sense of luxury. A wood fire burned under the white painted mantelpiece.

"I told my houseman to light a fire for you—it's to sleep when the wood falls into embers," Sharpe had said. "Besides, that room is large enough to be chilly on a snowy night like this—"

There was no chill now, however, and he put out the bedside light and lay watching the fire die while the snow beat softly against the windows and piled high upon the outer sills. He wanted to lie long awake so that he might think over all that Sharpe had talked of during the evening. He had felt his world enlarging, a wonderful world that he had seen heretofore only through books. But Sharpe had been everywhere himself. He had trod the streets of Indian bazaars, had lived in small inns in Japanese villages, had climbed Fujiyama and gazed into its sleeping crater. Yet later, on the isle of Oshima, he had looked into a living volcano and had felt the crust of earth tremble beneath his feet.

"Five days later the whole edge upon which I stood cracked off and fell into the smoking abyss," Sharpe had said.

His memory, always ready to present the total picture of whatever his thought summoned, roamed in kaleidoscope about the world. Why did he stay here in this little town, a dot upon the map, his life buried in books, when reality waited for him everywhere in the world? Time enough for books when he grew too old to wander!

"You need to know everything," Sharpe had said. "Whatever you can find in books is all to the good. Books are a shortcut to total knowledge. You can't learn everything by your own experience. Use experience to test what you have already learned in books—"

But why shouldn't he write books from experience? All his life he had read books. "I don't remember when you learned to read," his mother loved to tell him fondly. "I think you were born knowing how to read."

To write books—that would give meaning and purpose to all that he might experience! When he was five, he had wanted to learn to play the piano, and he played it well now, but it was not his work. Composition, perhaps, might be, but not merely to play the works of others, however great, and he had composed music just as he had written poetry. But books, solid books, putting into permanent and lasting form what he knew by experiences and could therefore communicate. He saw books, already written, standing in a stately row upon a shelf, living their own life long after he was dead. With this solemn and imposing vision clear in his mind, he drifted into sleep. The coals in the fireplace died to ashes and outside the snow continued to fall.

HE WAS WAKENED, SLOWLY AND GENTLY sometime in the night, by a hand stroking his thighs and moving, ever so slowly, ever so gently to his genitals. At first he thought it a dream. He was beginning to have strange new dreams, not often, for his rapid and extraordinary physical growth, combined with his incessant reading and studying, his obsession with learning everything as quickly as possible, had consumed his energy. But he wakened suddenly when he felt his body respond to the moving hands. He sat up abruptly, and by the light of a newly lighted fire, he was face-to-face with Sharpe. They stared at each other for a long instant, Sharpe smiling, his eyes half-closed. He was wrapped in a red satin robe.

"Leave me alone!" Rann muttered between his teeth.

"Do I frighten you, dear boy?" Sharpe asked softly.

"Just leave me alone," Rann repeated.

He pushed Sharpe from him and wrapped the blanket about his lower body.

"I introduce you to love," Sharpe said gently. "There are many kinds of love. All love is good. I learned that in India."

"I am going home," Rann said sternly. "Kindly leave the room so that I can dress."

Sharpe stood up. "Don't be absurd. The snow is two feet deep."

"I'll walk it."

"You are being childish," Sharpe said. "We were talking of experience. All evening—we were talking of the necessity of experience. When I offer it to you in the form of a sophisticated love, as old as Greece itself and of Plato, you are afraid. You want to run home to your mother."

"Perhaps you are right, Dr. Sharpe. Perhaps I am being childish. There is really no reason for me to go home in a snowstorm. It's just that this has taken me quite by surprise and I do not wish to pursue the subject any further, so it seems best that I leave."

Sharpe sat in the chair by the fireplace and watched Rann. "Again I say, don't be absurd. The snow is nearly two feet deep. You have said you don't wish to pursue the subject any further, so that's all there is to it. I'll go to bed and leave you quite alone. After all, I have my own pride, you know."

"I'm sure of that, Dr. Sharpe, and I'm equally sure I can believe you will not bother me again."

"You can be sure of that, Rann. Now I'll go to bed. Good night, dear boy, and I'm sorry, or perhaps I'm sorry for my sake and not for yours, that things cannot be different."

When Donald Sharpe left the room, Rann tried to put the events of the evening into some sort of order so he could understand what had happened. It was of no use, for he could not understand. He was desperately tired, he was sick with anger, with disappointment, and to his astonishment and horror, he burst into weeping as soon as he put out the light and drew the covers about his shoulders. He had not wept since his father died, but these were bitter tears too. He had been wounded, he had been insulted, his body violated—and he had lost the friend in whom he had believed with all his heart and soul. Moreover—and this shocked him to new knowledge of himself—his body, while he slept, had physically responded to the stimulation. He was angry with himself, too. Of course he could not continue now with college. What if Sharpe wanted to explain, apologize, try to establish some sort of relationship again? He, himself, was too embarrassed by his own response to even think of it.

He returned to his own home early the following day.

"I'm going away for a while," he said to his mother, trying to speak calmly.

His mother looked across the table at him, her blue eyes opened wide. "Now? In the middle of the school term?"

He was silent for a long moment. Suppose he told her about last night? He decided against it for now. The conflict within him was too great. He had to think through the whole relationship with Donald Sharpe—his admiration for the man quite apart from the experience of last night. Would he have told even his father, had he been alive? A year ago, yes, he would have told him. But now, maturing as he was, and he was mature enough to recognize how much of this was due to the many hours he had spent with Sharpe, he felt he would not have confided last night's experience even with his father. He recoiled from the physical disgust he felt for Sharpe as he thought of him and would recoil at any memory of it forever, but he wanted time to understand why a man of Sharpe's brilliance and, yes, goodness—could stoop to so physical an act. Perhaps he would never understand; if not, then he must try to understand himself, and why, hating the act, he was surprised to realize that he did not hate the man. But the shock, the horror, was too recent. He needed time to sort out his feelings.

"Yes, now," he said to his mother.

"Where will you go?" she asked.

He could see that she was trying to hide her consternation, perhaps even her fear. Her lower lip quivered.

"I don't know," he said. "Southward, perhaps, so that I can be out-of-doors."

She said no more and he knew why. Long ago he had heard his father tell her. "Don't push the boy with your questions. When he is ready to tell us, he will tell us."

He had been grateful many times for this advice, and never more grateful than now. He rose from the table.

"Thank you, Mother," he said gently, and went upstairs to his room.

IN THE NIGHT HE WAKED and lying quiet, his eyes opening wide, he saw his mother standing beside his bed, wrapped in her long white flannel robe. He turned on the bedside lamp and saw her looking at him.

"I can't sleep," she said wistfully.

He sat up in bed. "Aren't you feeling well?" he asked.

"I feel a heaviness here," she said, crossing her hands on her breast.

"A pain?"

"Not physical," she said. "A sadness, a loneliness. I could bear more easily your going away if I knew what had happened to make you want to go."

He was instantly wary. "What makes you think something has happened?"

"You're changed—you're very changed." She sat down on the bed so that they were face-to-face. "It was such a mistake that it was your father who died and not I," she went on in the same tone. She had a girlish voice, very young and gentle. But she was not old. She had been only twenty-two when he was born and she looked younger, especially now with her curly red-gold hair about her face and on her shoulders. "I should have been the one to die," she repeated mournfully. "I'm not capable of helping you. I know that. I can quite understand why you can't confide in me. It's probably true that I wouldn't know how to help you."

"It is not that I don't want to confide in you," he protested. "It's that I don't know how. It's so—unspeakable."

"Is it about a girl, darling? Because if it is, I've been a girl myself and sometimes—"

"That's just it. It's not about a girl."

"Is it about Donald Sharpe?"

"How did you know?"

"You've been so different since you knew him, Rannie—so wrapped up in your friendship. And I was glad. He's brilliant, everyone says. I've been happy that he was teaching you—being like an older brother, but—"

She broke off and sighed.

"But what?" he asked.

"I don't know," she said, her voice troubled, her face concerned, her eyes searching his face.

He yielded then, but uncertainly, word by word. He was compelled to tell her now that they were alone in the darkness of the night. He was compelled to share the weight of his memory of the night before, when Donald Sharpe had suddenly become a stranger from whom he must escape.

"Last night—," he began haltingly, and stopped.

"In Donald Sharpe's house?" she asked.

"Yes, I was in his guestroom. I was asleep. We'd had a wonderful evening talking about science and art and which direction I might want to take. It was long after midnight before we noticed. Then he took me to my room and we said good night. He came in to see that everything was all right. Then he went away. He'd had his Filipino manservant put a pair of his white silk pajamas on the bed—a huge four-poster bed. After my bath I put them on. I'd never worn silk next to my skin before—so soft, so smooth . . . I fell asleep soon. I must have slept quite a long time. The fire was burning when I went to bed—very brightly when I turned off the bed light. There was a volume of Keats on the bedside table, I think, but I didn't read. I just lay watching the fire die and I went to sleep. When I woke—"

He paused so long that she prompted him gently. "When you woke—"

He flung himself back on the pillow and closed his eyes.

"I was waked—"

"By *him*?" she asked.

"By someone—smoothing my thighs—and then . . . touching me . . . there. I felt—response. I thought it was one of those dreams—you know!"

"Yes, I know," she said, her voice very low.

"It wasn't a dream. By the light of a newly lighted fire I could see his face. I felt his hands . . . compelling me—against my will. I hated myself. I leaped out of bed. I was so angry—at myself, Mother! How can the body respond to what one hates and finds disgusting and repulsive? I was frightened—at *myself*, Mother!"

There—he had told her. He had put it into words. It would never again be a secret he had to carry alone. He lay, his hands clasped behind his head, he opened his eyes and met her tender, pitying gaze.

"Oh the poor, poor man!" she whispered.

He was astounded. "You're sorry for *him*?"

"And who could not be sorry for him?" she retorted. "He's in need of love where he can never find it—never truly find it because it's against human nature. Male and female God created us, and when a poor man tries to find that love with a man or a boy, he's doomed to sorrowfulness. However he excuses himself saying that to love and be loved is the importance in life, he knows he'll only find a poor warped sort of love. It's like a male dog mounting a male dog. There's no fulfillment. Oh yes, it's *him* I'm sorry for, my son. Thank God you weren't a little boy, beguiled by a toy or an ice-cream cone or something—perhaps just fear or even pleasure. Thank God you were old enough."

"But myself, Mother . . . how could I—my—my body respond to his . . . touch . . . when I hated it? That's what frightened me."

"Don't blame yourself, son. *You* didn't respond. The body has its own mechanism. You've learned a lesson—your body has its separate being and your mind, your will, must be in control, ceaselessly, until the time when it is right for body to have its way. Oh, how I wish your father were here to explain such things to you!"

"I understand already," he said, his voice very low.

"Then you must forgive Donald Sharpe," she said resolutely. "To forgive is understanding."

"Mother, I can't go back to school here."

"No, I can see that. Let's take a bit of time, though, to think. You could stay home a day or two. We mustn't decide too fast just where is the right place."

He sighed. "So long as you see I must go away—"

"We'll agree on that," she said. She leaned over him and kissed his forehead. "Now I can sleep, and you must sleep too."

She closed the door softly, and he lay for a few minutes, relieved of his anger, his shame, his sense of guilt. Though he felt now he never wanted to see Donald Sharpe again, he felt also a loss. He would miss him in spite of all. There had been communion between them, and he had supposed it would last forever. Now he felt a loss, a desolation. Who was his friend? His mother, of course, but he needed more. He needed friends.

Lying alone in his bed, his hands clasped behind his head on his pillow, he remembered a warning his father had given him shortly before he died. With his gift of envisioning, he remembered. He was sitting beside his father, lying on the living-room couch. His father's voice was weak, for he was near the end of his life and they both knew it. He knew, too, that his father was trying to tell him in that short time before death came that which he needed years to tell—the years that were not to be.

"You will be solitary, my son. The solitary creator is the source of all creation. He has produced all the most important ideas and works of art in human history. Lonely creators—you will be one of those. Never complain of being lonely. You are born to be lonely. But the world needs the solitary creator. Remember that. One-man creation—it shows that above all you are capable of greatness. What inspiration!"

LYING IN HIS BED, SLEEPLESS, he reviewed his life as he could remember it, a brief life in years, but somehow old. He had read so many books, he had thought so many thoughts, his mind constantly teeming with ideas—and here, with his ability to visualize, he suddenly remembered the goldfish in the pool under a willow tree in the garden, and how in the first warm days of spring when the sun shone, the water was moving and alive with flashing gold as the fish swarmed out of the mud where they had sheltered during the winter. That, so he thought, was a living picture of his mind, always flashing and moving with glittering thoughts, pushing for exploration. He was often exhausted by this mind of his from which he could find no rest except in sleep, and even his sleep was brief, though deep. Sometimes his mind waked him by its own activity. He envisioned his brain as a being separate from himself, a creature he must live with, an enchantment but also a burden. What was he born for? What was the meaning and the purpose? Why was he different from, say, Chris? He had not seen Chris since that brief visit shortly before his father had died. Some two years had passed since, years during which he had been pushing his way through college. Now, before he began again in some other place, if he began again, it occurred to him to go and find Chris, in curiosity and with a desire to return, however briefly, to the past. His mind thus resolved itself and allowed him at last to sleep.

"HI," CHRIS SAID, coming out of the garage. "What can I do for you?"

"Don't you know me?" he asked.

Chris stared at him. "I don't recollect you."

"Have I changed so much? I'm Rannie—Rann, nowadays."

Chris's face, grown round with added weight of years and food, broke into a grin.

"Well, I'll be damned," he said slowly, "I'll just be damned. But you're twice as tall as you was. You sure have shot up."

"Like my father," he said. "Remember how tall and thin he was?"

Chris looked concerned. "Say, I sure was sorry to hear about him. Come on in. I don't get real busy until around noon when the trucks come in on their way to New York."

He followed Chris into the garage. They sat down. "I'm the owner now," Chris said, trying to be offhand.

"Congratulations," he said.

"Yes," Chris continued. "Happened last year when Ruthie and I got married. Remember Ruthie?"

Did he not? He had never forgotten the glimpse he had had of that rosebud organ, in childish ignorance that was scarcely old enough to be curiosity. He wondered if Ruthie remembered.

"Of course I remember," he said. "She was so pretty."

"Yeah," Chris said proudly, but pretending carelessness. "I had to marry her to keep the crowd away. She's pretty, all right. In fact"—he paused for a short laugh—"she was so damned pretty that our kid's coming a little too soon. We had to hurry the wedding. Course, there was no question I wanted to marry her, but we had to hurry everything. This here garage—I might have waited another year or two—our folks had to help out. But—"

He slapped his knees. "It's done. I'm on my way, I'm makin' out. Business is good here on the truck route." He glanced at the open door. "Here comes Ruthie now, bringin' me a hot lunch. Have a bite with me? There's always plenty. She don't skimp on anything, Ruthie don't. She's a damned good kid."

Ruthie reached the door and hesitated, basket in hand.

"I didn't know you had company," she said.

"Come in, hon," Chris shouted. "Guess who this is!"

She came in, and set the basket on the table beside Chris, and stared.

"Did I see you before?" she asked.

Yes, she was pretty as ever, he thought, her face fuller but almost as childlike as he remembered. But her body was the body of a woman ready to give birth. The mystery of birth! He had scarcely thought of it yet. He had scarcely thought of women, his life so much the life of his mind.

"Yes, you have seen me before," he said.

They waited while she continued to stare at him. Then she shook her head.

"I don't remember you," she said.

He felt a quick relief. She did not remember him. Probably

there had been many episodes, none as childish as the one he remembered so vividly.

"He's Rannie!" Chris shouted, laughing at her puzzlement. "'Member little ole Rannie in school? Always knowin' all the answers? You sure were a damned know-it-all, Rann—makin' fools out of the rest of us. We didn't like you too well for it in them days either."

"You wouldn't like me any better now," he said in a quiet bitterness.

"Aw, it don't matter now," Chris said with kindly warmth. "I got my garage. I got my girl—what else do I need? I make good money."

Ruthie sat down, her eyes still gazing. "You've changed," she announced. "I wouldn't of known you anywhere. Didn't you used to be sort of runty?"

"Naw, he wasn't ever runty—he was just a kid besides us—too smart for us, I reckon. Well, it takes all kinds. What'd you bring? Pork and beans—enough for an army! Have some, Rannie."

He rose. "No, thanks, Chris. I must be on my way, I'm leaving town—"

"Goin' where?"

"New York first—Columbia, perhaps. I am to finish in another year. Then I may go on to my doctorate. I haven't decided."

Chris let his jaw drop. "Say, how old are you now?"

"Fifteen."

"Fifteen!" Chris echoed. "Hear that, Ruthie? Still a kid and talkin' about bein' a doctor!"

He opened his mouth to explain, "not a medical doctor," and then did not explain. What was the use? These were not his people.

"Good-bye," he said. He put out his hand to Chris and then to Ruthie. "I'm glad I came by before I went." They were warm, they were honest, they were kind, but they were not his people and he went away leaving them behind forever.

"WHEREVER YOU GO, SON," his mother had begged him, "stop and see my father—your grandfather—in New York City. He lives alone there in a little apartment in Brooklyn. I don't know why. He rarely writes to me now. When he came back to America after my mother died, he went to the city where he was born. He said he'd always wanted to live there and to live alone. I've felt badly about it—but he was never like anyone else. Sometimes I wonder if you take after him!"

He did not promise that he would seek out his grandfather. He did, however, go to New York and take a room at a small hotel—simple but to him horrifyingly expensive, although his mother had given him the money on which they had once planned to go to Europe before his father died. It was a long, narrow room, "self-contained," the landlord called it, because at one end there was a small gas stove, a smaller refrigerator, and a sink with a cold-water faucet. Down the dark and dusty hall upon which it opened there was a communal bathroom in which beside the toilet was an old four-legged bathtub. But the room itself was furnished after a fashion, and the bed was clean. The landlord, an ancient bearded Jew who wore a small black cap on his head, was proud of the room.

"You can see a tree outside the window when spring comes," he said. "A wild tree to be sure; no one planted it, but it grows bigger every year down there out of a crack in the cement."

This was to be his home then for how long he did not know. For he had not yet made up his mind to go to any school or college, in spite of what he had told Chris. Teachers were not to be trusted. No one was to be trusted. He would live alone and learn. Somewhere in this endless city there were books, a library, museum, and these would be his schoolrooms, these and the streets. There was everything here in the city. He was not ready even to see his grandfather. He had not realized how much he needed to be alone and free—free even of school and teachers. He decided not so much consciously as instinctively, that he would not go back to college nor think of doctorates and degrees. He wanted to learn about life, learn through living. Suddenly he realized that he knew nothing—nothing at all.

HE WAS NOT LONELY BEING ALONE, for all his life he had been lonely, and now he did not notice that he was any more so. Now, since there was no one who knew him and he knew no one, he could think his thoughts undisturbed. He did not so much think as wonder. Wonder was his atmosphere, wonder at all he saw and heard. The city enveloped him as the sea envelops a fish. He rose early, for in the early morning the city was different from the city at noon or in the evening and the night. The streets were clean, for all night great machines had marched ponderously to and fro, sweeping with great insulating brushes or spouting splashing falls of water that spread over the asphalt and ran gurgling down the drains. In the morning the air was cool. If the wind blew in from the sea, the air was almost pure, but that was before people poured into the streets, before great trucks came lumbering in from the highways, filled with food and goods and spewing out of their tails a foul, thick smoke, before cars and cabs raced each other against the changing streetlights.

He liked to go early to the river, which ran down to the sea. He enjoyed the fish markets and the sellers and buyers of fish of every kind. This was all so new to him, for he was an inlander, born and bred. Most of all he loved the ships. Someday he would sail in a ship across the Atlantic Ocean. But for now this city was huge enough for him to explore. With his already trained and disciplined mind, he divided the city into its parts, racially and nationally. Not all of these people spoke English, and he would try to find out from what part of the world they came—Puerto Ricans, speaking Spanish? It did not wound him, or even touch his real being when they cursed him with strange curses because he was white and different from them. He understood instinctively, with his envisioning mind, why they could naturally hate him. Why not? They had reason to hate him. And the blacks he studied with endless wonder, wandering through their streets, watching them, listening to them with their strange mouthing of the English language so that he found them more difficult to understand than the Puerto Ricans, even though the latter spoke an impure Spanish. The blacks were different from all the others. He felt it, he knew it. With his orderly, comprehending mind, he knew it.

DURING THOSE WEEKS, NOW FAST ACCUMULATING into months, he continued to live alone and yet not alone among the millions of people who surrounded him. He had a habit of talking with anyone who happened to be near him, asking his countless questions, storing the answers, short or long, into the bottomless wells of his memory, without thought of what use he would make of all he learned. He asked, he listened, he stored, and prompted by his endless capacity for wonder, he continued his life, knowing that this was only a passing moment in the many years. He wrote to his mother regularly, but, as he explained, he had not yet had time to look for his grandfather. His supply of money scarcely dwindled, for he was frugal, eating gargantuan meals but of simple and cheap food, and from time to time earning money by temporary jobs, usually on the wharves, loading and unloading ships. Still trusting no one, he kept his money in a few large bills, hidden on his person or under his pillow at night. He was friendly to his neighbors in passing, but he continued to make no friends. He did not miss friends now, for he had never had them, his thoughts always far beyond theirs.

So time might have continued for him, except for an experience he had one night, near midnight, which made him feel the need of someone to know, someone related to him. He had been to an opera at the Metropolitan, climbing to a seat high under the roof, from whence the figures moving upon the stage were dwarfs. But the music floated upward, the voices superb and pure, and this was what he had come to hear, standing in line for hours before to buy his ticket. He had stumbled downstairs at the end in a dream of delight, and alone in the masses of people pouring out of the doors, he decided against the subway and chose instead to walk, the night being clear and the moon full. At a corner of a dark, half-empty street he waited for the red light to change to green. Standing there, he became aware of a young man, almost a boy—so young he was—slender, his dark hair long over his pale face, approaching him.

"Hi," the boy said. "You goin' somewheres?"

"To my lodging," he replied.

"Haven't a quarter, have you?" the boy asked.

He felt in his right-hand pocket, found the coin, and gave it to the boy.

"Thanks," the fellow said. "This'll buy me a bite to eat."

"Don't you work?" he asked.

The boy laughed. "Call it work," he said carelessly. "I'm on my way now to where the nightclubs are. I'll pick up five dollars—maybe ten."

"How? If you don't work—"

"You mean you don't know? Where'd you come from?"

"Ohio."

"No wonder you don't know nothin'! See—this is how a feller does it. I pick a guy—rich, by himself—and I ast him for ten dollars, five if he ain't so rich. He looks at me like I'm crazy—maybe tells me to get outta his way or somepin. Then I tell him if he don't give it to me I will go to a policeman—always do it when I know there's a policeman 'round the corner—like. I tell him I'll tell the cop he propositioned me."

"Propositioned you?"

The boy laughed raucously. "Golly, you're only a kid! Don't you know? Some guys like girls, some like boys. On'y difference is, it's a crime to like a boy. So the guy knows this will make him big trouble so sooner than get into that kind of trouble, the guy'll give me the money first."

"You make your *living* like that?"

"Sure—easy and no work. Try it and see."

"Thanks—I'd rather work."

"Suit yourself. It ain't easy to get a job. You got folks?"

"Yes. My grandfather."

"Okay—so long. I see a guy comin'—"

The boy ran down the street to a restaurant, from whence a well-dressed man had just come. The man paused, shook his head, and the boy ran to the corner where a policeman stood.

Rann waited no longer. Suddenly he wanted to know his grandfather. Tomorrow, early, he would find him. He no longer wanted to be alone in this wilderness city.

THE ADDRESS WAS IN BROOKLYN and he had not yet been to Brooklyn. He disliked the subway and he liked to walk, especially in the early morning, when the air was still clean and the streets were almost empty. Only great trucks lumbered in from the countryside, bearing their loads of fowl and vegetables and fruits, eggs and meat. He stopped to saunter through Wall Street, that narrow center of the city's financial heart. He lingered to peer through the iron fence of an ancient cemetery set about an old smoke-blackened church, Fraunce's Tavern—he knew its history, and paused to stare at its sign, its doors not yet open for the day. And reaching at last to the great Brooklyn Bridge, he stood gazing into the flowing water beneath. The ships, the barges, were on their way. He saw it all in his usual, absorbed fashion, in his habit of wonder, each sight sinking into the depths of mind and memory, and deeper still, into his subconscious, somehow, sometime to emerge when he needed it, whole or in fragment.

Thus he followed one street and another, having studied his map well before he came. He did not like to ask his way, he liked to find it and for that he learned to memorize a map visually so that he always knew where he was. Thus in time, before the sun had reached the zenith of noon, he found himself standing before an old but very clean apartment house. The street was quiet and lined with trees now beginning the first autumn coloring.

He entered the building and found an old doorman in a gray uniform, asleep in an armchair, its brocaded upholstery rich and soft.

"Would you please—," he began.

Instantly the old man woke. "What do you want, boy?" he asked, his voice quavering with age.

"My grandfather lives here—Dr. James Harcourt."

"Does he expect you? He don't usually get up until afternoon."

"Will you tell him his grandson, Randolph Colfax, is here from Ohio?"

The old man heaved himself stiffly from his chair and went to the house telephone. In a few minutes he was back.

"He says he's still eatin' his breakfast but you can come up. Top floor, to the right, third door. I'll run you up. The elevator's over here."

The vehicle conveyed him to the top floor, and he turned to the right and knocked on the third door. There was an old-fashioned brass knocker and a small engraved card was fastened to the center panel of the mahogany door—JAMES HARCOURT, PHD, MD. And now the door opened and his grandfather stood before him, a white linen napkin in his hand.

"Come in, Randolph," he said, his voice surprisingly deep and strong. "I've been expecting you. Your mother wrote me you were coming. Have you had your breakfast?"

"Yes, sir. I got up early and walked."

"Then sit down and call it luncheon. I'll have some eggs scrambled freshly."

He followed the tall, very thin old figure into a small dining room. The oldest man he had ever seen, wearing a spotless white jacket over black trousers, came into the room.

"This is my grandson," his grandfather said. "And Randolph, this is my faithful manservant, Sung. He attached himself to me some years ago because I was able to—ah, do him a small favor. Now Sung takes good care of me. Eggs, Sung, scrambled, and fresh coffee and toast."

The old man bowed deeply and went away. Still standing, he met his grandfather's electric blue eyes.

"And why have you waited so long to come to me?" his grandfather demanded. "Sit down."

"I really don't know," he answered. "I think," he continued after a few seconds of thought, "I think I wanted to see everything—the city, the people—first for myself, so that I could always keep them, you know, inside me, as they are . . . to me, I mean. As one does with pictures, you know—laid away for what purpose I don't know, but that's my way of learning: first I see, then I wonder, then I know."

His grandfather listened attentively. "Very sound," he said. "An analytical mind—good! Well, here you are now. Where are your bags?"

"At the hotel, sir."

"You must fetch them at once. Of course we must live together. I have plenty of extra room, especially since my wife died. I live in her room, not my own. We believed in separate rooms, but after she went on her way I moved into her room, thinking it would be easier for her to visit me then—as seems to be the case. Not that she comes often—she's independent, always was—but when she feels the need, or understands my need, she comes quite promptly. We arranged for all that before she went."

He listened to this in amazement and with puzzlement. Was his grandmother dead or was she not? His grandfather was still talking.

"I would send Sung with you to get your bags, Randolph, but he is afraid to go to Manhattan. Ten years ago he was wanted by the police for jumping ship. Serena—that's my wife—and I were shopping on Fifth Avenue. I believe we were looking for a white mink stole for her Christmas gift that year, and he came dashing in, obviously escaping from someone. He couldn't speak a word of English, but luckily I'd been in Peking for some years doing research at the great Rockefeller Hospital there. I'm a medical doctor as well as a demographer—and my Chinese is fluent enough that I was able to ask him what was wrong. I am entirely out of sympathy with our immigration policies toward Asians, so I told him not to be afraid, for I'd take him as my servant. I gave him my overcoat to carry and took him at once to the men's department and bought him a decent black suit and had him put it on, and when the police came into the store, I was very angry with them for interfering with my manservant. He came home with us but he is still afraid to go to Manhattan, with which I have every sympathy, not because I am afraid, but because it is a hell hole. So leave it at once, my dear boy, and come here."

"But Grandfather, I hadn't planned—"

"Never plan, please. Just do the next thing that happens. You can always go your way. But it would please me to know my only grandson, even briefly."

How could he refuse? The old gentleman was charming. Sung brought in eggs scrambled with a dash of something delicious—

"Soy sauce," his grandfather explained.

He was always hungry; he ate heartily, drank three cups of coffee with sugar and thick, sweet cream, ate his way through a mound of buttered toast spread with English marmalade, and in an hour was on his way—"in a taxi," his grandfather said, stuffing a bill into his coat pocket. "I'm a poor one at waiting."

IT WAS NEARLY TWO HOURS before he was back with his bags, for the day's traffic had thickened and the streets, absurdly narrow for so huge a city, were crowded with every sort of vehicle. But he was back at last, excited by the adventure of an unknown grandfather—not permanent adventure, of course, for nothing was permanent except what he stored away in his deepest subconscious self, but something new and someone different from anyone he had ever known. Why had his mother never told him that his grandfather had lived in China, and in Peking, a city of which he had read with a perception of magic? And what was this about his grandfather's wife? Was she his grandmother? Serena! He could remember having heard that name at home. A beautiful name for a woman, he thought. And, his whole being alive with wonder, he was in the house again and Sung took his bags and began unpacking them and his grandfather led him to a huge window in the room which was to be his.

"This is the only room from which we can see the Statue of Liberty," his grandfather said. "For that reason Serena would not have this room. She said she simply could not argue with that great stone woman. 'Ha—Liberty!' That's the way she'd talk—Serena, I mean. She was always embroiled in other people's troubles. Just to read the newspaper would send her to Washington to protest or some such thing . . . Ellis Island! She was there day after day, trying to help some poor wretch or another. So I took this room. But she was right, you know. By the way, she wasn't your grandmother. Your mother's mother was my first wife, a sweet woman, gentle, perhaps ignorant—I was never quite sure how much she knew about anything. My poor Sarah! She's dead too, but she never comes back to visit me, even though I am now alone—I daresay Serena sees to that!"

He laughed high laughter and then was suddenly grave. "Of course, now that you're here, Serena may relent. I'll speak to her—no, I won't. There's no use in upsetting one's true love."

"My mother never told me anything about your wife, sir," he murmured, not knowing what to say.

"Oh, she wouldn't," his grandfather said cheerfully. "No need to, you know. Each of us has an independent life. Now you must amuse yourself for a while lad. I always sleep an hour before dinner, which is at seven. You see those shelves of books? From what your mother writes, I'm sure you can amuse yourself."

His grandfather left the room and he went to the bookshelves. There was a biography of Henry James there and he took it down and began to read.

* * *

"I SUPPOSE," HIS GRANDFATHER SAID CHEERFULLY at the dinner table, "that I ought to explain to you about Serena. To tell you the truth, your mother knows nothing about her. When her mother died—my first wife, Sarah—I was in Peking. Sarah had not wanted to go to China with me. She thought of it as a heathen country, instead of what it was, the oldest and most civilized country in the world. So I went alone. Your mother was then about three years old. Sarah went back to her own family. As a matter of fact, we never lived together again though we were not legally separated, but as I said, she died while I was in Peking. When I returned from China, I was a very different man from the brash young fellow I was when I went there, thinking I had so much to teach the Chinese. Instead, they taught me."

"How long were you there?" he asked.

"I went to stay a year and stayed seven," his grandfather replied. "When I came home again, I moved here. I had a job in a private foundation—a very wealthy man in Wall Street, who was interested in vital statistics and world population. My office was there, just across the bridge, on the forty-fourth floor of a skyscraper. I met Serena there—matter of fact, she was his daughter, a brilliant, beautiful, willful creature. She fell in love with me first. I hadn't thought of love. It embarrassed me—she was much younger than I. I went to him about it. He laughed, but he sent her to the Sorbonne for a couple of years. Then suddenly she was back again, standing there at my desk. 'Well, here I am,' she said, 'and I'm just the same.'"

He laughed that high old laughter. "Well, I said, 'I'll have to take you seriously.' Which I did, with the result that I married Serena in due course—or rather, she married me."

"My mother never told me," he said.

"No, she wouldn't, for, as I told you, she never saw Serena," his grandfather replied. "She continued to live with her aunt, and I went regularly twice a year to see her while she was growing up, but Serena felt she would be happier not to see my child. She always said emotions should never be confused. But little Sue always knew where I was and that she could depend on me, if needed. Nevertheless, I did not ask her to bring you here and live with me when your father died. I felt Serena would be confused, even after death. And I wasn't sure that Serena wouldn't come back now and then. I don't think she'll mind you—but two women—"

His grandfather shook his head doubtfully. Silence fell and neither of them broke it for several minutes. Then he spoke, his curiosity overwhelming him.

"Grandfather, do you mean she—Serena, your wife—really comes back to you . . . now?"

His grandfather, placidly eating an ice dessert, wiped his lips with his huge old-fashioned linen napkin before he spoke.

"Oh yes, indeed, dear boy," he said cheerfully. "I never know when, of course, any more than I knew when she'd come into my room at night when she was alive. And she didn't come at all for nearly four years after she died. I suppose it takes a certain length of time to become accustomed after the shock of death. It must be a shock to die, just as it is to be born. It takes time—it takes time. That's a very delicious sweet, Sung. I'll have a bit more."

His grandfather ate heartily and with enjoyment. He appeared so sane, so healthy, so alive in spite of his age, that Rann could not believe his mind was deranged. Indeed, he was sure it was not.

Then, his grandfather must have experiences not common to ordinary folk. But he himself was not ordinary either, and his sense of wonder would not let him rest.

"What I am trying now to discover," his grandfather continued, "strictly through the science of parapsychology, is just how she does it, or how I do it. It is probably a combination, which as yet with me is accidental. But in time, as I do more study, I shall discover the proper technique. I am a scientist, Randolph. I learned that in China. I don't know how much you know of my work. It began with my interest in the heart as the center of life."

"Nothing, I'm afraid, Grandfather."

"Ah well, that doesn't surprise me. My first wife was a dear, good woman, as your mother is, but she had an ordinary, though intelligent mind. I never knew your mother, my daughter, well enough to discuss my work with her. But you have an extraordinary mind. I can see that—indeed, I saw it the moment you walked in the door."

He was infused, inspired, impelled by his sense of wonder, his insatiable curiosity. "How did you know, Grandfather?"

His grandfather pushed away the plate from which he had been eating with such enjoyment, and Sung removed it and disappeared. They were alone.

"I will tell you what I have told no one since Serena died," his grandfather replied. "I was born with a rare ability. Serena had it to some degree, and I was able to discuss it with her frankly, as I did everything else. It may be you have some of the same ability, though possibly expressed in a different way. You may want to tell me. With me it is expressed in color."

"Color, Grandfather?"

"Yes, I don't like to use the word 'aura,' for that is the jargon of mediums and fraudulent people who make their living through a false mysticism and suchlike nonsense. I am a scientist, trained first in medicine then in electronics. I understand—to some extent—the interplay of electrical waves. We are all a part of such interplay. Given the right combination of forces, a human being is the result—a crystallization, if you like. Or a dog or fish or insect, or any manifestation. When we 'die,' as we call it, the combination is merely moving from that form to make another. *Change* is the word. There is constant movement in the universe, and we are part of that change. Nothing is destroyed, only changed. What the change is, which we call death, interests me very much at my age, naturally. I doubt I can find the real explanation until I undergo the change myself, which will not be soon, because I inherit longevity and health—as you do, too, through me."

Oh, his persistent mind! He was half-ashamed of it. "But color, Grandfather?"

"Ah yes," his grandfather said. "But I hadn't forgotten, dear boy! I never forget anything, any more than you do. I had to give the preliminary explanation. Well, all my life I have seen color about living creatures and most strongly, of course, about the concentrations we call human beings."

"Do you see color about me?"

"Oh, very strongly."

"What color, Grandfather?"

"More than one."

His grandfather studied his head, and was silent for a minute. "Green is predominant—in what I see in your emanation—a living, vital green, signifying that the life force in you is very strong.

This shades off into a rich blue—nothing pallid about you! And the blue fringes off into yellow. Yellow denotes intelligence, and blue denotes integrity. You won't have an easy life. Everything in you—your feelings, your determination, your idealism—all very strong. You'll suffer on all counts. But you know that, you're a creator."

"Of what, Grandfather? I feel the pressure in myself to create—but what?"

He spoke intensely, his elbows leaning on the white tablecloth, silver and china pushed aside, everything forgotten except what his grandfather was saying.

"It's too soon, boy!" his grandfather said gravely. "Much, much too soon! You've talents—but talent is a means, a tool to use. You must find your material, and that can only come out of knowing, learning and knowing. When you've learned enough, when you know enough, your own talent will guide you—no, force you, push you, compel you. So be at ease, dear boy! Wander the Earth, look and listen. But never waste yourself. Use your body as well as mind. Put it better—your body is the valuable container for the precious talent. Keep your body clean and free of disease."

Their eyes met, his grandfather's electric blue, his own dark and vividly penetrating in their gaze. His grandfather gave a deep, shaking sigh.

"Serena!" he murmured. "Do you see who has come to our house?"

They rose in silence then and went into the library and he sat, still silent and absorbed in thought while his grandfather played a small pipe organ at one end of the room. It was Bach—ordered, coordinated, scientifically beautiful music, a whole made up of controlled parts. Control, he thought. That was the key to life—control of self, of time, of will.

IT WAS PERHAPS A WEEK LATER. During the week he had seen very little of his grandfather. Each morning after breakfast his grandfather had told him briskly that he had work to do, and so he could wander about as he liked until dinnertime.

"Wandering is never waste, dear boy," he said. "While you wander you will find much to wonder about, and wonder is the first step to creation."

On this evening, upon finishing dinner they had as usual gone to the library, to talk, to read, to listen to music, or even to play chess. Upon a chess table made in Korea, his grandfather kept set in position a great set of chessmen carved in white and black marble. His grandfather was a superb chess player, and though his own father had taught him the game, he had yet to win over his grandfather.

"I could let you win, in order to avoid your possible discouragement, dear boy," his grandfather had said, "but out of respect for your intellect, I will not do so. In time you will surpass me, for you learn, I observe, from your mistakes, each time. You teach yourself, and that is true learning."

Tonight, however, there was to be no chess, it appeared. The evening was cold, the sky overcast and the first snowflakes were floating past the windows. Sung came in and drew the long velvet curtains over the windows, lit the fire, and went away again. His grandfather opened a small leather case and drew forth a magnifying glass—"a very fine one that I picked up in Paris, years ago," he observed. Then he opened a silver box.

"To prove to you, if you need proof, of Serena's visits," his grandfather said, "I've made these photographs of her. I've taken them regularly over the visits she has made. I rigged up a camera in my room and took a series of pictures while she was in the process of materializing. These are the photographs. Study each one carefully, please. You will see me seated in a chair in Serena's room. If my face seems strange to you it is because I am concentrating upon nothingness. Ordinarily this might be called trance. I learned in India how to enter into nothingness. I dislike the condition, for I lose myself. But I know that Serena cannot communicate with me otherwise. I daresay that others might communicate with me also if I cared to have them do so. But I do not care. In due time I shall be where they are. Serena, however, I need from time to time."

He took the photographs one by one from his grandfather's fine old hand. The first one showed only the aged man, sitting at ease in an armchair. The next showed a faint suggestion of mist descending behind the chair. In each picture the mist grew stronger and more defined, until in its center there appeared clearly and more clearly the lively face of a beautiful woman.

Her body remained mist, but the eyes, the features, were illuminated.

"You see her," his grandfather exclaimed triumphantly. "It is as she was when she was at her most beautiful, in health and maturity, before illness and age attacked."

"Does she speak to you, Grandfather?" he asked.

"I do not hear as I hear you," his grandfather replied, "but I am aware of communication—yes. I cannot explain it to you. It is an awareness. Whether you could hear a voice, were she to appear now, I cannot tell you. I do not know whether she would appear in that case. I rather imagine that it requires some effort on her part, just as it does on mine, for us to cross the barriers."

His grandfather spoke so naturally, with such acceptance and faith, that he asked no more questions.

"Thank you, Grandfather," he said.

His grandfather put the pictures carefully in their sequence and into the box. Then in a gentle voice, infused with love, he said quietly, "Dear boy, it is time for you to continue your travels. I have no right to hold you here in this old house, inhabited by an old man and the spirit of a woman who lives beyond. It has been joy to have you here. You must return many times. If I die, too soon, before your return, I have arranged that Sung will keep the house in order for you. If we both die, the house will still be kept. In each of the capital cities of countries you visit, money will be held for you. You must set forth and find the center of your interest. You are a creator, but you must find your interest and then dedicate yourself to that interest—not to the act of creativity. Merely to want to create will make it impossible for you to do so. You must find an interest greater than yourself—a love, perhaps—and then the power to create will set you on fire."

"I understand, Grandfather," he said quietly. "Thank you for sending me away. You set me free, even from myself."

HE WAS ON A SHIP, crossing the Atlantic Ocean, on his way eastward—a wandering, meandering way—to China, as once his grandfather had gone. He might have flown and been there in a few hours, but he wanted to know more, see more, much more, before he reached the ancient country that had meant and still meant so much to his grandfather. And so he chose the slow approach, hoping to see the old countries of the West, in order that he might have the contrast of Asia, and also because he wanted time in which to know the sea. His life had been spent inland, in a landlocked state, until he came to New York, and though he had often gone there to the harbor and watched the great ships draw anchor, he stood firm upon the land. Now he was upon a ship, the sea was rough, the sky gray. He had a small cabin to himself, and there were few passengers, for it was out of season.

Perhaps because it was out of season and the passengers so few, he came to know the captain and the first mate and some of the men. These seamen were different from land men. He wondered and watched them; he listened to their simple tales, simple in language but sometimes telling of fearful experiences of being lost at sea. Lost at sea! His imagination, always too quick, saw the piteously small lifeboats tossing upon the illimitable ocean, the beautiful, cruel ocean. And yet he came to love the sea, his favorite spot upon the ship the prow, where he stood hour after hour, leaning his elbows on the stout mahogany top rail, polished by the captain's command every day. There he stood, like a carved figurehead of youth, watching the ship's pointed bow divide the green waters into two huge white-topped waves. He watched and he felt, storing away the sights of the vivid changing sea, the purple sky, the white waves, remembering forever the clean cut of the ship, the feel of the fresh salt wind upon his face and in his hair, watching and feeling. He ate prodigious meals of simple, hearty food, he slept dreamlessly at night, soothed by the rise and fall of the ship, and woke again to another day, wishing the voyage would never end and then longing for it to end because there was so much to see beyond.

It was on the third day that he saw the woman. She had not appeared before, her place at the captain's table always empty. He had not known of her existence. She had perhaps been seasick and stayed in her cabin. The sea had been rough until this third day, a high wind in spite of sunshine and a clear sky, the wind perhaps the fringe of a distant storm. But the ship rolled easily, built narrow for its length for speed, perhaps? At any rate, the woman's place had been empty at the captain's table. Suddenly she appeared at the wide door of the dining saloon and there she stood, gazing somewhat uncertainly about her. She had dressed for dinner in a green gown, long-sleeved but low-necked and, fitting her slender figure, it fell straight and narrow to her feet. Even her shoes were green. Above her straightness her hair was swept back into a great knot at the back of her head, bright-red hair, shining in the lamplight like a casque of gold. He had never seen so beautiful a human being and he stared at her. But so did they all. A silence fell on the passengers. And she looked at them unsmiling, out of dark eyes, so brown they were almost black.

The captain got to his feet and pulled out her chair. "Come in, Lady Mary. It's good to see you at last. We've been waitin' these three days."

He was a Scotsman, the burr heavy on his tongue. She gave him a glint of a smile then and walked slowly toward his table. And suddenly, as she passed Rann's table, the ship gave a great lurch, hit by a huge wave, the seventh wave of a seventh wave, the second mate had told him, and she would have fallen had he not leaped to his feet to catch her in his arms and keep her steady.

"Thank you," she said in a clear soft voice.

She clung to his arm nevertheless until she reached her seat. Then he returned to his own place, aware only of the softness of her slender body under the green satin dress. Yet she was not very young, he thought, trying not to look at her though glancing at her out of the corner of his eye. Her profile was turned to him, a lovely profile, too strong perhaps for strict beauty, but somehow very beautiful. And if she was not young, neither was she old—perhaps thirty or thirty-five? But that was twice as old as he, though not old enough, not really, to be his mother. He could not imagine her being a mother. Lady Mary, the captain had called her, and that meant she was English and perhaps even lived in a castle somewhere. But it was not likely that she would notice a boy. Nor did he indeed wish for her notice. He was too young, too young except to see, as he saw everything, the vividness of her coloring and her supple grace. She was listening to something the captain was saying, a half smile on her lips. She was eating, too, with a frank appetite that somehow surprised him because she was so slender.

People were talking again, accustomed now to her presence, but he scarcely listened, except as he always listened, saying little himself but storing away unconsciously the sound of these voices, the changing expressions of their faces, their postures, their ways of eating, all details of life while though useless, it seemed, in themselves, he could not help accumulating because it was how he lived.

He would have forgotten Lady Mary, perhaps, as no more than part of the ship's life, this small contained world, confined between sea and sky, except that the next day, a windy bright morning, when he stood at his usual place at the ship's prow, he felt a hand on his arm, and turning saw her there, buttoned from neck to knees in a silver gray mackintosh.

"You have my place, boy," she said at his ear. "Whenever I'm on a ship, my place is here at the prow."

He was so startled that he stepped back and trod on her foot. She grimaced and then laughed.

"What a heavy-footed lad you are," she cried against the wind.

"I'm sorry—so sorry," he stammered, but she only laughed and, tucking her hand in his elbow, she drew him with her.

"There's room for the two of us, surely," she said, and held him there, her hand still in his arm and her bright hair flying back from her face.

He stood there then, linked to her, the strong west wind pressing her against him, and together and yet completely separate and in total silence they gazed across the sea. It might have been an hour before either of them moved or spoke, but he was conscious of her in a strange new way, shy and not shy together. Then she stepped back, releasing her hold on his arm.

"I'm going below," she said. "I've letters to write. I hate writing letters, don't you?"

"I have only my mother and my grandfather, and I haven't written them," he said.

"Ah, but you should and you must," she told him. "Put your letters in the ship's post and they'll be mailed as soon as we land. I'll give you some English stamps."

She nodded and turned away and left him standing there and feeling strangely alone and somehow restless. He did not want to stay there alone. It had not really occurred to him to write his mother or his grandfather until he reached England. There would then be so much more to tell—London, for example. But now he felt she was right—he should write them. The letters could be mailed that much earlier. He went below and found a quiet corner in the dining saloon and wrote two letters, each surprisingly long. There was something pleasurable in trying to put into written language some of the sights of the sea and sky and ship. Of Lady Mary he wrote not a word, not knowing, indeed, what to say. If he singled her out, what would they think? And for that matter, why should he single her out, a woman nearly old enough to be his mother? But not quite—

"AND SO WHERE WILL YOU BE GOING in England?" she inquired abruptly.

It was the last day on the ship. Next morning, before noon, they would be landing at Southampton. There he would take the train to London. His grandfather had given him specific directions.

"To London. My grandfather gave me the name of a place—a small hotel, very clean," he told her now.

"It's odd, your being alone," she said.

"My father and mother were coming too," he told her, "but he died. Then she thought he'd have wanted me to come anyway. I'm—rather young for college, you see."

"How old are you?" she asked in her pretty, silvery English voice.

"Sixteen," he said reluctantly, half-ashamed to be so young.

"Sixteen! Oh, I say—not really!" she cried. He nodded and she stared at him.

"But you're so—enormously tall! I'd have said twenty, at least. American men look so young anyway—yes, twenty—maybe twenty-two. Good Heavens, you *child*! Why, you can't go wandering about alone! Where are you bound for?"

"China," he said simply.

She gasped and then broke into bright laughter. "China! Oh, nonsense! Why ever China?"

"My grandfather lived there for seven years and he says they're the wisest, most civilized people on Earth."

"But you don't speak Chinese, surely?"

"I can learn languages very easily."

"What do you speak now?" she demanded.

"English, French, German, Italian—some Spanish. I was going to take it this year. I would have before, but my father thought the literatures in the other languages were more important. Besides, I might go to Spain. There it would be very easy for me to pick it up. Of course, I don't count Latin—it's basic anyway."

She looked at him with a curious, penetrating gaze, her eyes very dark.

"Look here," she said decisively. "You are not going to London to some small hotel alone. You are coming home with me. I've a place outside of London and you'll learn about England from there."

"But—"

"No buts—you'll do what I say! I live quite alone since my husband was killed in the war—Sir Moresby Seaton. It will cheer me up to have someone young in the house. I can't bear relatives. Who knows? I might even go to China with you. I went to America, and that's almost as odd. I went quite alone, too—and had a marvelous time. Americans are such talkers, aren't they—not you, though! You're a silent lad."

"I like listening," he said, "and watching."

"But it is a very old castle," she continued, "and it has quite a history in my husband's family. He was the last male, and we had no children, alas. His fault or mine, who knows—or cares? And he was rather old-fashioned—'traditional' would be a better word, perhaps, for he loved sports—hunting and all that sort of thing, but he believed if one had no children, well, one hadn't them. And so when I die the castle will go to a nephew—a nice chap, older than you by twenty years, married and with three sons, so there'll always be a Seaton in the castle, and that's all that matters. Curiously enough, I'm glad now that I have no children. I can be myself—not divided. Children do divide a woman, in an odd sort of way. One's never quite whole after the division. There's always something gone. And I shan't marry again—ever! I've made up my mind on that. Not sentimentally, either—but because I find I like being alone. I don't believe in a one-and-only—though I was frightfully in love with my husband. Oh, yes—I was happily married—happily enough, that is."

"Then why—," he began, but she interrupted him in her gently ruthless way.

"Why ask you to the castle? It's a question I can't answer. You're someone in yourself—though you're only a boy, yet. I don't know who you are. You're not very American. You're someone quite apart. I shan't bother about you, you know. You'll be free to come and go. And I'll be free, too. You'll understand that. I've a curious feeling that you understand everything. There's something about you . . . I don't know . . . something old and wise . . . and quiet—

very strange! I suppose you're what the people of India would call 'an old soul.' We went to India once, my husband and I. Actually, it was on our honeymoon. We wanted to see the Taj Mahal by moonlight together—banal, wasn't it? But I'm glad we did. I'll never forget. And then we got really interested in India. There's no other country, I'm sure, where one feels the people are born old and wise and—*knowing*. You have that same *knowing*."

He laughed. "And yet I don't even know what you mean by that word!"

"You're young, too," she retorted. "And you weren't born in India. You were born in a very new, brash young country—which was a great mistake, I fear!"

She laughed, and then they were silent again and for a very long time, but quite at ease, in spite of silence. That was what puzzled him. He was at ease with her, as though he had known her always. And yet she was a stranger, living a life entirely unlike his own. He felt excitement, more than the excitement of being in a new country.

IT WAS DUSK WHEN THEY DROVE through a small village and he saw, a few miles beyond, in the open countryside, softly rolling hills, the outline of a crenellated wall, and above it the turreted roofs of the castle.

"William the Conqueror built it," she explained, "and for five hundred years it was a royal seat. Then it was given to an ancestor of my husband as a reward for some feat of honor in war. And Seatons have been there ever since, until now, and I suppose it's only by the generosity of the nephew—no, my husband insisted I was to have the right to live here for my life, if I wished. I daresay someday I shall want to live somewhere else—perhaps even with someone though not married—or alone, if I still like being alone."

They were drawing near now, and suddenly all the lights of the castle flashed on, and it stood brightly outlined against the darkening sky.

"It *is* beautiful," she murmured, half to herself. "I always forget how beautiful it is until I've been away and then come back to it. I've always come back alone until now. It's rather nice having someone with me—which surprises me, somehow, since I've always wanted to come back alone after Moresby died—Morey, I called him."

"It's great luck for me," he said. "Much better than wandering about London by myself—though I'm used to being alone too, being an only child at home and always too young for my schoolmates."

"What did they do with you in school?" she asked curiously. "You must have been a brilliant little pigmy among big, stupid giants!"

He thought a moment, remembering. "I think they didn't like me," he said at last.

She laughed. "How could they? They hated you! Ordinary people always hate the rare few who have brains! Did you mind?"

"I didn't have time to think of it," he said. "I was always too busy—making something, reading about something—talking with my father—"

"Your father meant everything to you, didn't he—"

"Yes."

"Then he died."

"Yes."

"And there's been no one else?"

He hesitated, then replied. "Yes . . . a professor—a very brilliant man—but—"

"You're not friends anymore?"

She had a soft, persistent way with her. He wanted to tell her about Donald Sharpe and did not. He had resolutely tried to forget, and now to put that experience into words would make it all real again. That friendship, that affection—call it what he might—had gone very deep. There had been so much, so very much, about Donald Sharpe to like, even to love. There had been understanding such as he had not found since. It must not be recalled.

"No, we are not friends anymore," he said abruptly.

And before she could ask why, they were crossing the bridge over the moat, gates were thrown open, and they were at the castle itself.

"Welcome to my home," Lady Mary said.

THEY WERE IN THE GARDEN in the morning of this his first day in England. The previous night, after an early dinner, she had bade him good night almost coldly, and he had been shown to his room by a manservant, who drew his bath, turned down the bed covers, and laid out his pajamas. His suitcases had already been unpacked and his three suits hung in the closet of a dressing room. This he discovered when the man had left him after asking when he would like to be waked.

"What time is breakfast?" he had asked.

"Her Ladyship takes breakfast in her own rooms, sir," the man had replied.

He was a short young man of perhaps twenty, round-faced and pug-nosed, his hair blond and stubbly. There was something humorous about his solemnity, and Rann had smiled.

"What would you advise?" he asked. "Remember, I'm only an American."

The young man hid his own smile behind his hand and coughed slightly.

"As to that, sir, breakfast will be ready anytime after half past eight, sir, in the breakfast room just off the east terrace."

"I'll be there," he had replied, "at half past eight."

He had slept without waking until eight o'clock, and then was attacked by a monstrous hunger for food and, looking out the window, saw the morning sunny and warm in spite of the season. And after a breakfast vast enough, what with bacon and eggs and broiled kidneys, and much toast and marmalade and cups of coffee with thick cream, he saw Lady Mary in the garden, her slim figure very smart in a blue pantsuit, and her hair bright in the morning sun.

He left the table immediately and joined her, and without preliminaries she said, "Look at this exquisite piece of workmanship!"

She carried a thin bamboo walking stick with a carved ivory handle, and with it she pointed now at a spider's web, the largest he had ever seen. The spider had caught branches of a holly tree in its spinning, and dew hung in silver drops upon the delicate threads.

"Beautiful," he said, "and see how the drops of dew change their size—large on the periphery and infinitesimally small toward the center."

The spider was in the exact center and at rest, a small black spider, motionless and watchful.

"But how," she asked, "how does that bit of a creature know how to spin its web in mathematical perfection, the widening circles, the exact angles—"

"It's all built into his nervous system," he replied, "a sort of living computer."

She laughed, and looking down into those laughing dark eyes, he saw admiration.

"Now, how do you know that?" she demanded.

"Koestler," he replied simply. "Page thirty-eight, as I remember. *Act of Creation*—marvelous book."

"Is there anything you haven't read, you young monster?"

"I hope so—I'm longing now to get into the castle library."

"Oh, those old books—nobody's read them for generations! Morey's books are all upstairs in his rooms. Go on about the spider. He looks wicked indeed, in my opinion, sitting there pretending he's asleep while he waits for some poor harmless fly!"

"Well, I suppose it's wicked in a way," he agreed. "But then again it's his nature. And he's done his job perfectly. He's attached his web to twelve points—see? It's not always so many—depends on what he thinks necessary. But the pattern is always the same. The center of the web is always the center of gravity from the spider's point of view and the intersection of the threads always make the same angles and—"

"Oh, stop," she cried, "there's an insect caught there in the far corner. Oh, get it out, Rannie!"

He broke off a twig and tried delicately to free the struggling insect without breaking the web—a tiny film of a moth it was— but it was too distracted.

"I can't," he said, "I'll break the web."

"Break it then," she cried. "Oh, look at that nasty spider! He's rushed straight to the poor thing—he's wrapping his beastly little arms about it. Oh, I can't look!"

She lifted her cane suddenly and struck at the web and ruined it. Spider and moth dropped into the leaves of the shrub and she walked away.

"I won't let it spoil my morning," she said with resolution.

"Of course not," he agreed. "The spider was only acting according to its own built-in rules. Koestler points out that there is a 'fixed code of rules, which may be innate or learned,' though its functioning depends on the environment."

"Oh, be quiet!" she cried, flashing her eyes at him. "I don't want to hear any more of your old Koestler! Who is he, anyway?"

He was confounded, almost wounded, but he refused to yield to her. "A very great writer," he said quietly, and was silent for so long that suddenly she smiled at him coaxingly.

"Forgive me," she said. "I know you can't help it."

"Help what?" he inquired.

"Oh—being what you are—a brain, and all that. But you are so—so beautiful, too. Yes, you are, Rann—don't blush! Why can't I say you're beautiful to look at? Why must you be handsome as well as everything else? If I weren't such a kind, good-natured human being myself, I'd hate you for having everything—that curly hair, too! And blond! Why should you have exactly the color of hair I've always wanted—and blue eyes—not watery blue, but ocean blue? I think I do hate you!"

They were both laughing now, and suddenly she threw away her little cane and seized his hand.

"Let's run!" she cried. "I love to run in the morning!"

And to his astonishment he found himself running across the lawn, her hand in his, and they were laughing—laughing—as they ran.

HE WAS LINGERING FAR TOO LONG in England and he knew it. After a week—or was it two?—when he spoke of going on to France, she had protested.

"But you haven't seen anything! You sit here in this old library, reading these old books. You don't even go upstairs to Morey's library."

It was true. He had gone upstairs once, her leading the way, to a suite of rooms quite modern in their decor, and then in her abrupt fashion she had left him. He had stayed to read the titles of shelves of books about ships and guns and the history of wars and travels, and then had stood for a while before the portrait of a young man. It was life-size, painted by a modern artist as he could see from the technique, and it was set in a flat frame of gold—Sir Moresby Seaton, a man still young, very powerful in build, dark and strong and smiling, the cheeks ruddy, the eyes alive. Indeed, the portrait was so vivid that, gazing at it, he felt a presence in the room and was made uncomfortable by it. The eyes were insistent, demanding. "Why are you here?" He seemed almost to hear the question hanging in the air. Why, indeed? He had left the room without answer and, going down the great curving stairway, he returned to the old library, where there was no presence except his own and there he evoked life from the books.

"You can't see England just from books," Lady Mary was saying, "and so I shall drag you right away. We'll go to Scotland before it snows, and to the Cotswolds—such charming stone houses in the Cotswolds—and perhaps get into Ireland for a day or two . . . green Ireland, where I'm always more myself than anywhere else in the world. I've a bit of Ireland in me through my grandmother. The O'Hares have a castle or two of their own in Ireland."

And obedient always to her demanding, willful, pretty ways, they had made their journey, Coates driving them, and he drank in the scenery and the change, marveling at so much variety in so small a space, always engirdled by the sea. But for him there was wonder everywhere, and he spent hours engrossed in accumulating impressions of faces and places, villages and towns and the rare city of Dublin, and she accused him of forgetting that she was even with him.

"I might as well have stayed home," she cried one day, petulant and laughing.

"Oh, no indeed, Lady Mary," he had protested. They were in some ancient cathedral, and he had been absorbed in a small book the vendor handed him, giving the story of a knight encased in a coffin of brass, in a crypt there, his image also of brass lying upon the coffin. He put the book down on the image.

"No, indeed, Lady Mary," he had protested again, and had been about to explain when she broke in.

"And don't you think you might call me Mary, after all this time of knowing me?"

"I always think of you as Lady Mary," he replied in all innocence, in such innocence indeed that she had gone into a fit of laughter.

"Why are you laughing?" he inquired gravely.

She had only laughed the more and he was puzzled, but he wanted to know the end of the dead knight's story too, and so he had taken up the book again and she wandered away.

So had passed one lovely day after another until they came back to the castle, just escaping the first snowstorm. And still he marveled how much green there was in the gardens, the late chrysanthemums still blooming, too, though near their end, and sank back into the old life easily and yet uneasily, because he knew he should be moving on his way, for there was a dangerous charm in the ancient and idyllic setting.

Now here she stood before him in the old library on this day in early December. It was twilight and a coal fire was burning in the grate. She had changed for the evening and wore a long skirt of black velvet with a scarlet bodice and pearls about her neck.

"And still you are reading," she scolded, "and even without turning on the lights! What is the book now?"

"Darwin—his voyages—"

He had been far away, so far away that she saw how far, and slowly she came and stood before him and gently she put her two palms on his cheeks.

"Do you ever see me?" she demanded, and moving away she turned on the lights, all the lights, so that suddenly all was dark outside and bright within.

"Yes, of course," he said. "You're beautiful."

He looked up at her, smiling, and suddenly she stooped, and he felt on his mouth the pressure of her lips, light at first and then with a quick pressure.

"Now do you see me better?" she demanded, and drew back.

He could not speak. He felt his cheeks get hot, his heart begin beating in his breast, hard and quick.

"Have you never had a woman kiss you?" she asked softly.

"No," he said in a half whisper.

"Well, now you have," she said. "You'll have learned something new in England—something to wonder about—you who are always wondering! So—how do you like it?"

She spoke in so downright a way, her voice half-laughing, almost scornful, that he could only shake his head.

"I don't know."

"Don't know or don't want to know?"

He did not reply, indeed he could not. He was in a tangle of feeling, repelled and yet enchanted. But the enchantment was in himself. He was not enchanted by her. In a strange way he wanted her to kiss him again.

"You are shocked," she said. "It was nothing—just fun. Come along to dinner."

She drew him to his feet by her hand on his and then walked with him into the dining room, her hand now in the crook of his elbow.

HE COULD NOT FORGET. That night, when they sat late side by side on a small curved couch before the dying embers, the servants gone to bed, he could not forget that warm sweet pressure on his mouth. They had been talking, not steadily but in a desultory, half conversation, her head leaning against the high back of the couch as she talked now of her childhood, of Berlin and Paris, of the rounded hills of Italy, crowned by small old cities, and he sat turned toward her, listening and not listening, remembering the kiss. Suddenly in a long moment of silence he felt impelled by that deepening enchantment in himself, by his quickening heart impelled, and he leaned toward her and to his own surprise he kissed her mouth. Immediately her arms went about his neck. He felt her hand pressing his head down—down, so that his lips clung to hers, clung until he could not breathe. Then slowly she drew back her hands on his shoulders.

"How quickly you learn! Oh, darling—is this wicked of me? But some woman must teach you, darling—and why not I? Eh, Rann? Why not I? You're a man—your body a man's body—so tall, so strong. Haven't you—known it? Or has your head been so full of your books—"

He did not answer. He scarcely heard her. Instead he was kissing her again, madly, wildly, her cheeks, her neck, the cleft of her bosom where her low-cut gown revealed the shape of her breasts. And when he kissed her there, she loosened a button and another, and in a foam of fragrant lace he saw her breasts, rounded and firm, her two little breasts, pink-tipped. He gazed at them, fascinated, shy, his blood rising to tempest pitch and concentrating in his rising center.

"Poor darling," she whispered. "Why not? Of course—of course—"

And under her guiding touch, he sought her and found her and with great gusts in that warm receiving place he was released and knew himself.

When they parted at last, her good night kiss as light as a child's now, when he had bathed and put on clean garments, his body sanctified, when he lay alone in the great bed, his exultation was for himself. He did not think of her, he did not think even of love.

"I am a man," he said aloud in the darkness of the night. "I am a man—I am a man—"

And when he slept it was the sweetest sleep he had ever known, the sweetest and most deep.

* * *

MORNING WOKE HIM and he lay for a long moment, recalling himself. So this was he, a new person, and she was new, a woman. She would never seem the same to him again, any more than he was the same. They had met in a new world. They had stepped across a threshold. It was a reality he had never known before.

He was shy when she came down to breakfast in a dark-green jacket suit that brought alive the vivid color of her hair and eyes. To his surprise she was quite herself, quieter perhaps, giving him a smile instead of a greeting. When the butler left the room, she yawned behind her narrow white hand with its diamond and emerald rings.

"How I slept," she said. "Of course, I'm a natural sleepyhead, but last night I didn't even dream. Just slept. And you?"

"I slept very well, thanks."

He was formal because now he was shy. He did not know what to say to her. Should anything be said? And how would they proceed from here? Perhaps he should go away. What was the next step? She was twice his age, but she looked no more than twenty. He had never seen her look so young, so fresh. She was smiling at him, not in the least shy, her bright eyes teasing.

"You're ten years older than you were yesterday," she said. "I can't explain it, but you are. And I am ten years younger. Of course, I *can* explain it, but I won't. I'll leave you to realize it for yourself. You don't know me—or yourself. You've spent your life learning about everything except yourself."

"I'm—more than one person," he said stiffly, not looking at her.

"Of course," she agreed with gaiety. "You're an unknown number of persons. But I wanted to confirm what I guessed—that you are also very much of a man. Now I know."

Her voice dropped almost to a whisper. "You were wonderful, Rann—so instinctively wonderful. I knew as soon as I met you that you were a genius. I've known geniuses—a few. What I didn't know was whether you were—something more—something that would make you complete. Well, you are. And that something completes even your genius."

"I don't understand."

"I don't expect you to understand. That will come slowly. But someday, at some moment, you will know yourself wholly. This is a time of learning."

They were looking into each other's eyes, his drawn to hers by her steady, honest gaze.

"Will you trust me?" she asked.

"Yes," he said.

HE TRUSTED HER and he learned how readily he obeyed. He was amazed and sometimes shocked that he was ready, and at all times, to obey her slightest touch. Standing behind his chair, she leaned over him, her cheek against his and he turned instantly, instinctively, passionately to seek her mouth. One touch, one movement, led to the next until they were in each other's arms. They tried to be wary of the servants and this led to their night hours together. When the house was quiet, the servants sleeping in their distant quarters, they would steal to each other's rooms, she to his at first but soon he to hers. She preferred him to come to her, and when he discovered her preference, he always went to her. He lay awake, impatient with longing, until the clock in the hall struck one. Then he rose and put on his robe and, barefoot on the thick carpets, he went down across the hall to her rooms. Sometimes she was sitting before the fire, wrapped carelessly in a silk robe, her body naked beneath it, and soon, how soon, he learned to slip it away, at first shy, his hands trembling, but after a few nights boldly and quickly, revealing all her white loveliness. He never tired of looking at her, not until he could no longer wait, and then lying on the wide bed, looking at her again, his head supported on one hand, the other free to touch, to feel, to examine.

"Did you ever really see a woman before?" she asked one night smiling at him.

"Yes, once," he said. "When I was a little boy on my first day at school. We were coming home together and she wanted to see me . . . my—my penis, I mean. My father had told me about myself—a penis is a planter, he said. And then she offered to show me herself, and did. And I saw something like a flower holding a pink tip. We were as ignorant—and innocent—as the babes we were. But some woman saw us and, evil-minded, she told Ruthie's mother and Ruthie's desk was moved far from mine in school. I didn't know why."

"Were your parents angry?"

"Mine? Oh, no—they understood a boy's curiosity—"

"Which grows into a man's—doesn't it?"

"Yes—but I didn't know it. I'm so grateful to you. It might have been so—horrible. Instead it's—beautiful—with you. Because you are so beautiful yourself."

"What will happen to us, Rann?"

"What do you mean?"

"This can't go on forever, you know."

He had not thought of this. Go on forever?

"Do you want it to?" he asked.

"I might—if you were even ten years older. But you're not."

"I don't think I've been thinking. For the first time in my life—I've been feeling, only feeling. No, I don't suppose it can go on forever. You aren't asking me to leave you? Because I can't—"

It was true. He could not imagine himself leaving this lovely body of a woman. He had come to needing her as a man needs to drink. His flesh clamored for her. He responded viscerally and physically. He was impatient for the night. If they walked in the loneliness of the deep forest surrounding the castle, he could not wait for the night. He was inappeasable. Satiated at one moment, in an hour he was hungry again. He did not know himself now. He was yet another person. Where was that studious, book-loving boy? He rarely went into the library now. The more he knew her, the more he wanted her—not her mind, not her laughter, not even her companionship, but her body.

"Are all men like me?" he demanded at three o'clock in the morning.

"No one is like you," she replied. She looked white in the lamplight, exhausted yet strangely, sweetly beautiful.

"But I mean it," he said impatiently. "I'm like a man who can't get enough to drink—again and again and again—I exhaust you."

"And, loving you, I love it," she said.

"Then are all women like you?"

"I don't know. Women never know each other—not where men are concerned."

"Shall I always be like this?" he demanded.

"No," she said half-sadly. "Perhaps only with me. Every experience is the same—it can never be repeated."

He pondered this, lying on his back, and gazing unseeing into the shadows flickering on the ceiling. There was a wisdom in her words that he could not immediately grasp. After a moment he turned and kissed her abruptly.

And then he got up, wrapped himself in his robe, and went back to his own room, conscious of her quiet gaze following him until the door closed between them.

WINTER HAD COME SLOWLY over the landscape. He was accustomed to the abrupt weather of his own country, and the mild approach of cold and chill rather than cold, he scarcely noticed. The autumn had been mild, the flowers bloomed late, the trees changed their colors gently, and the first snowstorms were mere flurries, edging the outlines of the landscape, house roofs in the village, the slow rise of the hills, the lines of tree trunks and branches rather than the violence of wind and snowstorms.

He was conscious of change not so much in his outer world as in himself. He read very little nowadays. Books, instead of being sources of discovery, made him impatient; instead of enjoying the long quiet hours alone in the vast old library, he found himself wondering where she was. Impossible of course to concentrate if she was in the library with him, it was even more impossible to concentrate if she was not there. Or, if she told him that she would be away for an hour or several hours, for she kept her independence, then time was interminable and he was too restless to read.

Instead he walked about the grounds or the moors, glancing often at his watch, timing his return to hers.

Yet theirs was no rational relationship. They seldom talked, and never for long; willful, amusing, even brilliant as her talk could be, he found himself not listening, and scarcely answering. Instead his whole being was concentrated upon the inevitable meeting of their bodies—inevitable but without schedule, so he never knew whether, when he took her in his arms, she would allow him to proceed or whether she would merely give him a gentle kiss and withdraw herself. She teased him, she tantalized him, she made him happier than he could imagine, she cast him into anger or despair. He did not understand her, nor did he want to understand her as a person. He wanted only to know her mood. Would she receive him this day, this night, or would she reject him? Nor could he even call it rejection. She was too tender, too courteous perhaps to reject him. Even when she withdrew, it was after a kiss, a touch, a reassurance.

"But why?" he demanded.

"I just—don't feel like it today," she might say, or she would say, "I love you, I always love you, but tonight I love you quietly."

If he sulked, and he was surprised to discover that he could sulk, she laughed at him. When she laughed, he left her and went away and she never followed him. She never mentioned the difference in their ages, but she could make him feel sometimes, though always subtly, by her amusement, that she was indeed far older than he, far wiser or at least more knowing, and that it was possible that she could tire of him.

They celebrated Christmas with a dinner of roast goose and an exchange of token gifts and greeted the New Year from the white satin canopied bed toasting each other and taking what each had to offer the other until dawn was breaking over the horizon as Rann crept back to his own rooms careful not to attract attention from the already-stirring household. He thought of this year ahead of him, yet another year in his young life, and of what he knew he must do. There was still the world beyond the castle, beyond even Lady Mary, waiting for his discovery, but could any discovery be as sweet, as complete, as all-encompassing as the discovery of himself that he had made here within the ancient walls of this castle under the gentle but wise guidance of this beautiful woman? Questions that would remain unanswered, he knew, until he himself went forth to find the answers. But the answers would not change, would they? Eternal truths would remain as they were for him to find, and he was still so young. There was time, plenty of time for all that he wished to do and this, too.

The winter passed into spring with one day folding into another, their outlines dim, his waking thoughts, and often his dreams as well, filled only with contemplation of her and when they would be together again in her huge old bed while the servants slept, unknowing, in their own beds in a remote wing of the castle.

It was the day after his seventeenth birthday that brought him back to himself at long last. Even so, the return was not immediate. Two incidents compelled his return. The first was a long letter from his mother. She did not write often, nor were her letters usually long.

"Your life is so full," she wrote, "that I feel there is nothing here which would interest you. I do sometimes wonder, darling, if you are limiting yourself too much in your present life. I know the castle must be very interesting with its wonderful library and I don't worry about the academic side of your education, for your father always told me you would educate yourself with books, provided you had enough of them, which now it seems you have. But the world is made up of people as well as books, and while I don't expect you to be really interested in people of your own age, still they are people. I don't want to be unkind to Lady Mary, for she has been and is so kind to you, but I do just ask myself sometimes if she is lonely and in some way is using you to alleviate her loneliness, whereas perhaps it would be better for her, darling, if she, too, found companionship with people of her own age—not that she is using you, of course, or if she is, I am sure she does not mean it that way."

She wrote from another world. The small American college town was no longer his home. He belonged now to a different world, not a geographical world but one of emotion and sensation, centered in himself. Was Lady Mary using him? Rather, he was using her—using her to explore himself. Until now he had not dreamed of the depths of feeling, physical and emotional, of which his body was capable. His body—he had not thought of it before as separate from himself. Now it occurred to him that it was indeed separate, each part separate, each with its own function, his legs, his feet, his means of movement and motion; his hands his tools; his inner organs part of the machinery that sustained and made possible the life of his brain; and now the center of his being, his sex! And yet each part mechanically performing its duty, conveyed more than a mechanism. They conveyed the awareness of shape, the feeling of touch upon the skin, of scent and sound that some part of him received, delighted in, or rejected—an emotional part, separate from the body sensation and even from brain, something that was pure emotion. It was emotion that was the core of his being—emotion so volatile that it could convey the keenest delight or be cast into disappointment and even despair. The focal point of this emotion was, at present, his penis in its useful aspects. But when it became what his father had called "the planter," it became the conveyor of a delight so inexplicable that he could not describe it, although he tried to do so in words and more than once.

> *The slow rise, the swelling joy,*
> *Filling vein and pulse until*
> *Desire, flooding to its full height*
> *Breaks—as breaks the wave upon the sea.*
> *Then am I you, Love, and you are me.*

He was not satisfied with the words. Moreover, they did not express the truth. For a brief moment, yes, they were one, he and she, and at that instant he thought of love. But it was only for a moment. When it was over, and inevitably it was over, they were separate again, he and she. His penis, shrinking, was symbolic of his whole being. He shrank away from her. He had given what he had to give. And she, too, had given what she had to give. And what was this except a momentary spasm of delight? And then what? Nothing, except perhaps a relief, also a matter of moments, a few hours, no more—for there the desire was, back again, always—inevitable and stronger, perhaps, even than before.

"Make the most of your age, my young lover," she had said one day almost wistfully.

"Why do you say that?" he had demanded.

"Because even desire doesn't last," she had replied. "It becomes habit, and then—well, it's only habit. That's why I like my lovers young."

"Lovers?" he had inquired.

"And are you not my lover?" she said, laughing.

He considered this thoughtfully and she waited, watching his face with a teasing smile.

"I am not sure I know what love is," he said at last.

She opened her eyes wide. "Then you give a very good imitation of it!"

"No," he said slowly, still thinking, "it's not imitation, because I don't really love you. In a way, it's more like loving myself— or loving the opportunity you give me of loving myself. Perhaps that's all I give you, too."

For she had made it a fair exchange. She had taught him how to exchange delight, an exchange he had not understood at first until she revealed to him the secrets of her own body and made them his, until he understood the fulfillments of mutuality. Ah yes, she had taught him very much. But when it was over, each time now, there was no more to learn. They returned to what they had been before, two separate beings—himself, herself. And was this all there was to love? Was separateness inevitable and eternal between human beings? Then what was the use of love if it was only endless physical repetition? Was there no more?

"What are you thinking?" she demanded.

He looked at her. They were here in her room afterward, long after midnight. She was lying on the white satin canopied bed beside him, naked.

"What does this mean to you?" he asked in reply.

She put up her arms and drew his head to her warm breasts.

"It keeps me young," she said.

IT WAS A SIMPLE STATEMENT, simply made, and with it she had given him her lovely smile. At the moment it had seemed no more. But he woke before dawn, alone in his own room. The moonlight had wakened him and, as though that cold light illumined his mind, the full enormity of what she had said revealed itself to him. His mother was right. He was being used. He pondered upon this truth. Lady Mary needed a male body to stimulate and satisfy her own need. He was young, physically he was in the full fresh vigor of his sexual manhood. Into that narrow passage of her body his strong thrust excited, exalted, and satisfied her. That was all he was to her, an instrument of gratification. He was used as a machine might be used and was he not more than a machine? Was he not also spirit?

Yet let him be just a machine, if this was what she wished. Did he in turn demand more of her? He was fastidious in his own way, nevertheless. He could never have lent the use of his body, of which he was proud, if not indeed even somewhat vain, to a mere Ruthie, any more than he had been able to accept the strange caresses of Donald Sharpe. He did not love Lady Mary, but her beauty charmed him—her beauty and her breeding. In a way, he supposed, it was a sort of love. But was there anything lasting, or even meaningful for him about such love? Still, perhaps, it was more than she felt for him. She had spoken only of herself, and for such ends, that he felt at this lonely moment degraded and therefore outraged. He would not be used. He would not have his body used. His body was his own possession—solely his own. And then he had made up his mind. It was time for him to move on his way. Beyond this castle the whole world still waited. It was the world to which he belonged. All people were his people. No one woman was his only woman, no one man his only friend. He was going his own way, where he did not know, but onward. His world was in readiness somewhere beyond this castle.

THE FAREWELL WAS EASY, AFTER ALL. He had dreaded it, though only a little because he was resolute, and yet somewhat because in his own way he was also tender of heart. She had been kind, in her English, offhand fashion, and he was not sure whether after all she had an attachment. Even though she might replace him, undoubtedly would replace him in time, still a vague sort of fondness held them lightly together. He felt it in himself. She was lovely in her cool fashion, delicate even in her passion—no, "delicate" was not the word. She could be abandoned but always with taste; if the words were not too contradictory. She could not offend. Her very frankness was never offensive. Her clarity of expressed desire was pure.

Then when, he had pondered, was the suitable hour for the farewell? Now that he had decided upon it, he was impatient for it to be over. One night he packed his bags, the third night after the decision. He had avoided going to her room, and so delicate was her perception that she had seemed also indifferent to him. By this very indifference, studied and graceful, he knew she was preparing herself for the unavoidable separation. The next morning, his bags packed and breakfast over, although they had lingered at the breakfast table that had been laid for them outside on the terrace, it being a perfect early spring morning, he began, not abruptly, but as though they had spoken before of his departure.

"I shall never be able to thank you enough," he said.

"When are you going?" she asked.

"Today," he said.

"And where?" she asked. She sipped her coffee and did not look at him.

"To London and then to France, and then southward across Italy and perhaps even to India. I shan't stay anywhere—as I have stayed here."

"Ah, you'll like India," she said almost indifferently. Still she did not look at him.

"What shall I find there?" he asked.

"Whatever it is you are looking for," she said. She touched a bell and the butler appeared.

"Have a car ready to take Mr. Colfax to the station at once. He'll catch a train for London."

"Yes, madam," the butler said, and disappeared.

Mr. Colfax! She had never called him that before and he looked at her, his eyebrows lifted in question.

"Aren't you going?" she said.

"Yes," he said. "But—"

She rose from the table. "I'm not sending you away," she continued. "It's only that I've learned that if something is over, it's better to have it over at once."

"Yes," he said.

He rose too, and they stood facing each other, he taller than she. Yonder in the rose garden where a fountain played, a bird sang three clear notes, a cadence, and stopped abruptly.

"Oh, Rann," she said in a whisper.

And suddenly he saw that she was sad. But what could he say except to stammer his thanks?

"I do thank you—I thank you most awfully—"

She did not hear him. She was talking to herself.

"I'd give anything to be your age—I'd give all I've ever had—I would and I would; I would indeed!"

She put her arms about him and held him and then pushed him away. "I'm going to the village for shopping. When I come back, you'll be gone."

He stood watching her as she walked away in her usual light, quick fashion. She did not turn her head, and he knew now that she was gone from him forever, and he was returned to himself— free as perhaps he had never before been free.

WHEN HE ARRIVED IN LONDON he took a taxi to the small hotel his grandfather had told him about.

"We had expected you much earlier, Mr. Colfax," the desk clerk said to him. "Your grandfather had led us to believe you would be here some months ago. There is a letter here from some solicitors but nothing more than that."

"I've been visiting a friend I met on the ship on the way over," he said by way of explanation. "Now I'll be here for a few days, then I'll be going to Paris."

"Very good, sir," the clerk said. "Your room is all ready."

The letter from his grandfather's London legal firm told him of funds his grandfather had made available for him, and by telephone he told them he would not be needing the money in London and they insisted he take the name and address of the firm in Paris where it would be forwarded to him. He walked around London for a while and found it much the same as New York and other cities he had visited and decided the sooner he went on to Paris the better for him. He had heard that Paris was a city with a soul, unlike any other city in the world.

PARIS WAS IN THE MIDST OF AUGUST HEAT. It was a changeable city, and he had loved it immediately, partly because it was changeable and difficult to understand and therefore enchanting. In June it had been like a young girl his own age. Indeed, it had swarmed with young girls. They were new to him and he was fascinated by them but not more by them than he was by the beauty of the city itself, its history, which led him into libraries; its paintings, which led him to weeks in the Louvre; its magnificence—which led him into Versailles, and cathedrals. But now there were days when he simply wandered about the streets, stopping at outdoor cafés, sometimes walking as far as the Bois de Boulogne to throw himself on the ancient French earth and lie there, submitting himself to it. He imagined, or felt, emanation from that earth, as indeed he had felt too in England. Lady Mary more than a few times had stopped the small car she drove herself, when she was alone with him, when they were out merely to enjoy a fine mild day, or when she wanted to show him an old village, or open a picnic basket or make excuse, he now suspected—at any rate, she had stopped the car in some remote spot, shielded by hedgerows, and declaring herself weary, had spread a car rug, usually folded in the backseat, and there in the hedges, in the warm glow of approaching spring, she had stirred him to make love. Make love! He disliked the phrase. Could one *make* love? There was a compulsion hidden in the word "make." Now, today, far away from her, and lying alone under the trees in this French forest, he admitted his own too-ready response to her physical stimulation. He had allowed himself to be overcome not by her so much as by himself. He carried within himself his own constant temptation and therefore he must blame himself. But was there need to blame himself for his male nature? No, his reason replied, for he was not responsible for his own parts. His responsibility lay only in the choice of which part of him was to be his master. There was far more to him, he knew, than the enjoyment of his physical being. His world was still not in himself. Or else, he was only a small single world, however composite, in a world of other worlds, and his undying sense of curiosity and wonder—that powerful inner force that impelled him to every adventure—made him a part of every other world. Knowledge was his deepest hunger and now especially the knowledge of people, of what they were and thought, and did. And when he was replete with this knowledge, if ever he were, what would he do with it?

Lying there on the warm French earth, his cheek pressed against its green moss, he pondered his own question, adding to it his eternal why. Why was he as he was? What was his compound? Without vanity, he accepted the fact of his own superiority, his own self-confidence. He knew that whatever he chose to do he would do superbly well. He did not think of fame—indeed, he did not care for it. His own need to live in freedom, to learn in his own way, at his own speed, was now his supreme desire. How he would express his self-gained knowledge was as yet unknown to him. But there was a way, waiting, and he would find it.

He turned on his back, head on his clasped hands, and gazed into the leaf-flecked blue sky and waited while slowly a decision found itself invincibly in his own being. It was not only in his mind. It was a decision forming throughout his whole being. He would never again go to school—not to college—ever! Others could not teach him what he wanted now to know. Books he would always learn from, for people, great people, put the best of themselves into books. Books were a distillation of people. But people would be his teachers, and people were not in schoolrooms. People were everywhere.

Decision! He had decided. He recognized finality and a deep peace pervaded his being, as real as though he had drunk an elixir, a wine, had eaten a consecrated bread. Whatever came to him was good. It was life. It was knowledge. He sprang up from the earth. He brushed the leaves from his hair and with his handkerchief he brushed the dampness of moss from his cheek. Then he walked back into the city.

FROM THAT DAY ON, he devoted his time to the new learning. He who had spent his life as long as he could remember with books, still read as a matter of habit and necessity. On any fair afternoon he wandered to the book stalls of the Left Bank and spent hours there, browsing, searching, tasting one book and another to take an armful of books back with him to the big attic room that in its fashion had become home to him. For he came to perceive that since people were his study, his teachers, the objects through which he could satisfy his persistent wonder about life itself, his own being among others, wherever he lived for the moment, there was his home. It was as though he had reached a place that he had been seeking all his life, a point of knowing himself first, and where he was meant to be and what he was meant to do. Now he could satisfy his hunger to know, his eternal sense of persistent wonder about life, its reason, its purpose, for now he had found his teachers, and these teachers were wherever he happened to be. A new and delicious joy filled his entire being. He had no sense of compulsion. He was entirely and truly free.

Therefore on this August morning, a hot and sunny morning, a day of quiet in the city, for this was the month of holiday and many people were away at seaside and country resorts, he lingered at the bookstalls and fell into conversation with the wizened old woman who was dusting her stall. He had seen her often, had always replied to her cheerful greetings, her chirping comments, her sly, suggestive remarks on certain books a young man might like, especially one, this morning, which she said an American might like.

"And why especially an American?" he asked.

He spoke French easily now, being long past the stage where he was compelled to translate French mentally into English before he could converse.

The old woman was only too ready to converse. He was her first customer, August being a poor business month, and she was as cheerful as a cricket.

"Ah, the Americans," she exclaimed. "So young, so full of sex—always the sex! Me, I remember—ah yes, I remember—my husband was a real man in such matters . . . but Americans are so young—even white hairs don't mean age when it comes to sex—the men—the women—I tell you—"

She shook her tousled white head and cackled laughter. Then she sighed. "Alas! We French! It is soon over with us. Is it because we are poor? Too soon we must think of how to earn a loaf of bread, a bottle of cheap red wine! From birth to death—behold me, myself, old as an ancient crab—yet rain or sun I am here, am I not? Ah, truly!"

"Have you no children?" he asked.

The question was mild, almost abstracted, for he had his eyes on a book in another stall, but it loosed her complete concern. She beat her breast.

"I have the best son on the Earth," she declared. "He is married to a seamstress, a good young woman. They both work. There are two children. Her mother cares for them during the day. But I—I am proud to work. I have a room next to their apartment. They have two rooms—well, call it three. My son is clever. He has put up a small wall, behind which her mother sleeps. The wife leaves very early for work—also my son. He is a guard at a factory. We eat our evening meal together. But I am independent, you understand? Two evenings in the seven I buy food and cook dinner. They make me welcome, ah yes—I am still welcome!"

"Will you not always be welcome?"

She shook her head. "One does not ask too much of life. I pray the good God that when my hour comes it will be quick. If He is merciful, it will come in my sleep, after a day's work. Ah yes, that would be happiness—to lie asleep in my bed—I have a good bed. That I saved. When we were married, my husband said, 'At least let us have a good bed.' So we had it. And I kept it. There, pray God, let me die in peace. The bed where I first knew love, where my children were born, where my husband died—" She wiped her rheumy eyes with ends of the black scarf that hung about her neck.

"You had more children?"

"A daughter who died at birth—"

He put his hand on her shoulder, forgetting the book.

"Don't cry—I cannot bear it because I don't know how to comfort you!"

She smiled up at him through her tears. "I thought I had done with weeping long ago. But no one asks me such questions now—only the price of a book and trying to buy it cheaper!"

"But to me you are a human being," he said, and smiled at her and went away, putting the coins for the book in her dry old palm.

That night he did not go out on the streets as he usually did for his long evening walks. Instead he sat on the low windowsill and looked out over the city until the twilight faded into night and the electric globes sparkled as far as the horizon. He kept thinking of the old woman. It was a life. Poor as it was, it was a human life: birth and childhood, a woman and a man in marriage, children—one dead, one alive. Then death splitting a life in half, and now what was life for this human being except work? Except work and still life itself—waking in the morning to another day—life itself!

He rose and lit the small lamp on the table and, as though impelled, he wrote down the story of the old woman. It was only a shred of a story, a shred of a life, but writing it down as he remembered it, as he felt it, brought him a new sort of relief—not physical, as he felt after an orgasm with Lady Mary, but something deep—very deep, which was so new to him that he did not try to fathom it or explain it. Instead he laid himself upon his bed and fell quickly asleep.

IT WAS A HOT DAY in early September. People were coming back to the city. He sat down at a small round metal table under the awning outside a café. It was late morning, too early for luncheon, but he was hungry. He was growing, still growing, now well over six feet and his skeleton bare of flesh. His skin was smooth and clear, and although he had always kept his auburn red hair cut short, now that the new style was coming in that men, at least young men, were beginning to wear their hair longer, he was letting his own hair grow, washing it daily, for to be clean was a passion, yes, and there was little time for anything more. If women looked at him with more than a glance, he was not aware of it. If his eyes caught hers, he met the look with such blankness she went on and he did not notice it. He knew, or thought he knew, all about women; Lady Mary was a woman, was she not? He had not forgotten her, but she belonged to his past. But everything belonged to his past, once he had lived through it. He lived intensely in the moment, in every day as it came, without planning or preparation. He was always consumed in thinking. About what? About what he had learned today merely in living—the people who had come and gone, the people with whom he had talked or had not wanted to talk so that he could simply study their faces, their hands, their behavior. He stored them away in his memory and this he did unconsciously. They remained with him. Though they came and went, these people he collected stayed with him. He thought of them with wonder and question. He asked questions if they were willing to answer him, as usually they were, for most people he met were interested in themselves and he had a concern to know, which he himself could not yet understand. These strangers—why did he want to know where they came from and went, what they did and thought, any scrap of information they were ready to give him?

He never asked their names. He did not care to know their names.

They were human beings and that was enough for him. It was an endless pursuit, one continuing wonder. Meanwhile he had little interest in himself beyond this accumulating knowledge of human beings.

Today, being fine, the sidewalks were crowded as they had not been in recent weeks. His gaze moved swiftly from one face to another, until a girl passed and her eyes met his. For an instant their eyes caught and held and this time he smiled. She hesitated, then stopped.

"You are keeping this chair for a friend?" she asked.

The tables were filling and the question was a natural one. She was an unusual-looking girl—an Oriental, or at least partly so. Her dark eyes were long and slanted.

"No, mademoiselle," he replied. "Please seat yourself."

She sat down and drew off her short white gloves. That was unusual too, the gloves—most girls no longer wore them, even in Paris. She studied the menu and did not look at him. He looked at her with his usual frank curiosity, wondering if she would be willing to talk. Her oval face was interestingly different from the usual pretty girl's face. The features were delicate, the nose low-bridged and straight, the lips delicately cut, the skin cream-colored and very fine. Her hands, as she drew off the gloves, were long and narrow. When she had given her order, she caught his steady gaze and gave him a slight, quick smile and looked away.

"Forgive me," he said, "but you are not French, mademoiselle?"

"I am a French citizen," she said, "but my father is Chinese. That is, he was born in China, where his father's family remains— that is, as many as are still alive."

She paused to reflect, and then went on, slightly frowning. "I suppose that even the dead still remain there, but we do not know where. Certainly not in the family burial grounds, since they were—since they died in . . . unusual ways."

She took a sip of wine from the glass that had been brought her. He studied her face, a thoughtful, abstract face, not thinking of him, but certainly of something very far away, having nothing to do with him. He was overcome with his usual wondering curiosity.

"China," he repeated. "I have not been there but my grandfather was there, long ago, and he has told me many things."

"Your grandfather is—American?"

"How did you know?"

"Your French is perfect—but almost too perfect for a Frenchman! You understand?"

He laughed with her laughter. "Is it a compliment or not?"

"Take it for what you please," she said. "The fact is we are both somewhat foreign, on opposite sides of the world. But you have the advantage, I think. You have lived in your ancestral country. I have never been in China. I speak Chinese, but badly I fear, though my father has tried to teach me. But my mother, who was an American, talked with me when I was a child more than my father did, and so I know English also. Would you prefer we speak English?"

"Would you?"

She hesitated. "I am more easy in French. Besides, even my American mother spent a lot of time here in Paris and she also spoke fluent French, even to me sometimes. Alas, she never learned Chinese. There was a prejudice. I never understood it. But my father has taught me Chinese also after—well! I have little chance to speak English. But I speak English also. Let us speak in English, for my practice! I don't have any English-speaking friends."

"What does your father do here?" he asked in English.

She replied in his language, a trifle slowly but precisely. "He is a collector and dealer of Oriental art objects, but of course especially of the Chinese. Unfortunately it is not so easy now to get art objects out of China. But he knows the necessary people in Hong Kong."

"Have you been in Hong Kong?"

"Oh, yes—I travel with my father. Of course, being Chinese, he hoped I'd be a son. When I wasn't, still being very Chinese, he made the best of it. But then I've tried, too."

"You have tried—"

"To take the place of a son."

"Very difficult, I should say—when a girl is as beautiful as you are!"

She smiled but did not reply to this obvious small talk.

He discerned in her something of his own aloofness and remained silent. Now it was her turn to ask questions if she had any curiosity about him—that is to say, if she were interested in him. He wondered how old she was and resolved to conceal his own age. He was in years so distressingly young. How often he would have liked to lie about his age, to say, for example, that he was twenty-two or -three! He was never able to lie. Honesty was an absolute—but then he could be silent. He watched her as she sipped her drink meditatively, meanwhile gazing about her at the people.

She was looking at him now. "It is your first visit here?"

"Yes."

"And you came from—"

"I was in England all winter."

"You have a slight English accent but not quite English!"

He laughed. "That's clever of you! No, as I said, I'm American—from the very heart of my country."

"Where is that heart?"

"The Midwest—if we're speaking geographically."

"You are here to study something?"

"I suppose one could say so."

She lifted her delicate eyebrows. "You are very mysterious!"

He was smiling at her serious eyes, dark eyes, set in long straight black lashes. "Am I? But you are rather mysterious yourself, half-American, half-Chinese, but speaking perfect French, too, with only the slightest accent—an accent I can't recognize."

She shrugged. "It's my own. We Chinese speak languages easily—not like Japanese, who have thick tongues. I speak also German and Italian and Spanish. It is possible for me to understand other languages—we live so close here in Europe."

"Do you consider yourself Chinese?"

"As my father's daughter, of course I am Chinese. But—"

Again the slight shrug, and he leaned his elbows on the table the more closely to examine her exquisite face.

"But what do you feel you are, inside yourself?"

Unconsciously he was back in his old habit of asking questions. Yet how did it indeed feel to be the child of nations and peoples, speaking many tongues as one's own?

"How you do ask questions!" she exclaimed, half laughing. Then suddenly she was serious. The lovely mouth closed; her eyes were thoughtful and she looked away from him. "How do I feel inside—," she murmured as though asking herself. "I suppose I feel I belong nowhere and everywhere."

"That means you are unique—you are a new kind of person," he declared.

She shook her head. "How can an American say such a thing? Are not Americans something of everything? I have heard my father say that Americans are the most difficult people to understand. When I asked why, he said it is because they are all so mixed, having roots in every country. That is what he says. Is it true?"

He reflected, gazing straight into her eyes as he did so. "Historically, yes, individually, no. Each of us belongs, beyond family, to his own region, his own state, and to the conglomerate, the nation. We are a new people, but we have our own country."

"How intelligent you are," she exclaimed. "It is so pleasant to speak with an intelligent man!"

He was laughing at her again. "You don't find men intelligent?"

She gave the characteristic little shrug, very pretty, very French, "Not usually! It is customary for men to remark on one's face, et cetera. Always the looks!"

"And then?"

"Then? Oh, something like where is one going, where does one live, will one have a drink and so on. Always the same! But you, although we are strangers, not meeting until fifteen minutes or so before now, you have given me a sensible thought. I know more about Americans. Thank you, monsieur—"

She was entirely serious, as he could see. And he might have thought of her sexually, with that lovely face and the long narrow hands she used with unconscious grace, except that somehow Lady Mary had helped him to put sex in its place. She had given him nothing but sex and in so doing she had made it extraneous, having nothing to do with anything else in life, an act merely physical. She had surfeited him until he knew that sex was not enough for him. Healthy male that he was, he knew the limitations of sex. There were many other aspects of life for the human animal, and these he must explore. His curiosities were far beyond sex, and in this Lady Mary had served him well. He did not hate her but he doubted that he would ever return to her or indeed ever see her again. Meanwhile here, facing him, was a new and beautiful female creature, one for whom he had not sought but had found as one accidentally finds a jewel.

"And you," she was saying. "Tell me who you are and truly why you are here. It seems to me that I can like you as a friend, and I don't find many."

How could he explain himself to her? And yet he wished very much to be able to do so. It was the first time in his life that he really wished to explain himself to someone else. For that matter, he had never tried to explain himself even to himself. Driven by question and wonder and the insatiable hunger to know everything, he had omitted explanations even to himself!

"I don't know what to tell you," he said slowly. "I have not had time to think much about myself. Wherever I have been—at least until now, I have been mostly alone. The others were always much bigger—much older." He paused to consider himself in the past. "Older in years, that is," he amended. "I've always been too old for myself."

She looked at him thoughtfully. "Then you have an old soul. We know about such things in my father's country. Would you like to meet him? I think he would like you. Usually he doesn't like young men—especially Americans."

"Then why me?"

"You are different from the others. You've said so yourself—in effect. Even your English isn't American."

He thought again of the many months he had spent with Lady Mary. Had she indeed left even the mark of her language upon his tongue? Yet why should he speak of her to this girl? He did not want even to think of Lady Mary.

"I would like very much to meet your father," he said.

"Then let us go," she said. "He will be wondering where I am. When he sees you he will understand. At least he will forget to ask me why I am late!"

THE HOUSE WAS ENORMOUS. It was on the outskirts of Paris and on the borders of a wood, a man-made forest, as he could see, so orderly the trees stood, with shrubbery massed at their feet.

"My father loves his gardens," she said. "Not flowers—only trees and rocks and water—flowers are for pots and vases in the house. He's very old-fashioned—formal and all that. You'll see when you meet him. Yet he's very good with people—not everyone, of course, but with special people."

She circled the drive smartly in her small Mercedes and drew up in front of the house. A wide walk of marble led to the front door, which opened, it seemed, automatically until he saw the slender black-robed figure of a Chinese manservant.

"Father brought his own servants to Paris," she said. "Of course, that was before I was born. Their children have grown up here and some of them still serve us in the house. Others of them help my father in the business. He doesn't trust white people."

"Though your mother is American?"

"I didn't tell you," she said almost casually. "She left us when I was six. She went away with an American—a very rich man's son, younger than she. He divorced her later—several years later—and she asked my father to take her back. He refused."

"And you?" he asked.

Against his will he asked, for what right had he to inquire into her personal life? But the old insistent demand to know, to know everything about life and people, impelled him. The demand was not mere curiosity. It was a necessity to follow action through reaction to final resolution. He had to know the end of the story.

"I have not seen her since she left. I have not forgiven her, I suppose, for leaving us, and my father has provided all I have ever needed and I am entirely loyal to him. It is as though she were dead, to me, and indeed she could be for all I know," she said.

They were at the top of the several steps leading to the marble terrace before the great door, now open and waiting to receive them. She paused and they stood looking out over the formal gardens through which they had passed.

"And?" he asked remorselessly.

"My father said I might go to her if I wished, but if I went I must know I could never see him again. So I stayed."

"Because?"

"I've always known I was more Chinese than anything else—because I want to be, I suppose. Come—let's go in!"

They entered a wide hall facing a great stairway that divided at its upper half into left and right. Now he saw a tall, slender man in a long Chinese robe of silver-gray satin descending from the right, to the main stairway.

"Stephanie!" he said, and then followed words in Chinese.

He listened to the unknown language, a mellifluous flow of vowels they seemed, and he looked at the handsome, silver-haired Chinese gentleman who spoke them and noticed his strong, beautiful hands. Then it occurred to him that he now heard her name, and at the same instant she turned to him, laughing.

"I want to introduce you to my father—and I don't know your name!"

"And I have heard yours for the first time!" he said, laughing. Then he turned to the father.

"Sir, I am Randolph Colfax—Rann, for short. I must admit to being an American, for your daughter says you don't like us, but my grandfather was in China in his youth, and he has taught me to admire your people—and so your daughter and I became acquainted today, and she told me about you and was so kind as to—" Here he turned helplessly to her. "How *did* you?"

"I feel he is different, somehow, Father."

French was the language again, and the father answered in that tongue, a stilted accented French.

"And you asked him, not even knowing his name?"

"He doesn't know mine, either," she retorted, and began laughing again as she turned to him. "How stupid I am and you are so polite, asking nothing! I am Stephanie Kung. You will ask why Stephanie instead of Michelle or some such name, but as I told you I was supposed to be a boy, who was to be named Stephen."

"Quiet!" her father commanded.

She stopped, looked at her father, and then went on. "Well, as you see, I disappointed my father and he punished me with this long name!"

"Be silent, my little one! And why are we standing here in the hall instead of proceeding into the library? Besides, it grows late. It will be better if we prepare ourselves for dinner. You, sir, will you spend the night with us?"

"Oh, yes—Rann Colfax, is it? Do stay the night! We will have so much good talk together, the three of us!"

He was bewitched, he was enchanted, he felt as though he were being led into another country—one unknown and perhaps long sought.

"It is too good to be true," he said. "And of course I will stay, at least for dinner. But I have nothing with me—no change of clothes. I shall have to go back to the hotel to get my things."

"That is easily mended for now," Mr. Kung said. "I have clothes—suits I wear to business—we are not too different in height, or weight. I can guess we can enjoy tonight with no thought to details and then tomorrow my car can take you to pick up your bags."

He turned to the waiting servant and spoke a few words in Chinese and then again to Rann.

"This man will take you to a guestroom and bring you anything you need. In an hour he will come back for you and lead you to the dining room."

"Thank you, sir," Rann said, and knew that he was indeed entering another world.

TIME HAD PASSED, DAYS MOVED INTO WEEKS, and now months. Even as he had stayed timelessly in the castle in England, he now stayed in this old French château on the borders of Paris. Wherever he found life he stayed in this timeless fashion and felt himself welcome. As long as he felt himself welcome he would stay, and yet even this was not conscious and perhaps not even true. As long as he was learning, as long as he was satisfying his insatiable wonder about the world, people, everything, there he stayed.

They were sitting in Mr. Kung's library, where usually they spent the evenings. The windows were open to the soft evening air. The city was almost quiet in the distance, its many voices no more than a murmur afar off. It was late autumn but the weather was dry and warm, holding the promise of another mild winter in Europe. The walls were solidly books, except for the windows. Here and there a few small tables held priceless jade statues and vases or lamps, objects with which Mr. Kung could not part unless he found something he liked even better, in which case the rejected article went into his enormous shop on the rue de la Paix—a museum of a place—replaced by the new, more favored object until yet another more favored object appeared. It was an endless sifting process, only the more choice works of art remaining here.

Rann had noticed the subtle changes taking place constantly and Stephanie had explained the process to him.

"Mr. Kung," Rann asked, "how did you become so deeply interested in these works of art?"

"Ah, art is the free man's dream," Mr. Kung said, "and a man's life begins and ends with his work—that is, if he is an artist. Each of these works represents the best in a man's life to that point, for an artist is forever striving to improve and he leaves a piece of himself behind each time as he grows. If one, in a generation long past his, collects carefully then he can know the artist and follow his development even as if he lived in the same day. The artist can never escape his work, and if he is good it is his stamp on the future."

"I wish I knew where my work begins," Rann said. "I think of it constantly. I prepare for it without knowing what it is. Meanwhile I ask questions—I cannot keep myself from the necessity of knowing—everything!"

Stephanie laughed. She was curled in the seat under the open window that overlooked the rock garden. "It's true—nine-tenths of everything you say is questions."

She was giving him lessons in Chinese now, claiming that teaching the language would help her to improve her own abilities. It was the most profound and fascinating language he had yet learned, and the most difficult, perhaps because it was the most difficult both to speak and to write. He found himself learning it primarily through the writing, the brushing of characters in their manifold design, and every stroke with design and meaning. Each written word was a work of art unto itself, a picture of its meaning, a signal of its sound, carrying within sight and sound a conveyance of feeling. "House," for example, was only a building, walls and a roof, which might be used for any purpose. But if people lived in that house, "house" became another word, brushed differently and with different sound and meaning. It became "home." Therefore each written character was a work of art, carefully brushed with precision, each stroke taken in exact order.

It was in discussing the Chinese language that he was learning this winter evening, after dinner, the conversation had moved so easily to the subject of art again, a subject that always drew Mr. Kung's concentrated thought and attention, since his life's work was the accumulation and dispersing of objects of art. It was a lucrative business as well, but somehow he could not think of Mr. Kung in connection with business or money. He had more than once been in the shop and had seen and heard Mr. Kung refuse to sell some favorite piece to a customer willing and waiting to pay its price.

"It is not for sale," Mr. Kung said with dignity upon such occasions.

"But why—"

"I reserve it without explanation," Mr. Kung said.

"My father," Stephanie had explained later when they were alone, "my father will not sell a beautiful object which has caught his soul unless the buyer has the soul for it too."

Later that evening while they enjoyed the warmth of the fire in the library after dinner, Mr. Kung held in his right hand a round piece of priceless jade, a pure soft green, which he rolled in his palm with his fingers. He seldom sat in his Chinese Windsor chair without such a piece of jade in his right palm, turning it slowly but constantly. Sometimes it was a ball of white jade, or the red one. It depended on the color of the satin robe he wore. Tonight his robe was silver-gray, again, his favorite and most often worn color.

"Why do I hold the jade piece in my hand?" he had repeated when Rann had put the question to him. "There is more than one reason. Jade is cool—always cool to the touch. And turning it is my habit. It relieves any tension I may feel. It brings me calm. Moreover, not least, it keeps my fingers supple. It is a sort of unconscious play. But it is more than that. I hold beauty in my hand. In art there is always something deeper than play. The artist knows this. Perhaps his art is a sort of play, an overflow of the spirit, but it is more—it is a revelation of human nature, varying with its time. That is why it is so necessary to know the age of a beautiful object, in order that we may know the creator and what is revealed, through him, of the times in which he lived—the times and therefore the people. If they loved beauty then they were civilized. Art must serve more than a functional purpose. We can judge the cultural stage of a people by the art of its architecture, the style of its literature as well as its content, the manner of its painting, for painting describes the human mind of its times."

Mr. Kung spoke slowly, reflectively, thinking as he talked, his mellow, gentle voice distinct in the silent room. His two listeners did not speak. Stephanie's head was turned to the window as she sat silent; the spotlights on the garden created a dramatic effect on the trees and rocks. Rann followed her gaze but looked at nothing and saw nothing, for he was absorbed in a strange new consciousness, a perception of the meaning of beauty that was deeper than any he had known before. Art—he saw it now in its totality—could be expressed in many ways, concretely through many facets of expression, but also in living—just living. The life in this house was based on love and comprehension of the beauty of art and the art of living.

Suddenly he comprehended art as an incentive in life, a call to labor, and yet at the same time a joy. But was there not contradiction here? He put it to Mr. Kung.

"Sir, is the purpose of art the enjoyment of beauty, or is it to provide a sort of work, even though enjoyable, for the artist?"

Mr. Kung replied immediately as though he had already asked himself the question many times before. "Both—art is both labor and pleasure for the creator. It is a compulsion and it is a release, a joy and a demand. It is both male in its aggression into life, and it is female in its acceptance into life. It is one's destiny, if he be the creator. It is the appointment of heaven when one has the gift. Art condemns no one. It portrays. What does it portray? The deepest truth, and in doing so attains beauty."

The quiet, steady voice, rich in its mellow tones, reached to his soul. Something crystallized in him, a form, a desire, almost clear enough to be defined as purpose. His range of possibilities assumed boundaries. As yet he had never said to himself that he would become this certain person or that certain person. He had taken each day, each experience, each revelation of new knowledge through a book or a human being or by his own discovery for enough in itself. The impact was never of his own making. It came and he made the most of it. Now he was stunned at the sudden knowledge of himself. Before he could break the pit of silence into which he had fallen, Mr. Kung spoke.

"I am tired, my children. I must leave you."

He struck a small brass gong on the table beside his chair. The door opened; a Chinese manservant entered and, approaching Mr. Kung, he held out his arm. Hand upon this arm, Mr. Kung smiled at the two who rose to their feet, and left the room.

They sat down again, Stephanie now upon a hassock before the dying fire. She did not speak nor did he. How could he speak when he was so dazed within himself, such questions pressing him—art, yes but which art? How to discover his own talent, if he had a talent? He had never spoken to anyone out of his own depths. He had always been the listener, the learner. With Lady Mary no speech beyond the most casual had ever been necessary. Their communication was always physical, without the necessity of words, each absorbed in individual ways. Besides, he did not know if he wanted to speak to anyone. What was there yet to be put into words? I want to create—what? Something of beauty, something of meaning, something to relieve the terrible inner pressure of this need! How could he put this into words? And would she understand? They had never talked of inward feelings, thoughts, desires—

"I will tell you something very strange," she said. Her voice was dreamlike.

"Yes?" he said.

"Never has my father left me alone with a man before. Man or boy, I have never been left alone with him. I wonder why he leaves me alone with you?"

"I hope—because he trusts me."

"Oh, there is more to it than that," she said positively.

She lifted her head to fling back her long, straight black hair and looked at him.

"Why do you think so?" he asked.

"He is planning something," she said. "I don't know what it is, but he is planning. He has been very different since you came into this house. I know him. He is very different."

"In what way?"

"Not his usual arrogant self. Oh, he has never been loud, you know, always quiet—absorbed in his art collections—but arrogant. It was necessary for me to tell him everything I did, where I was going—he always managed to keep me too busy with what he needed done—I've had little time to myself since I grew too old for a governess. He's always watched me—or had people watching me."

"How can you bear that?" he demanded.

"I understand him," she said simply.

She was looking at the fire and her hair was hanging over her face again. He saw only the lovely profile. Until now he had not truly examined it, but now he noticed each detail, not because it was her profile but because it was lovely. An awareness had awakened in him since he had been in this house. An awareness of beauty. There was more to know than knowledge. There was beauty. The awareness swelled again into a yearning to create beauty of his own. Again how? And what?

Out of the sheer need, he spoke. "Stephanie!"

She did not look up. "Yes?"

"Do you think you know me? Even a little!"

She shook the long dark hair. "No."

"Why not?" he pleaded.

"Because I have never known anyone like you," she said, lifting her head and looking at him straightly.

"Am I so—difficult?"

"Yes—because you know everything already."

"Except myself."

"You don't know what you want to do?"

"Do you?"

"Of course. I want to help my father in his business, but above all I want to learn how to be independent."

"Surely you'll marry!"

"I've never seen anyone I want to marry."

"There's time—you're only as old as I am!"

"Do you want to marry?"

"No!"

"Then there's the two of us. And now I can tell you safely what my father wants and why he won't let you go when you talk of leaving. I suppose you've noticed that?"

"Yes, but I haven't wanted to go—not really! I learn so much from him—and there are all these books! I haven't needed much persuasion to stay. Haven't you noticed?"

"My father has his own way of getting people to do what he wants—gentle but relentless."

"So what does he want?"

"He wants us to marry each other, of course."

He was shocked. "But why?"

"So that he'll have a son, stupid!"

"But I thought he didn't like Americans!"

"He likes you."

"Wouldn't he rather have a Chinese?"

"He knows I won't marry a Chinese—ever!"

"No?"

"No!"

"Why not?"

"Because there's too much in me that's not Chinese. And yet there's too much Chinese in me to marry a Frenchman—or any white man. So—I won't marry."

"Does he know that?"

"No, and it's not necessary for him to know it. It would be to refuse him a son forever. He wants me to marry a man who will take our family name and carry it on. It's the legal way—the custom—in the China he knew. For him there's no other China."

He was silent, trying to sort out his feelings. Shocked, vaguely alarmed and then reassured because neither of them wanted marriage, and yet somehow fascinated—no, that was too strong a word—somehow stirred, in ways that were a result of what Lady Mary had taught him. . . .

"Well," he exclaimed abruptly and, recognizing Lady Mary symptoms in himself, he rose to his feet. "At least we understand each other, but we'll be friends, eh? I like you enormously, of course—more than any other girl I've ever known, though in a way you're the only girl I've ever known."

"You're the only man—young, that is—I've ever known. Someone living in the house, that is—"

"So we'll just go on being friends," he decided.

Then he remembered his own previous confession and sat down again.

"Since you don't really know me," he said, "but you do know others and you are wise for your years with your father, what do you see me as—tentatively, I mean, and perhaps far in the future . . . very far?"

She looked at him again, for she had kept subsiding into gazing into the dying fire. Now, looking at him with a peculiar clairvoyance, she answered with astonishing assurance.

"Oh, a writer, of course. Yes, indeed, from our very first meeting. In fact, you know, I thought that's what you were, sitting at the little table staring at everyone as though you'd never seen people before."

"A writer!" he repeated, his voice a whisper. "I've been told this before and of course I've thought of it a great deal myself but I've never reached a concrete decision. And you've known all along!"

"Oh, yes, definitely!"

He was sobered by a stab of doubt. "You might be wrong!"

"I am right. You'll see."

But he could not be sure all at once like that. "Well," he said slowly. "I'll have to think. It will take a deal of thinking—a great, great deal. Of course I've thought of it, as I said, but only among many other possibilities. But to have you so sure—well, it's upsetting in a way. Almost compulsive—"

"You asked me!"

"And I'm not blaming you—but to have you come at me like that!"

"I'm always straight-out. I suppose that's the American in me."

"You're much more American than you know. There's a world of difference between you and your father."

"I do know—sometimes too well! *He* doesn't."

"That's because he's all Chinese."

They were silent then and for so long that he rose. "You've given me too much to think about. I'll say good night, Stephanie."

"Good night, Rann."

He stooped and upon a sudden impulse he kissed the crown of her dark hair. He had never done such a thing before. But she did not move. Perhaps she did not even know what he had done.

* * *

IT WAS, HOWEVER, A GERMINAL MEANING. In his bed he lay sleepless, thinking first of what Mr. Kung might be planning for him and then for hours thinking with excitement that perhaps indeed he would be a writer. He had written many short pieces, verse and prose, but usually questions he was asking himself. He thought of these as questions, not writing, and merely putting them down clarified the possible answers in his mind if he was unable to find answers in books or from people. The trouble was that people, even the best of them, really knew so little and of books there were so many that he wasted time in searching and scanning. And when he was alone the questions often came in rhythm, especially if he were alone outdoors. He remembered that dewy autumn morning at the castle when, unable to sleep and excited from the night before, he had risen at dawn and gone out into the garden at sunrise. There, caught among the blooming roses in the rose garden he had seen an elaborate cobweb, glittering with dew drops, every drop a diamond in the sunshine and in the center of it the creator, a small black spider, and questions came rhyming out of his mind:

> *Diamond web of silver dew.*
> *Beauty from your evil shape?*
> *Angel? Devil? Which are you?*
> *Or one? Or two?*

And at this moment he had been interrupted by Lady Mary. She was in her morning mood, distant and even cold. It had been bewildering at first, the frightening heat of her physical passion, and when that was satisfied to exhaustion, her chill reserve. No one but he knew that within her slender, erect frame there lived two such diverse beings. He had learned to accept both, the one who fell upon him with total abandon and the other distant and dignified in the conventional, almost traditional English manner. He had learned a great deal from Lady Mary. It all seemed useless now in the light of what Stephanie had declared last night. He thought of it again with a sense of illuminating capacity. Yes, he could do it. He could be a writer, devoting himself to the art of writing. "A man's life begins with his work," Mr. Kung had said. Then that was why he had not felt his own life begin—had not chosen his work until now. Had he really chosen even now? Could one choose one's life so quickly?

Not answering his own questions, he fell asleep before dawn broke.

"TO SEE PARIS," STEPHANIE WAS SAYING, "you must walk— walk—walk, unless you are sitting beside a little table somewhere on the sidewalk, drinking an aperitif and watching the people pass by, for the people are Paris too. Of course, we won't walk every-where—say, for example, to Montmartre! There's a funicular—or even the subway, though I hate going underground. It's sinister."

"Am I never to spend more time in the Louvre?" he inquired.

They were exactly the same as they had been before the conver-sation late that night, now four nights ago, in the library. He had not forgotten for a waking moment, however, what she had said, but neither had referred to it again. And subtly he had changed his manner toward Mr. Kung. He did not so obviously sit at his feet, metaphorically speaking. Instead he took books to his room to read or he went on walks. Yesterday, Mr. Kung had seen him on one of these walks and this morning before he left the house, he had summoned Stephanie.

"My child," he said reprovingly. "Why do you allow our young friend to prowl about the streets alone? Accompany him today!"

"I would like that, Papa," Stephanie said. "And you, Rann?"

They had exchanged knowing smiles. "I'd love it," he said with true enthusiasm.

"Then it is arranged," Mr. Kung said with satisfaction, and so departed.

"Never the Louvre with me!" Stephanie was saying now.

"And why not?" he demanded. "I've spent weeks there and have only scratched the surface of all there is to see."

"That's just it," Stephanie replied, "it is too, too big."

He was inclined to argue, for he felt he had not spent enough time in the Louvre and besides bigness did not frighten him. In many ways Stephanie was very French. She had a delicacy of approach. Or perhaps that was Chinese? He did not know. At any rate, she was delicate in her tastes. She did not like too much of anything at once.

"So," he continued, "how am I to see the treasures of Paris?"

"One by one, shall we not?" Stephanie said, coaxing. And then she ticked off the fingers of her left hand with her right forefinger. "I will take you to the Cluny medieval treasures; to Arts et Métiers because you are interested in science; to the Carnavalet for everything about Paris herself. As for art, I will take you first to Jeu de Paume. That's impressionist, of course. And I don't know anything more satisfying for Oriental art than my father's collections. But no! I will be generous, I will take you to the Guimet."

"And Versailles," he hinted.

She put both delicate hands over her face. "Oh, please! Let us choose Chartres—so much lovelier—and then Rouen! But I want to take you too to the Mouffe."

"What is the Mouffe?" he demanded, never having heard of it.

"A wonderful old market, hundreds of years old, with such people, such faces, all quarreling over prices at the top of their voices—such fun! We could buy some bread and cheese and go to the Jardin des Plantes and see the fountain."

They set off with the joy of sunshine and morning and their own youth. He felt free with her, at ease and happier than he had been in his life before. Ever since the night in the library when she had told him she did not want to marry he had been at ease with her. Her independence, her wish to be completely free of marriage and men freed him, too. The months with Lady Mary, a bondage exciting at first and ending in repulsion, had put a shadow upon him, a burden of secret knowledge that faded on this bright summer's day and the days to follow.

HE KNEW, OF COURSE, that this life could not be endless. That a day slipped so easily into another day was only because he was learning so much every day. Stephanie knew many places, many people of many sorts, people among whom she moved without intimacy and yet with knowledge of their personal histories and peculiarities, all of which she recounted to him in such vivid detail that he felt he knew each one, and this though she seldom introduced any by name. He absorbed facts complete with colorful detail.

"Monsieur Lelong," she announced, "is an excellent teacher in the school I attended as a small child. Unfortunately, he has severe halitosis due to a deranged liver, but he is the soul of goodness."

They were about to pass at this moment a tall, excessively thin, yellow-faced man in a shabby black suit. She hailed him with the utmost friendliness.

"*Bonjour, Monsieur Lelong! Comment allez-vous?*"

A few minutes of rapid exchange, and this done, she allowed him to proceed while she described the aging Frenchman's history in detail, his unrequited love for a much younger teacher who had married another man, and—

He laughed. "It's you who should write the books, Stephanie—not I!"

"Ah, I could never have the patience," she told him. "But you—you must know people. You must know all kinds of people, not only what has happened to them but why they are as they are."

Each day was indeed new learning and he might have accepted this without planning its end, except that one evening Mr. Kung asked him to come the next morning to his shop. There in his office he had a matter to discuss with him. He had of course been many times in Mr. Kung's vast shop, a museum indeed of every variety of art object. Stephanie had led him thither whenever a new shipment came in from an Asian country, and he had learned the history of one country and another and one century and another. He learned the many qualities of jade and topaz, ivory and rubies and emeralds. He had never, however, seen Mr. Kung's private office, far in the back of the treasure-filled rooms.

"Shall I come too, Father?" Stephanie asked.

"No, it is not necessary," Mr. Kung replied.

It was the end of an evening. Winter was over, the city was crowded again, and the spring season had begun. He and Stephanie had been to the opening of a new play and, returning, had found Mr. Kung waiting for them in the library, where, magnifying glass in his hand, he had been examining a long hand scroll of Chinese landscape. When they came in he had put scroll and glass aside and, having made his invitation to the shop, he was mounting the stairs to his own rooms.

They watched him from the foot of these stairs, and Stephanie's face grew sad.

"Do you see how feebly he walks now?" she whispered. "He has been failing all winter. Yes, he never complains. What has he to say to you tomorrow, I wonder?"

"I wonder too," he said. "But I think we know."

She looked at him with sorrowful eyes, but she spoke resolutely. "Whatever he asks of you, Rann, you must not do it unless it suits your life. You have your own genius!"

"PLEASE SEAT YOURSELF," Mr. Kung said affably.

He sat down in the chair Mr. Kung indicated with a wave of his long, thin hand. It was a Chinese chair, armless and straight-backed, of polished dark wood. The back was decorated with an inset of landscape marble. Mr. Kung explained the marble inset in the chair, a special marble from the province of Yunnan in South China, which, when cut crosswise in thin slabs, was so veined that the dark streaks seemed to compose a landscape and sometimes even a seascape. The room was entirely Chinese. Scrolls hung on the walls and tall potted plants stood in the corners.

The chair Mr. Kung had assigned to him was on the left of the square table that stood in the center of the inner back wall of the room. Mr. Kung, as the elder, sat in the opposite chair on the right of the table. A Chinese manservant in a long blue Chinese robe entered silently with a teapot and two covered tea bowls. He set the tray on a side table, removed the covers from the bowls, filled the bowls with tea, covered them again, and with both hands placed one bowl before Mr. Kung and the other before the guest. Then silently he left the room.

"Drink," Mr. Kung said, and lifting his bowl he put aside the cover, sipped the hot tea, and set the bowl down again.

"My daughter tells me she has shown you many sights," Mr. Kung said.

"We've had a wonderful time together," he replied, and waited.

Mr. Kung was silent for a few minutes, as though in meditation, then abruptly began to speak.

"I am Chinese. My family in China is very ancient and honorable. We are Mandarins. I do not know how many of my brothers are still living. Nor do I know where, except for my youngest brother who escaped to Hong Kong. He lives there under another name and he does business for me there. I came to Paris many years ago, but before I could complete my studies the government in my country changed. At that I might even have returned had it not been that my honored parents were among the first to be killed. We were landowners and my parents were killed by our own farm tenants, who were land-hungry peasants. Without parents, I was compelled to arrange my own life. It was not possible for me to return to my country to marry the woman to whom I had been betrothed by my parents when we were both children. Her parents too, and she herself, probably, were also killed. Therefore I arranged my life. I had an American—what do you call it—an 'amie.' You understand?"

He nodded in reply, and Mr. Kung continued.

"I should have known better—but she wished me to marry her because she was pregnant and I did so. I wanted a family. I had a duty to carry on my family. A son would have been Chinese, though he had foreign blood. He would have borne my name. Therefore I married. As it turned out, she had been pregnant but she lost the first child through a miscarriage. I've always thought she caused it deliberately and at the time I was very angry. When she became pregnant the second time, a year later, I myself saw to the details of her care. My daughter was that child. Then later, the mother—the woman—became enamored of an American, an artist, not even a good artist, either. She left me when the child was only six years old. But she has been a good child, very intelligent. Yet she is a daughter. You also find her intelligent?"

"Very intelligent," Rann said.

"And—beautiful?" Mr. Kung asked.

"And beautiful," he agreed.

Mr. Kung sipped his tea again and set the bowl down as before. He cleared his throat and proceeded.

"I am encouraged, then, to go on with what I am about to propose. First, let me say that of all the young men I have seen, you are the only one I would choose as my son to be born to me. You have an old soul. I am too modern to believe in reincarnation—and yet I am old enough that I believe. I wish you were my natural son. It could have been so. Your mind is pure intelligence. You speak little but you understand everything. When I tell you something—anything—I can see you already know."

What could he say? He remained silent.

"In my country," Mr. Kung went on, "we have an ancient custom. Where there is no heir, no son to carry on the family name, the favorite son-in-law, the husband of a favored daughter, is adopted as the true son. He assumes the family name. He becomes the son, the heir."

Mr. Kung held up his hand to stop reply, for he had lifted his head, he had opened his mouth to speak. "Wait! I said *heir*. I am a very rich man. I am even famous. My word is trusted in this foreign country. I am an authority in the highest forms of Oriental art. I will teach you everything. You will inherit my business— when you marry my daughter."

"Sir," he said, "have you talked with your daughter about this?"

For a thought had crept into his mind as he listened to Mr. Kung's mellifluous, gentle voice, that father and daughter might have planned together this proposal. Perhaps Stephanie had even prepared for it by declaring to him previously that she did not wish to marry. Perhaps in fact she did. He had learned from Lady Mary that a woman could pretend indifference when in truth her heart was set upon something—upon someone.

"I have not spoken with my daughter," Mr. Kung now said. "It would not have been fitting until I had your word. If you are willing—if you would even consider becoming my son, then my heart rejoices. I will go to my daughter at once. But no—you are American—I must not forget that. After I have spoken to her you shall speak to her yourself. I am not old-fashioned. I will permit it. I must remember she also is partly American. It is difficult for me to remember that. And yet I never forget it either. Now I will be silent. I await your answer."

Mr. Kung smiled at him, a warm, welcoming smile, a smile of expectant happiness. He did not know how to begin. He understood by God-given instinct all that this good man, this aging Chinese father, was feeling. He shrank from hurting him, and yet he had his own life to fulfill in ways that were only just beginning to clarify. He had not faced marriage even as a possibility. Lady Mary had made the very thought of it impossible. She had ravaged some part of him. He was damaged somewhere in his inner soul. She had forced something in him too soon. What might have developed in him with natural beauty had been torn open. True, too, true, he had yielded when he should have resisted but what had at first been a physical surprise of delight had become a repulsive demand. He had indeed been used and therefore misused. Where, even if he married, it must be so different that the past would be cleansed.

"Sir," he began with resolution that was at the same time difficult. "I am honored. Indeed, sir, I don't know a man whom I would be more honored to call my father. But sir, I am not ready to marry. I have a family too—a mother, a grandfather—"

Mr. Kung interrupted. "You will be able to care for both."

"But sir," he said with urgency, "I have myself. I must consider that for which I was born—my own destiny, my fate . . . my—my job, sir!"

"You mean—you mean—you *decline?*"

"I must, sir!"

He rose, and Mr. Kung rose too. He put out his right hand but the Chinese did not take it. The Chinese face grew cold and stern.

"Don't you understand, sir?" he pleaded.

Mr. Kung glanced at his wristwatch. "Excuse me," he said. "I see that I have another appointment."

He bowed and left the room.

AN HOUR LATER Rann was in the beautiful rooms where he had been so happy for all these months. He was packing his bag, he was gathering together the few things he had brought with him, leaving all else behind, and Stephanie was with him. The bus left for the airport in half an hour.

"I must go home," he kept muttering. "I want to go home. I want to get back where I began. I have to be alone there."

He heard himself and stopped. He turned to Stephanie. She stood there, pale and silent.

"Do you understand, Stephanie?"

She nodded. Suddenly he realized he was leaving her. "Shall we ever meet again?"

"If it is our fate," she said.

"Do you believe in fate, Stephanie?"

"Of course I do. At least the Chinese part of me does."

"And the other—the American?"

She shook her head. "You'll miss the airport bus. The taxi is waiting."

"Aren't you coming with me?"

"No. I'm not coming with you. I'd only have to come home alone. Besides, I want to be here when my father comes home."

She turned her cheek and he kissed its cool, smooth paleness.

"Good-bye, Stephanie. We'll write?"

"Of course. Now, be on your way!"

PART II

PART II

When he reached New York, Rann was impatient to leave at once for home. Yet here was his grandfather and he had not the heart to go without inquiring of him so that he could tell his mother how the aged man did. A lifetime, it seemed, had passed during this trip. He had gone away a boy in experience and he had come back a man. But he had been compelled too quickly. Lady Mary had done him a damage. She forced a physical maturity upon him. What would it have been like, he wondered, if he had loved a girl, shy and young, someone his own age or even younger, and had made his own sexual way, leading instead of being led, hesitating instead of being hurried, wondering instead of being impelled? But there had been no young girl. Stephanie—no, Stephanie somehow belonged to the future. Yet if there had been no Lady Mary, might it have been Stephanie?

He was too tired to answer his own question. A deep weariness, a mental lethargy, overcame him. He had grown too quickly. His mind was too crowded. He needed time for the approach to manhood, time in which to study his own nature, divine his own needs. The thought of the quiet house in which he had been born and where he spent his childhood, yet that also always too quickly he now felt, nevertheless presented peace to his troubled spirit. No, he would not blame others. It was he who hurried himself, his restless mind, his instant imagination his masters. He would sleep, he would eat, he would rest in his mother's calm presence and gradually he would know what to do. Meanwhile he must consider the matter of military service. Those years loomed ahead—shadow or opportunity? He did not know.

He traveled the crowded, litter-strewn streets of Manhattan with a sense of distaste after the immaculate streets of England and France, seeing the people anew—his people, though they seemed strange to him for the moment. How little he knew them and how much there was to know, how much to learn! He had learned something, in a fashion, about himself, but what he had learned he now did not like. He had learned in fact that body and mind were at war in his big frame and that he had conquered neither. Indeed, he had not fed or satisfied either being, for here was his clamorous body, its passions roused, its instincts alive, and here his mind, hostile against that body. He did not want to see a girl's shapeliness or imagine her unclothed, and yet he was compelled thus to see and to imagine. He rebelled against his body, for his mind was hungry and impatient for its own satisfaction. The war was within his own members, and somewhere a third part of him hovered—his will, hesitating between body and mind. Body was tyrant and somehow it must be subdued so that he could assuage the deeper and perpetual hunger of his mind.

In this troubled state he left his modest hotel room on his first morning in New York and journeyed toward Brooklyn, intending to stay a day or two with his grandfather and then proceed westward. It was a fair morning, sunny and clear, the sky cloudless, the people walking briskly in the warm, pure air. He took a cab and watched the scene that moved slowly outside the window. Strange, strange how a people shapes its world! This could not be any other city on Earth than it was. Dropping haphazard from the sky, he would still know at once that it was American and New York. The car trundled finally over the Brooklyn Bridge and wound its way through streets until it reached his destination and stopped. He paid the driver, greeted the white-haired doorman who remembered him, and went into the elevator to the twelfth floor.

Then he pressed the doorbell and waited. Impatient, he pressed again. The door opened a few inches and he saw Sung's frightened face peering at him.

"Sung!" he cried.

Sung put his finger on his lip. "Very sick—your grandfather."

He pushed his way in, past Sung, and hastened to his grandfather's room. There, stretched upon the bed his grandfather lay, his hands crossed on his bosom, his eyes closed.

"Grandfather!" Rann cried, and leaning, he put his hand on the folded old hands.

His grandfather opened his eyes. "I am waiting for Serena," he murmured. "She is coming for me."

He closed his eyes again, and Rann gazed at him, frightened and awed. How beautiful this aged face, the waxen skin, the white hair, the carved lips above the elegant hands! Suddenly he could not bear to lose his grandfather.

"Sung!" he called sharply. "Has a doctor seen him?"

Sung was at his elbow. "He not want doctor."

"But he must have a doctor!"

"He talk he wishing die. He begin die last night—maybe five, six o'clock. He talk some lady only I don't see, and he talk he too tired waiting her and must go her side somewhere—I don't know. So no more eating, he talk me, but I make soup anyhow. He no eat. Just lying there all night talking this lady. I sit here all night too, not seeing lady, just hear him talk like she here."

"He is wishing himself to die," Rann declared.

"Maybe," Sung agreed. "Man wishing die, he die, in China same."

He shook his head, resigned and calm, but Rann went to the telephone and dialed. His mother's voice answered.

"Yes?"

"Mother, it's I," he called.

"Rannie, where are you? What—I didn't know you—"

He broke across her joyful surprise.

"I am with Grandfather—got in yesterday from Paris. Mother, he's dying—he won't see a doctor. He just lies here in his bed, waiting."

"I'll take the next flight out," she said.

RANN AND HIS MOTHER spent the summer in New York doing all that they could to instill in his grandfather some will to return to living. Each doctor who came conducted extensive examinations and at last declared that there was nothing really wrong with the old man.

"It seems he simply has no wish to go on," the last one had said with finality.

He refused any medical care and feeding him was a matter of forcing hot broth between his thin lips.

Autumn passed quickly into winter and on a brisk day with the feeling of snow in the air Rann's mother had gone into Manhattan to purchase a few warm clothes, for she had brought none with her to New York and hesitated to return home with her father so ill.

When she returned, Rann met her at the door. "Grandfather died an hour ago, Mother," he told her.

Tears came quickly to her eyes and she gave him a quick embrace and kiss. "We have been through this before, Rann, and we know life must go on."

"But there's so much I don't know how to do," Rann said. "What—"

"I'll get the proper things going. You look tired and you need to rest. Have you eaten? No? You really should, you know, we both should. There is no need to make ourselves ill."

Sung hovered about them. "I fix. I know. Soup maybe with sandwich. Coffee."

He went away, soundless in his felt slippers and Rann put his arms about his mother.

"I'd forgotten," he muttered. "I'd forgotten what death is like. But he wanted to die. He kept hearing—someone—call him." He remembered then that his grandfather had not told his mother about Serena.

"My mother—," she broke in.

He sat down in a carved chair. No, he would not speak of Serena. If his grandfather had wanted his daughter to know, he would have told her. Now he would keep the secrets of the dead.

"He simply willed himself out of life," he said.

* * *

THEY WERE IN THE JET flying westward. A few days and it was as though his grandfather had not lived. Yet both of them were conscious of the urn of ashes they had left behind. It was macabre. The ashes were so meager, a handful of chemicals that a quick wind could blow away.

"I'll send the urn to you in a couple of weeks, if you'll give me the address," the man at the crematory had said.

They had looked at each other, mother and son.

"He's never left New York after he returned from Peking," his mother said.

"He was happy here," Rann said, and thought of Serena.

"You can rent—or buy—an alcove here," the man suggested.

In the end that was what they had done. They had left the final dismantling of the apartment to Sung, and then suddenly his mother had changed her mind.

"Your grandfather left everything to you, son, even this apartment which he owned. Why not keep it? Sung can take care of it. You may not want to stay in a little Midwestern town. You will want a place of your own, someday, if not now, and in New York, doubtless. He has left you very comfortably well off. You can certainly afford it."

So they had left the apartment to Sung, and just as it was. The thought of it pleased him. He could come back.

"I will come back," he had told Sung.

"Please, sir—soon," Sung had begged.

Now sitting next to the window in the airplane he watched the clouds floating about them in the sky. He was aware of monstrous bewilderment, shock, weariness. When his father died it had been expected and prepared for. His mother had prepared him and so indeed had his father.

"Your father is approaching his next life," his mother had told him.

"Is there another life?" he had asked.

"I want to believe there is," she had said firmly.

He had accepted this, as in those days he had accepted everything, it seemed to him now. And his father had spoken easily of his future beyond Earth.

"Of course, we don't know, but with the passionate will to live that we humans seem to have, there's the probability that life continues. It's all right with me either way. I've had a wonderful time here—love and work and you, my son. What a glorious life *you* will have! Joy to you—"

"Don't," he had whispered, fighting off his tears. "Don't talk about it!"

His father had only smiled, but they had never talked of death again. One of these days when he was ready to face it, he must think it all through—gather all the evidence. Now he wanted only to live. He leaned back in his seat and fell suddenly asleep. The plane was jarring to the ground before he woke.

THE OLD LIFE FELL INTO PLACE. The house enfolded him. Here he had been infant and child. Here he had learned to walk and talk and wonder. For a few days, even weeks, it was comfort to fall into a familiar niche, to wake in the morning in his old room, to go downstairs to the logs blazing in the fireplace, the gentle clatter of his mother preparing breakfast, to know the day lay ahead of him, his to possess. Neighbors came in to greet him. After a while even Donald Sharpe called on the telephone.

"Well, Rann—back from your jaunt abroad? What's next?"

"I don't know, sir—I suppose military service somewhere. My induction notice has arrived and I'm to go on Thursday for the preliminaries."

"No idea where, I suppose?"

"No, sir."

"Try to come and see me before you leave!"

"Thank you, sir."

He would not go. He knew too much now. He was no longer a boy. And yet he was not quite a man. There were these years facing him, a barrier between past and future, years when he must lend his body to his country, years which he must spend in some unknown place, performing an unknown duty. There was no use in planning until these years were over, and still he could not keep from planning.

He listened, without hearing, to his mother's determinedly cheerful chatter. There was a comfort in being with her but that was all. Yet though he knew his life had now proceeded beyond her ken or reach, he was aware that she, too, knew this and so she did not question him about Lady Mary or about Stephanie. Of Lady Mary he did not speak, but he told her of Stephanie, briefly and casually, at breakfast one morning.

"The sort of girl who is—well, one of a kind. She isn't French, nor is she Chinese, and certainly not American, and yet somewhat each."

He was silent for so long that his mother encouraged him.

"She sounds interesting, at least!"

"Yes," he agreed. "Yes, certainly she is interesting. Very complex, perhaps! I feel I'd have to be a good deal older before I'd understand her."

He paused again, undecided, and then went on.

"You'll be amused by this, Mother! Her father is an old-fashioned Chinese, though he's lived in Paris for so many years. He has no son, and it seems that when this is the case a Chinese may ask his son-in-law to become his son and take his name. Well, he asked me to be that son-in-law!"

He was half-laughing, in some embarrassment, and she laughed aloud. "How could you refuse such an offer?"

"Well, Stephanie had warned me. She told me she didn't want to marry at all. And certainly I don't . . . not at this point in my life when I don't know—can't know—my future."

She grew suddenly serious. "Have you any idea inside yourself, Rannie? Of what you want to do—and be?"

"No, except that I don't want to work for anyone. I don't want to be part of a corporation or in any organization I can't control. I want to work by myself, for myself. It's the only way to ensure my independence. I know, of course, that whatever else I do, I will also write. It's already sort of a compulsion in me."

She looked at him with troubled eyes. "You're taking a great risk, aren't you?"

"But on myself," he said.

They were silent for a moment. He piled pancakes on his plate again. His appetite was enormous.

"Eat," she always said. "You have a big body and very little flesh on your bones."

"Well," she said now, "you're lucky in one way, at least. Your grandfather left you all he had. We won't know yet just how much it is, but he wrote me that you wouldn't starve, and that you would always be comfortable if you were careful."

"He wrote that?"

"Yes, before you came home. I think he knew he hadn't much time."

"We liked each other, Mother—though I didn't know what to make of him."

He hesitated and then told her what he had not planned to tell her.

"You don't know it—but he married again, after Grandmother died."

He watched her face and suddenly it grew hard. "It was never a marriage. She simply moved in—Serena Woolcotte. Oh, there was some sort of civil ceremony but not a proper marriage. We knew about her."

"We?"

"My aunt and I."

"But he never told—"

"There are things one doesn't need to be told. Everyone knew Serena."

"What was she?"

"A woman whose father had too much money and too little time and left her to meddle in men's lives."

"Mother!"

"Well, she did!"

"But that doesn't tell me anything—meddle in men's lives!"

"She had nothing else to do and that's why I warned you against your Lady Mary!"

He stopped short, not wanting to talk about his Lady Mary. He got up from the breakfast table. He had been notified to report for induction, and this was the day.

SEVERAL MONTHS LATER HE WAS IN KOREA, stationed at a base on the line between north and south. Behind him lay the crowded miles of South Korea. In front of him were the mountains of North Korea. A bridge toward the left as he faced north was connection and prevention. If he crossed that bridge, he would be shot down. He had no intention of crossing it; indeed, he had a horror of it. At night he woke himself out of the nightmare that unwittingly he had crossed it. Day after day he patrolled the line between north and south, he and others with him, a dull, dangerous, mechanical task from which there was no relief or recreation—or at least recreation that attracted him.

"Get yourself a girl," the nasal-voiced sergeant had drawled the first night his company had arrived at the base camp. "Don't pick up with these broads that talk English. They've been around a lot and they're rotten with disease. You'll have to fight 'em off, though. They're bold as brass—walk up to you and pull down your zipper before you know it! Naw, you find yourself a nice little country girl and shack up with her. She'll look after you—they all know how, these little gooks!"

He had not taken up with anyone. He had simply watched the other fellows, laughing, shamefaced, apologetic, boasting as they found girls. He had no desire to imitate them. In a way he could not explain, he now comprehended that Lady Mary had instilled in him a certain good taste. At least they had made love in beautiful surroundings. She herself had been fastidious, clean, and perfumed. Now it was impossible for him to imagine lying with one of these crude Korean whores, unwashed and stinking of garlic, or even the girls in Seoul, whither he had gone on his first three-day leave. He saw them in bars and recreation rooms, aping the garb and the mannerisms of Hollywood stars of an earlier generation, and he could scarcely be courteous when one and another coaxed and wheedled as he sat apart and alone.

"You, nice boy! Lonesome, maybe? You dance, please? I like dance very much."

"Thanks, no. I'm just here for a nightcap."

"Nightcap?"

"A drink before I go to bed."

"Where you sleep, big boy?"

"I am staying here in the hotel."

"What room number?"

"I—forget."

"Look your key."

"I—left it at the desk."

"I think you not liking girls. Maybe you only liking boys."

"Certainly not!"

"Why you not dance, big boy?"

"Not tonight."

One by one they tried and one by one they went away and he was alone and yet not lonely. That was the strange element of his life—he was never lonely because he was beginning to write. He had discovered that in communing with his own mind he was in communication with life. There was a certain permanence in putting down words on paper even in his letters to his mother. They were there in the morning, his thoughts of the night before. He was relieved of inward pressure. He could endure the stupidities of his life in this wild, strange country where he had no business to be. The people were like none he had ever known, basically a nomad people although they lived in villages centuries old. He found books about them in an English bookshop in Seoul and with his insatiable desire to learn and to know, he became absorbed in the mere comprehension of the Korean people. From learning he began to write his private conclusions: "They have never ceased to be nomads at heart, these Koreans! They began as a nomad people long ago in Central Asia and they wandered in search of a place to rest, being persecuted by warrior tribes. This explains their coming finally to this tail end of land, this peninsula, hanging between China, Russia, and Japan. There was nowhere to go from here, except to push northward into Russia, and across the Bering Strait, which then was a land bridge to what is now Canada and thence southward, who knows how far? It is no accident that Americans and Koreans are so much alike. Indeed today when the Korean mess boy was cleaning the tables he muttered something about one of the fellows being Choctaw, and when I asked what that word meant, he said 'too-short man.' Whereupon I remembered that we have a tribe of American Indians, the Choctaw, who are short men. Coincidence? There is more than coincidence."

And again, on a hot August night: "Today I was on border duty. I marched for hours on our side of the line, gun on my shoulder and staring into the sullen face of the North Korean guard on the other side. One step toward him, one step across the line, and he would have shot me. One step over the line toward me and— would I have shot him? No—I'd have thrown him back where he belongs. What absurdity! He is about my age—not a bad-looking fellow. I wonder what he thinks about while he is staring at my white face. Perhaps he is wondering what I am thinking about him. There is no possible communication. Yet under ordinary circumstances, were we not enemies we would have many questions to ask each other. Now we'll never ask them. That is what I hate most about this war game. It cuts off communication between peoples. We cannot ask questions and so we cannot get answers.

"Tonight there was a breakthrough. Three North Koreans in the dark of the moon crossed the border. We caught them at once, but not before I shot one of them. Thank God I did not kill him—only a shoulder wound, but it bled horribly. Of course he was taken to the hospital here at the base. I suppose he will be turned over to the Korean command—probably shot after he is patched up. I can't think about these irrationalities."

And again, after his next period of rest and recreation: "I can't understand, in spite of my own clamoring flesh, how our fellows can penetrate the bodies of these worm-ridden, germ-infested Korean girls! There must be decent girls but we don't meet them, of course. I don't want to meet them—any of them."

And still later: "Today I met the general's wife. She happened to be in his office unexpectedly. I have been appointed his aide as of last week and it was the first time I had seen her. She is between forty and fifty and still kittenish. I don't know what to make of her. Fortunately, I don't have to make anything of her, but she kept looking at me—bluntly put, at my crotch. Whereupon I looked above her head."

The next day after this meeting the general sent for him. He stood before the desk and saluted smartly.

The general threw an order over his shoulder while he sorted papers. "A senator on a fact-finding trip arrives day after tomorrow. As if we didn't have enough to do with meetings now every few days with these damned Reds! My wife called me to send you to our quarters today—she needs some sort of help about something—better go over there for an hour or so and see what it is she wants."

"I will, sir," he said.

When he reached the general's bungalow, however, there seemed little for him to do and, vaguely uneasy, he left as soon as he could.

The next day the general invited him to a dinner party being given for the senator and he attended, feeling he must accept an invitation from the general. The night after the dinner party he wrote:

"Am I imagining this nonsense? I swear I am not. The general's wife put me at her left at the dining table tonight. The senator, a lanky fellow from some western state, sat at her right. She said to me, laughing when I hesitated to sit down, 'I'm putting you where you'll be handy in case I need something.' So I sat down. The table was crowded and her left knee touched my right knee under the table. I moved immediately, but in a few minutes I felt her foot pressing between my feet, her leg against mine. I could not believe it. I moved again, and again she moved against me. And all the time she was chattering to the senator. But as I moved she turned her head toward me and gave me a coy little smile and pressed her foot further between my feet, her leg almost over my knee. I moved my chair and was out of reach. She did not speak to me again. It's nothing, but I don't like it."

The next morning he was on duty in the general's office. When he entered, the general gave him a frosty look. He saluted and stood at attention, awaiting orders as usual.

"At ease," the general said.

He dropped his hand and stood waiting.

"Sit down," the general said.

He sat down, surprised.

"I'll be frank with you," the general said abruptly. "I like you. I've counted on you. You're old for your age. You're officer material. Have you ever thought of a military career?"

"No sir," he said.

"Well, think of it, because I'm going to kick you upstairs, Colfax. I'm going to see that you get promoted."

"I'm quite happy as I am, sir," he said.

"I'm going to promote you anyway," the general insisted.

He was a kindly man, his blue eyes friendly under his graying hair, a handsome man, his face, the features clean-cut, was kind yet somehow sad in unsmiling firmness. He went on speaking, leaning back in his chair, his left hand playing with a silver paper knife, its handle studded with Korean topaz.

"I have to move you out on my wife's demand, but I'll move you up, at least."

Rann was astounded. "But what have I done, sir?"

The general shrugged. "I understand, of course—you young men are here for months on end and nothing but these Korean girls around—you are men, after all—" The general paused, flushing slightly, and pressed his lips together. The silver paper knife slipped from his fingers, and he took it up again and gripped it in his right hand.

"But I still don't understand," he said, bewildered.

The general put down the paper knife. "Bluntly, Colfax, my wife told me that last night you made obscene gestures to her under the table during dinner."

"I? Obscene—" He broke off, the blood rushing to his head.

"Don't apologize—or even explain," the general said. "She's still a pretty woman."

Silence fell between them, intolerable silence. He could not endure it.

"Be silent," the general commanded. "You will get your orders tomorrow."

"Yes sir."

The next day, as the general had told him, Rann received his orders. He was distressed that he had been unable to argue the accusation made by the general's wife, but to argue with a superior would have been to lose, and perhaps it was best to take his orders and let matters rest. He had been promoted and transferred to Ascom, a base southwest of Seoul, and was put in charge of the supply station there. It was the main supply station for the American military forces in South Korea and his position was responsible and detailed enough that it kept him busy for a few weeks until he discovered all that was expected of him. Then he found he had even more time than before for pursuing his own unquenchable thirst for knowledge.

He began to speak Korean, a strange guttural language, unlike anything he had ever heard or spoken before, unlike even the little Chinese he had learned from Stephanie. He asked questions of all Koreans he came in contact with during his daily work, and read books on Korean history long into each night. He began to realize how little Americans knew of these strange people in their geographically strategic country and how, unknowing, his own people had seriously affected their history, indeed were affecting it now, with the American military in South Korea and the truce, American-imposed, at the 38th parallel. He had watched the UN group, including American and South Korean delegates, at the peace talks as they read long lists of infractions of the truce agreement at the meetings there, and had watched the North Korean delegates and their Chinese advisors completely ignore all that was said. Indeed, more than once he had seen these enemy delegates, with their haughty bearing, sit and read comic books throughout the entire proceedings.

In his job in supply he became aware, also, of the well-organized black-market operations, with some Americans getting rich passing out supplies to Koreans to sell on the black market long before the supplies could reach his own warehouses. Rann saw all of this and much more. He saw the American men, many of them officers, involved with Korean girls and he saw the inevitable children who were born. Beautiful children, half-American, and yet doomed to live on the lowest level of Korean society because of their racial mixture. He had never heard of any of this before he came to Korea though he had read the daily newspapers and all of the newsmagazines.

Months passed and yet Rann could not learn enough of Korea, and while he wrote something each night, in the form of a diary, he still felt he had not exhausted the wealth of knowledge he gathered. Then a strange phenomenon began to take place in Rann's fertile imagination—at least, strange for him as it had never happened to him before. From all of the Koreans he knew, a man well known to him, a composite, came to Rann in his imagination. He was no one person, actually, and yet he was all Koreans and all of Korea was his background. He began to speak to Rann and he told Rann the story of his life. He was a very old man, his life beginning in the late 1800s and continuing through the Japanese occupation of Korea, World War II, and the Korean War. He told of the four sons he had, two of them killed in the war, one of them now in the government, and the other, the youngest one, deeply involved in the black market.

Soon after the old man began to speak in his imagination, Rann carefully wrote down everything he said. He reported every conversation exactly as he heard it, each detail in the long life of the old Korean. Page after page he wrote, night after night, until he saw in his imagination the old man as he lay dying, his two sons standing by his bed, and Rann wrote what he saw and heard. After this night the old man never came upon his imagination again, and Rann felt somehow satisfied in his knowledge of Korea, his thirst quenched for the first time in his life that he could remember. He bundled the pages carefully and mailed them to his mother, thinking that in this way she could share some of his life here. He had not written to her often while he was writing these pages, and perhaps she would be less concerned when she saw all he had learned.

His mother's letter surprised him. "Darling," she wrote, "you didn't tell me what to do with your book when you sent it to me, and I didn't know what to do. The first thing I did was read it and, darling, it is very, very good. It is so good, in fact, that I knew I was not truly capable of doing anything with it, so, and I do hope you won't mind, darling, I took it to your old professor, Donald

Sharpe. He was so excited when he read it that he called a friend of his in the publishing business in New York and took a plane to the city the next day with the manuscript. Well, darling, you have begun, at last. The publisher has called me three times in two days. He feels the book is very timely and they want to rush it into print right away.

"They are offering you a twenty-five-thousand-dollar advance, and Donald Sharpe thinks that's very good for a new author, and they also want the rights to your next book. Anyway, darling, congratulations! Your father would be so very proud of you, as, of course, I am. I gave the publisher your address and they will send the contract on to you."

Indeed, the contract was in the same mail as the letter from his mother. Mingled with his surprise, Rann could not suppress a feeling of deep pleasure pervading his being. He had considered revising the papers he had written at some future time and possibly for publication, but that his writings were considered publishable as they were pleased him greatly. He signed the contract and mailed it back to the publisher with instructions to deposit his earnings to his New York account and then he wrote to his mother.

"You did the right thing under the circumstances, you may be sure. I do not know why I wrote those many pages except that my character, the old Korean man, haunted my imagination and writing down what he had to say seemed the only way to rid myself of him. I am free of him now that it is done. That the pages can be published as they are pleases me, of course, though I did not write them with publication in mind. It is just that the story is true, though the characters are mine, and the Korean people have no one to tell the story for them. Somehow I had to tell someone."

Rann had no close friends in Korea and so he told no one of his book. The publisher consulted him about the title and Rann could think of none better than *Choi*, the family name of the old man of his imagination.

In the weeks that followed he read and returned the galley proofs. It wasn't long before a neat package arrived for him containing a copy of the book itself: *Choi*, by Rann Colfax.

Rann sat down and read it through and then he placed the book on the shelf containing his other books about Korea.

It is a good job, he thought to himself. Indeed, he had said what he had to say, and there was no more. He wondered if Americans would read what he had written and if they did, would they understand it?

A few days later Jason Cox, another supply sergeant and one of the men who worked with Rann, came running into the office waving a copy of the military newspaper frantically over his head.

"Rann, you old son of a gun, when did you do it?" he shouted.

"What?"

"This!" The man banged a copy of the newspaper down on Rann's desk and pointed at the front page.

Rann stared at the headline, COLFAX WRITES EXPOSÉ. The article continued. "Rann Colfax, a supply sergeant now stationed at Ascom supply base in South Korea, and a surprisingly young newcomer to the literary scene, has, in spite of his youth, produced what will undoubtedly prove to be one of the most beautifully written novels of this century. His characters have been drawn straight from life and are presented with such tender understanding that long before the last page has been finished one feels one knows the Korean people as human beings rather than 'gooks.' He traces the life of a Korean man of the upper classes from the late 1800s through the Japanese occupation, the Second World War, the Korean War, and up to our present military involvement in South Korea. Aye, and therein lies the rub—Sergeant Colfax has written of the military entanglement with the black market and prostitution rings in South Korea with such realism it is obvious he must have had firsthand knowledge of his subject. It remains only for Sergeant Colfax to give the true names of his characters for the arrests to be made. He has left a lot of questions as yet unanswered, and I will not be surprised if they must be answered to the proper authorities in the future. If I were in authority, I would certainly want to know where and how he gets his information, for he seems to be doing a better job than any of our so-called intelligence agencies. It will be interesting to see what follows.

"In the meantime, all thinking Americans should go out and get this book and read it and then reread it, for it is probably the greatest book about a people that has ever been or ever will be written. Definitely recommended!"

"Come on, Colfax," Jason urged. "Give! I've already ordered your book along with dozens of other people down at the bookstore this morning and we are supposed to have it in about ten days, but meanwhile, ole buddy, you can tell me. Who are all of these people you've written about and not named?" An exaggerated shrewd look came on his face. "You'll be going home soon and maybe I could put the info to good use."

"I really don't know what you are talking about, any more than I know what this newspaper is talking about. No one in my book is taken from life, and I couldn't name one of the characters in it if

I had to. The people are real enough to me, but it stops there. They came out of my imagination."

"That's a good story for the higher-ups," Jason said, winking his eye and turning up the corner of his mouth. "But you don't have to keep it up with me. After all, we've worked together all these months and we're buddies. You can tell me anything. It won't go any further."

Rann was grateful when the phone on his desk rang and he waved good-bye to Jason as he answered, "Good morning, Ascom supply depot."

"Sergeant Colfax, please," the voice on the other end of the line purred.

"This is he."

"Yes, Sergeant Colfax. General Appleby would like you to be in his office tomorrow morning at ten o'clock. He says he would like to read what you have written and asks that you bring a copy along. We will see you at ten a.m., Sergeant Colfax."

A metallic click ended the conversation before Rann could ask any questions.

The rest of the day was taken up with the telephone and with people stopping by the office to discuss the article with him. Rann could not understand all of the excitement since no one here had read his book anyway. Everyone seemed slyly "in" on the information about which he had written. He was invited to several parties during the afternoon but Rann declined, preferring to get to bed early to be fresh for the interview with the general the next morning.

The general's office looked different when he entered the reception room. He must have appeared surprised as he wondered if he had made a mistake, for the girl at the desk explained, "Go in. You are in the right place. The requisition finally came through last week for our new carpet. We waited two years for it. The red looks nice, but it makes me nervous."

Rann looked at the room. Yes, it was the same except for the bright-red carpet in stark contrast with the black teakwood desk and black leather couches.

The same carpet was in the general's office and gave a rose cast to the beige grass paper on the walls.

"I didn't actually write the book for publication, sir," Rann explained to the general. "I wrote it more or less as a personal record of the Korea I've come to know since I've been here."

"I'll have to read this and talk to you again," the general said. "I suspect with all this publicity that the pressure will be on me to look into this black-market business and come up with some answers. Where did you get your information?"

"That's just it," Rann explained. "I don't have any information. All I did was look at all that was going on, and what I have written is the only logical way it could be done."

"Well, I'll read this and get back to you. In the meantime, don't talk to anyone about any of this. The whole damned country is buzzing as it is. Why don't you take a few days off and go down to Pusan and lie in the sun for a while. It will give me a chance to boil this whole thing over and I'll call you down there. There are some reporters from the local papers in the outer office now and I think the best thing to say is that you have no comment until they have had a chance to read the book. That should stall things for a while."

* * *

IN PUSAN, THE BEACHES WERE WIDE, the sky clear above a sparkling blue sea, the soft green hills blending into the gray, rugged mountains in the background. Rann had been there for three days when the general called him.

"Well, Colfax, you've written quite a book. The only thing is, from the looks of it, you had to be mixed in the black market to have written it. Now, don't get me wrong. I don't think you were, it just looks bad. We have to think of how to explain it." The general waited.

"All I can do, sir, is to tell the truth," Rann told him.

"Of course, of course," the general agreed. "It's a question of how and where that must be decided. Meanwhile, you had better get back up here. There is a meeting in my office tomorrow afternoon at two o'clock. Most of the more important officers concerned will be here and I'd like you here for that. Maybe we can clear everything up then. By the way, Colfax, Mrs. Appleby is having a little cocktail party get-together for the officers' wives' club at our house tomorrow afternoon and she would like for you to come. I thought we could go directly from my office if that's all right with you?"

"Your wife, sir?" Rann knew he could not refuse, but he felt his face flush as the memory of his anger came back to him.

"Yes, certainly, fine woman, my boy, never holds anything against anyone. You will come, of course?"

"Yes sir, of course." Rann took the next train back to Seoul.

The general started the meeting the next day. "Gentlemen," he said, "I don't believe Colfax has had anything to do with all of this. I think he is just young and has a fertile imagination. However, in what he calls his logical way he just may have hit on a few things that can help us. I think we should ask him all the questions we can think of and then start a full-scale investigation before his book hits Korea. I am giving Colfax an early discharge, and I'm sending him back to the United States now. He can wait there. I don't want the wrong people to get hold of him while he is here."

For nearly three hours Rann answered questions as carefully and as completely as he could, being careful also each time to state that his answers were his own opinions.

"You don't think we should keep Sergeant Colfax here, General, until this whole mess is cleared up?" one of the officers inquired.

"No, I don't think that will be necessary at all," the general replied, his expression thoughtful. "I think the sergeant has told us everything he actually knows, and his suppositions are repeated in his book. I'm convinced he had no involvement in it himself, so I see no need to hold him up. It's his first book and probably won't be very widely read and I feel sure we can clear all of this up in a few weeks anyway. Perhaps it's best to have him out of the way so no one can get to him. No one else knows as yet exactly what his book says, and we can hold up release for a while here until we finish our work. He should be on his way back to the States as quickly as possible. Now, gentlemen, if there are no more questions I think the ladies are waiting for us."

The general's bungalow had been recently repainted also and the stucco was now soft yellow, causing it to stand out from the other houses all painted apple green in the American sector called Little Scarsdale. The split-level interior was the same, however, all in rose pink. "Mrs. Appleby's favorite color," he had heard guests told on his former visit here.

"Well, Sergeant Colfax." Mrs. Appleby moved across the room toward him, both hands outstretched to greet him.

She seemed to have lost some weight since Rann had last seen her, though she was still a plump woman. She wore a deep-rose hostess gown of crushed velvet that brushed the carpet, the toes of her gold slippers kicking up the front hem as she walked. She still wore too much makeup and her bleached hair was styled in tight, stiff waves that reminded Rann of a corrugated tin roof.

"You really surprised everyone but me. I knew you would do something really great and you certainly have. Girls! This is the Rann Colfax simply everyone is talking about, and just wait until you read his marvelous book and you will certainly see why everyone is talking. I just knew he was going to do something and be famous and all, and I told the general the first time I saw him he was an extra-special person and he should keep him at headquarters. But, well, you all know how jealous he always is so he transferred him right on down to Ascom supply anyway."

"Now, Minnie," the general interrupted. "You know you—"

"Oh, now hush, dear," his wife scolded the general. "We all make mistakes, even you. Besides, you're all forgiven so we don't need to talk about it anymore. Tell me, Rann Colfax, where do you go from here?"

"Well, Mrs. Appleby, I guess I'll go back to New York. Perhaps I'll stop for a few days with my mother in Ohio, but only for a few days."

"Oh, I know that, silly. The general tells me you leave in a couple of days. That's why I simply had to have you here tonight. After all, it isn't every day we have a celebrity born right in our midst, is it? What I mean is, where do you go in your career?

Come on over and have a drink and tell us all about it. Here he is, girls. The most exciting man of the day and he is almost a civilian, so I guess we can all call him Rann. That will be all right, won't it, Rann?"

Rann made excuses to leave as early as he could easily do so and returned to his quarters to begin packing for his journey home. Two days later he was on his way to the United States.

SAN FRANCISCO WAS A BEAUTIFUL CITY to Rann, perhaps indeed, at this point, the most beautiful he had seen outside of Paris. In some ways the city on the hill, surrounded by the San Francisco Bay and linked to its outer parts by the beautiful Golden Gate and Bay Bridges, surpassed even Paris. His entrance into the city by military transport from Tokyo had been quiet, his name appearing on no passenger lists, and his two weeks of mustering out of the service passed without difficulty.

Rann found himself in possession of considerable free time, which he spent in the museums and parks of the city learning what he could of his surroundings for the brief time he was there. He lingered an extra week in the city after his discharge, and then he began to long for the comfort of the apartment in Brooklyn and the presence of Sung. He decided to forgo the planned visit with his mother in favor of her visiting him in New York, and one clear morning he boarded a commercial jet out of San Francisco for Idlewild Airport on Long Island.

"Are you Rann Colfax, sir?" the ticket agent had asked when he had booked his flight.

"Yes, I am," Rann answered quietly.

"Well, I certainly am glad to meet you, sir. I have just finished *Choi* and I must say it's the best book I have ever read."

The woman behind him in line as this conversation transpired sought out the seat next to him on the plane.

"I haven't had a chance to read your book yet, Mr. Colfax."

The woman was middle-aged, Rann surmised, and spoke with the accent of generations of ancestry in New England. She was slender and small and wore a black suit. The stewardess had put the matching hat and coat into the rack over the seat.

"I'm just returning from a year in Japan, so I feel a bit left out. Of course, you have created quite a stir in all of the English newspapers. I suppose in all of the papers, but we never quite know what these foreigners say about us, do we? It's unfair, in a way, so many of them speaking English when their own languages are so impossible for us to learn. I've done little but travel for the five years since my poor husband passed on, so I feel quite out of things as far as books and the theatre are concerned. I have a great deal of catching up to do and I'm certainly putting your book as number one on my list. My, you do appear young to have caused such a stir. Why did you decide to write, Mr. Colfax?"

Rann thought for a moment before he answered. "I don't know that I've ever really considered why before," he said truthfully. "I suppose I could say simply that I'm a writer."

"But of course you are, you would have to be a writer to have made such a success. But what I mean is that everyone doesn't write, and there must be some mysterious quality that turns one man into a writer and another man not. Certainly I could never write."

"I suppose it's some sort of compulsion to put things down on paper."

Rann gave up and let himself be engaged in conversation. There was no escape in such close quarters. Soon, however, he began to ask questions of his own. He found the woman eager to talk of herself.

"I'm Rita Benson," she told him. "My husband was very, very successful in the oil business and while he was alive we played around with backing shows as a sort of hobby. I've continued it since he died. As a matter of fact, I have two on Broadway now. I shall step right back into that life, I suppose. God knows there is no reason why I shouldn't. He has left me with more money than I could ever spend and I do so enjoy the people of the theatre and the parties and all of that. Do you enjoy that sort of thing, Rann? Surely I may call you Rann—and of course you will remember my name is Rita?"

The conversation continued with her extracting his promise that he would let her introduce him to the theatre crowd in New York and as the plane landed they had exchanged addresses and phone numbers and promised to meet again in a few days.

When they rose from their seats, Rann took her carry-on bag from her and they proceeded together to the baggage claim area. Photographers' flashes blinded him as they entered the terminal.

"This must be Rita Benson and Rann Colfax," the reporter spoke in an excited voice. "How very interesting. How did the two of you meet?"

They explained they had met on the plane and Rann helped her into her car.

"Are you sure you won't let me drop you off, dear boy? It won't be out of my way as I'm staying in New York a few days before going on to Connecticut."

Rann agreed, taxies difficult at this hour, and her long black limousine glided easily through the traffic and the chauffeur put his luggage on the elevator of his apartment building. Rita Benson offered him her hand through the window of the car and he held it for a moment in his own. Her hand was warm and soft and well cared for.

"Don't forget, dear boy, you will hear from me soon. I have your promise now."

The car moved away from the curb and into traffic and Rann stood for a moment on the sidewalk before entering his building.

"It's nice to have you back, sir," the ancient doorman greeted him with enthusiasm.

"Thank you," Rann told him, and rode the elevator to his own floor. He banged the knocker and Sung opened the door, a dusting cloth in his hand. His round, usually expressionless face creased into a wide smile.

"Very glad seeing you home, master. I waiting very long time here."

"I'm home at last," he replied.

Yes, he was at home, his own home. Sung unpacked the bags while Rann telephoned his mother.

"Rann! Where are you?" Her voice sounded young and fresh over the air.

"Where I belong—in Grandfather's—no, in my apartment."

"You aren't coming home?"

"This is home now. You'll come and visit me."

"Rann—but I suppose you're right. Are you well?"

"Yes."

"You sound as if something were wrong."

"I've learned a lot during these months."

"You're back sooner than I expected. Do you have plans, son?"

"Yes, I shall write books—and books and books, sometime, that is—"

"Your father always said that's what you would do. When shall I come?"

"As soon as you like."

"Let me see—next week, Thursday? My club meets here on Wednesday."

"Perfect. Until then—"

"Oh, Rann, I'm happy!"

"So am I."

"And Rann, I almost forgot. Your publisher wants you to call as soon as you can. I told him you would call right away. You won't forget, will you?"

"No, I won't forget, Mother. Thank you."

He hung up, fell into thought, and then in sudden resolution rang France, Paris, and Stephanie. At this hour, reckoning time, she'd be home. At home she was. A Chinese answered in French that if he would wait only one moment, mademoiselle would be at the telephone. She had only just arrived with her honored father.

He waited the moment, which lengthened to several, and then heard Stephanie's clear voice speaking English.

"But Rann, I thought you yet in Korea!"

"Returned to New York only today, Stephanie! How are you?"

"As ever—well. Working very hard to speak good English. Am I not speaking quite well?"

"Excellent, now what will become of my French?"

"Ah, you will forget nothing! When are you coming to Paris?"

"When are you coming to New York? I have a place of my own—remember I wrote you?"

"Ah you! Writing me one letter—two, maybe!"

"I couldn't write letters in Korea—too much to do, to see, to learn. I repeat, when are you—"

"Yes, yes, I heard the first time. Well, in truth, my father is opening a shop in New York. For which case we come, perhaps in a few months."

"How can I wait?"

She laughed. "You are being polite like a Frenchman now! Well, we must both wait and while we wait we will write letters. Are you well?"

"Yes. Do you think of me sometimes?"

"Of course, I not only think of you I read about you. Your book is very famous, and it is to be in French next week. Then I can read it and see why everyone in the English papers talks so much."

"Do not expect too much of me. It's only my first book. There will be others. Now, Stephanie, I really must see you. You are a jewel in my memory!"

She laughed. "Perhaps you will not think so now that you have seen beautiful girls in Asia!"

"Not one—do you hear me, Stephanie? Not one!"

"I hear you. Now we must say good-bye. Time is money, telephoning so far."

"Will you write me?"

"Of course."

"Today, I mean."

"Today."

He heard the receiver put down and there was silence. Suddenly he wanted to see her now, at once. A few months? It was intolerable. He considered flying to Paris tomorrow. No, it would not do. He had much to arrange in his own mind. He had to order his own life, begin his work, plan his time. What was ahead of him now?

Rann decided to postpone the call to his publisher until the following morning. The flight had not been restful, though he had enjoyed Rita Benson's endless chatter, in a way. He felt now the need of a hot bath and clean, fresh garments and an evening of relaxation under the care of Sung. When he entered the large master bedroom where he had moved when his grandfather died, he found that Sung, the faithful man, had unpacked his luggage putting everything in its place and had laid a comfortable silk robe and pajamas on the bed for him. At home, Rann thought as he ran steaming water into the tub. If Serena had visited his grandfather in these rooms, Rann had experienced no such invasion of privacy. Indeed, nothing interrupted his comfort here and he thought of his gratitude to his grandfather as he rested in the tub. He dried himself vigorously and, deciding he was not quite ready for the pajamas, he selected a pair of trunks from a drawer and went out upon the terrace for the warmth of the sun.

"You have slept, young sir, and I fear you might chill in the late air."

Thus Sung had waked him. The sun was gone and Rann moved into the library where Sung had left a cocktail on his desk next to the paper.

Rann sipped the cool drink and glanced at the front page of each section of the paper. In the theatre section the headline arrested his attention.

RITA BENSON ADDS RANN COLFAX TO STABLE. Rann read on. "Broadway's brightest angel, Rita Benson, widow of oil tycoon George Benson, arrived in New York today from Tokyo with none other in tow than Rann Colfax, whirlwind young author of best-seller *Choi*. Rita certainly wastes no time in gathering up the eligible young men around town. . . ."

Rann could read no more. He picked up the telephone and called the St. Regis, where Rita Benson said she was staying.

"Of course I haven't read it, dear boy," she said when he was put through to her room. "But you mustn't pay any attention to what they say. They have to have something to say. You are new to all of this as yet, but you must learn that we simply go on with our lives no matter what the press might write. Now, how about dinner here with me tomorrow. Then we can go to a show. Of course they will talk, but let them, I say! I cannot start at this stage to base my life on what others may say, and you would be wise to feel the same. Anyone important to you or to me will know the truth and who else matters? Of course I enjoy a handsome young escort. That's why I do business with handsome young men. I don't haul them off to bed, dear one, but if I have a choice between a handsome young man and a wrinkled-up old one for an evening, I don't see that there is any choice. They will soon run out of things to say and it will all die down anyway, and don't you worry about it."

Rann was comforted by her light acceptance of the article. He put on cool linen slacks and a slip-over shirt and enjoyed an excellent dinner of sweet and sour chicken, one of Sung's specialties. After dinner he put on the pajamas and robe that had been laid out for him earlier and went to his favorite room, the library, where the thoughtful Sung had placed his favorite nightcap on his desk. He selected a book from the shelves, a biography of Thomas Edison, and settled into the comfortable chair. He never tired of the lives of great people, and while he knew well the life of Thomas Edison, this biographer he had not read and he approached the book with pleasure.

"Will you be needing anything else, young sir?" Sung inquired of him later in the evening.

"No, thank you, Sung. I shall be going to bed soon."

He rose and went into his bedroom, where his bed had been turned down and all had been made ready for his comfort on his first night home.

RANN OPENED HIS EYES in the morning, roused by the sunlight streaming through the window opened earlier by Sung. It was the man's way of waking Rann.

"One must never wake one quickly," he had explained. "The soul wanders over the Earth while body sleeps and if one is waked too quickly soul has no time to find its way home."

Sung now stood beside Rann's bed waiting for him to wake, a pot of hot coffee on a silver tray held in his hands.

"So sorry to wake you, young sir," he said. "But there is a man call three times in hour, say he must talk to you. Sounds important. His name Pearce. Say he publisher."

"That's all right, Sung." Rann accepted the coffee the man poured for him. "What time is it?"

"Ten o'clock, young sir."

Rann was mildly surprised at himself for sleeping so late. The telephone rang again as he was putting on his robe. He took his coffee to the library.

"Yes, sir. One moment, sir. He come now." Sung handed Rann the instrument. It was his publisher, George Pearce.

"Quite some article in the paper, Colfax. Now we must keep your name before the public. Where did you meet Rita Benson?"

Rann explained the meeting.

"Damn good stroke of luck, if you ask me. Otherwise you might have slipped into New York with no notice. You should have let me know your flight, then I could have arranged a reception for you and had full coverage."

"I didn't think of it," Rann said truthfully.

"Well, we have to think of it from now on. You're a bestselling author but the public is fickle. Can't let you slip out of sight. No harm done, though. Rita to the rescue. Can you have luncheon with us today?"

"Yes, of course."

"Good. We will meet at the Pierre at noon. My public relations people will be with me and afterward we may invite the press for a few drinks and see if we can drum up a headline or two. I think we had better play up the playboy angle now that they've started it."

"I'm afraid I don't know anything about such things, sir."

"You will . . . right after luncheon. Just leave everything to us. I've got the best PR in the business."

Rann ate the hearty breakfast Sung prepared for him and bathed and dressed leisurely and took a taxi into Manhattan to the Pierre.

"Well, well, well," George Pearce greeted him in the lobby of the hotel.

He was a tall man, stylishly dressed, a shock of blond hair falling across his forehead. Rann judged him to be in his forties, though he appeared ageless.

"So, this is Rann Colfax. And you are a handsome one too. Your photographs don't do you justice. Must get some new ones. Margie, make a note of that, new publicity photos right away."

The woman with him scribbled frantically in her notebook while he talked. They were seated in the comfortable dining room.

"I've ordered my favorite meal and I hope you will like it."

The man's assurance impressed Rann. He had never met anyone like him and found himself liking him.

"The PR people will join us in a while, but there are some things we should settle first," he went on. "Margie, he will need new clothes. These are nice but too traditional for the image. Got a tailor, Rann?"

Rann shook his head.

"Mine will take good care of you. Not cheap, but worth it. The best. Margie, make an appointment and tell that Italian to put a rush on everything. Sports clothes, suits, dinner jackets, the works, all the latest styles. And get an appointment with that barber on Fifth Avenue. You know the one. Rann's haircut looks too much like leftover GI. Oh well, we can change that."

"Mr. Pearce—," Rann began.

"Call me George," the publisher interrupted. "We are going to be working closely together. No time for formalities."

Rann continued. "All right, George, but I think I should be perfectly honest with you. I have always been just myself. I come from a university town in Ohio. I know nothing about styles and haircuts and press conferences and playboys and all of that, and I don't know that I really want to learn."

The older man studied his face carefully. "Rann, suppose I give it to you straight. You are a very young man, too young, in fact, to have written as good a book as you have. Nevertheless, you did it. We took a big chance on you when we published your book and now we have to make it pay off. Nothing personal, understand. I like you fine. I had thought of building you up as boy genius, intellectual and all of that, but that takes time. Your book will establish your brain—if people read it. That's where we come in. If people want to read the kind of drivel that was in the papers about you last night and will buy your book as a result of it, then it's up to us to give 'em lots to read in the papers. It's as simple as that. You are a property first and a person second so far as I'm concerned. Your sales have risen steadily and you are now number five on the list. Let's grab the number-one spot and see how long we can hold it. We have to sell you to the smart set in New York. They set the trend, and the smart sets of Wichita and El Paso and hundreds of other places will follow. It's a matter of promotion."

As the luncheon progressed, Rann found himself reluctantly agreeing with what the publisher had to say. The press conference had been set for five o'clock and Margie arranged a barber's appointment for him beforehand. They were joined for the dessert course by three people from the public relations department. When George Pearce explained his plan, the senior of the three spoke.

"Well, George, at least this one is going to be a lot easier than the last one you gave us. That was a dog if I ever saw one. When are you seeing Rita Benson again?" The question was directed to Rann.

"As a matter of fact, I'm having dinner with Mrs. Benson—"

The public relations man interrupted him. "Call her Rita, especially to the press. She will love it and the press will eat it up. Where do you go afterward?"

"We had planned the theatre."

"Good, then where?"

"Well, home I guess. I hadn't planned anything."

"That's good. You don't plan. We plan. Go to Sardi's. We will have a columnist there. That should keep us going for a couple of days. Now, there is a movie premier, an important one, on Thursday night. I've got some extra celebrity tickets. Do you think Rita will go with you?"

"I don't know, I'll ask her."

"Well, if she won't, we will get someone else important. Now . . ."

The conversation continued for an hour and Rann found his evening time taken up with social events at least every other evening for the rest of the month.

"Gentlemen, I hate to break this up, but we have an appointment with a barber." It was Margie who spoke. "We will see you at five."

George Pearce rose. "I'll go along with you," he said. "And we will all meet back here at five."

They arrived back at the Pierre at ten minutes before five. Rann's hair was trimmed into one of the new styles and a new black suit of a stylish cut had replaced his more conservative one. George Pearce had used his influence with a fashionable haberdasher to get the suit altered for him, as well as a dinner jacket for him to wear that evening. He had even had time for a short visit to the tailor for his measurements to be taken and George Pearce assured Rann he should leave everything else to the tailor, and Rann had agreed to do so.

Now that his first press conference was so near taking place, Rann expressed some shyness. "I've never done anything like this before," he repeated.

George Pearce seemed prepared for anything. "Margie, you take Rann in for a drink and settle him down. Wait about thirty minutes, then come on up. I'll go on and be sure everything is ready."

"You must trust him, Rann," Margie said to him when they were settled into a comfortable booth in the rear of the cocktail lounge. "You are very lucky, George Pearce is the best in the business. No one in the world knows publishing as well as he does, and with the start you've already got, you are off and running. What are you working on now?"

"I really hadn't thought about it yet, and from the looks of the schedule I've been handed I won't have much chance to think about it for a while."

"They will ask you upstairs, and it shows lack of promise for an author not to be writing, so just say you are not ready to comment on it yet. That should hold them for a while—till you can get something started."

Rann began to relax with Margie. "I really have no idea what I will write or even if I will write anything publishable again. There is a compulsion to put things down on paper, but not necessarily a compulsion to write things to publish. Do you know what I mean?"

"Certainly, I know exactly what you mean." Margie was matter-of-fact as she went on. "The best thing to do is not to worry about it. You will write again and there is no way to prevent it if you wanted to. You are a writer. From my experience in this business, I would say that writers fall into two categories. The first is one who studies his crafts of expression and description, knows his word tools perfectly, studies what comprises a novel or a story, devises a plot from beginning to end, and then sits down and applies his knowledge and does his work. He is frequently very good. This kind of writer can be trained. The other type is one who is haunted by an idea or a situation in existence and who cannot rid himself of it until he puts it down on paper. He may only write down the situation and present no solution, for there may not be one in existence. He may not know grammar or punctuation or even spelling, but that doesn't matter. Someone can be hired to punctuate and spell or correct these, but no one can be hired or trained to do what he does. He writes only out of existence, and his stories are made up of the situations of which life is made, the constant sights and sounds and smells and emotions of which every day is made. His work is alive, it breathes. This man must write. He cannot help it. He is a writer. The first one can write news or advertisements or manuals or not write at all, if he chooses. Not true for our second man. He writes only out of himself. He cannot have a writing task assigned to him, or even assign one to himself, and sit down and perform it as a duty. You are this second type. They are not always genius, but here is where genius comes along. You may not be a genius. It is too soon to know. You are a writer, however, it's not too soon to know that, and you are a darned good one too!" She glanced at her watch. "Oops! Drink up. God will be angry if we are late."

Rann left his drink unfinished and followed her to the elevator. He could not control a chuckle when he recalled her reference to George Pearce as "God." He felt he was entering into yet another new world with an entirely different kind of people than he had ever known. It was exciting to him and he felt the excitement throughout his being. They were alone in the elevator.

"Incidentally," he said, "thank you for what you had to say. It was not only a compliment but quite a vote of confidence."

"Don't even think about that angle." She gave him a broad smile. "I tell only the truth in my life. Not that I'm moralistic, either, but it's simpler if you only tell the truth. That way you don't always have to keep up with yourself. I told the truth. Know it, and now let's let the press know it. George Pearce is talking to them now about what a great guy you are and how smart you are and all that, which is why he wanted you to be a few minutes late. He has also given them a biographical sketch we drew up for this purpose. Just relax and be yourself. You've nothing to worry about."

Rann looked at her while she spoke. An attractive woman, thirty to thirty-five, difficult to judge, smart, pearl-gray business suit, matching shoes, an interesting oval face with lines of mirth at the corners of her eyes, her dark hair gathered on the back of her head neatly into a bun, the ever-present notebook and pencil in her hand.

Rann also smiled at her instruction to relax and be himself after all the talk at luncheon about his image and the new clothes and haircut and his schedule for the rest of the month.

The elevator door opened and they stepped into a red-carpeted hall, an open door at one end. George Pearce came down the hall to greet them.

"I didn't expect this good a turnout." His face crinkled into a grin. "Yesterday's blurb must have helped. This is going to be easy for you, Rann. Just remember that most of these are top people and they are friends."

There were about forty men and women with their backs to the door when they entered the room, besides the public relations men Rann had met at luncheon. A table had been set up as a bar on the left wall of the room and the senior public relations man stood there. Another table had been set up facing the door. Behind the table were floor-to-ceiling French windows draped in crimson velvet exactly matching the carpets. It was to this table Rann, Margie, and George Pearce made their way. The man from the bar came over with three drinks and everyone watched them in expectant silence while George Pearce referred to his notes. He cleared his throat and rose.

"Ladies and gentlemen, you all have your biographical notes, which should eliminate a lot of questions except that I will tell you they were written by Mr. Colfax's mother while he was out of the country and his information may very well differ from hers on some points. So don't hesitate to ask any questions you may have."

The reporters responded to this with a laugh.

"I'm going to ask that Mr. Colfax remain seated throughout the interview and that you do the same and that the waiter keep everyone's glass filled. Hands? Yes, Miss Brown." George Pearce took his seat and sipped his highball.

"Mr. Colfax, I have for some time wondered how one so young could write a book such as *Choi*. Now I notice in our notes that you were ready for college at twelve. Could you elaborate on this for us, please?"

Their questions for the next forty-five minutes dealt mostly with his background and his reference work regarding his book, and Rann answered them all as completely but as briefly as possible.

A young woman in the back row who had not spoken before raised her hand. George Pearce consulted Margie before he spoke.

"Yes, Miss Adams. I'm sorry, I don't believe I've met you before."

"No." The woman's voice was well modulated. "I'm just in from the West Coast. I'm Nancy Adams from the *Trib*. Mr. Colfax, how is it you know so much detail about the black market in Korea?"

Rann felt his neck redden. "Miss Adams, I don't know anything about the black market in Korea."

"But you wrote of it so realistically. How could you do so if you do not know anything about it."

"I have been asked not to discuss that."

George Pearce cleared his throat and pinched his lower lip between his thumb and forefinger, about to speak.

"Asked by whom, Mr. Colfax?" Nancy Adams went on, hurriedly.

"One of the officers in charge."

"In charge of what, Mr. Colfax? Were you tried for involvement in the black market?"

"No, I was cleared of any involvement."

"But cleared by whom, Mr. Colfax, if not by trial?"

"By a group of officers in charge."

"Not a court-martial?"

"No."

"Just a group of officers?"

"Yes."

"Mr. Colfax, in your book there are some ranking officers involved in the black market. Couldn't it be possible that the ones who gave you a clean bill were those you wrote about?"

"No."

"But how do we know, Mr. Colfax, if, as you say, you don't know? What was the name of the officer in charge?"

"He was not involved."

"Then if you were not involved and he was not involved, why not give his name?"

"It was General Appleby." Rann wished he hadn't spoken the name, but the woman had made him nervous with her persistence.

George Pearce rose. "Ladies and gentlemen, I hate to break this up but I know Mr. Colfax has to dress for dinner. Thank you very much and I hope that this has been helpful."

"Mr. Colfax, one more short question, please." It was the first woman who had questioned him. "I think my readers would be interested in knowing what a young serviceman would choose to do on his first night out in New York after being away for so long. Do you mind?"

"Simple for me. Dinner and the theatre."

"With anyone special?"

"Rita, Rita Benson."

"Oh, I see. *Very* special! Thank you, Mr. Colfax."

George Pearce and Margie seemed pleased with the afternoon and parted from Rann in the lobby and Rann took a taxi home to change for dinner.

"Why, young sir, you look so different." Sung's smile showed his enthusiasm. "You so all new from morning. Looks nice like, different but nice." He took the package Rann was carrying.

"Thank you, Sung. I'll be dressing right away and I'll wear the jacket in that box."

"Your mother called, young sir. She sound upset. She ask you call."

"All right, I'll call her now, but I'll have to make it quick. I don't have any time to spare. Turn the water on in the bathtub, will you, and not too hot."

Rann sat at the desk in the library.

"How are you, Mother? Is anything wrong?" His call went through quickly.

"Oh Rann, I'm so glad you called. I don't know if anything's wrong or not until you tell me. There was this very insinuating article in this morning's paper. Rann, who is Rita Benson?" His mother sounded anxious.

Rann laughed. "No one you need to worry about. She's just a lady I met on the plane."

"Not according to this article."

"Mother, I can only tell you what I have been told, which is pay no attention to stuff like that you read in the papers. She is a nice lady, that's all."

"As long as you are sure you haven't been added to someone's stable, though I suppose that's all right too, if that's what you want."

"I'm not in anyone's stable and I'm not going to be. There is nothing to worry about. Now, Mother, I have to run or I'll be late for a dinner date."

"With her?"

"Yes, Mother," Rann laughed again. "With Mrs. Benson."

"Well, all right. We'll talk again soon."

"And I'll see you soon, Mother, and you will enjoy Mrs. Benson when you meet her."

Rann sat, thoughtful, for a moment after he hung up. He could not resent her concern. She was not actually prying. It was honest, natural concern. It was a comfort to him, in a way, to have her there in the background of his life, always concerned for his happiness.

"MY DEAR BOY, you are not late," Rita Benson said when he telephoned her room at the St. Regis forty-five minutes later.

"And never apologize. In this world anything under a half hour is on time. Do you want to come to my suite for cocktails or, in view of the papers, shall I meet you in the lounge? I must say, however, that if this is a stable, I'm paying dearly for it."

"I'll meet you in the lounge, Rita," Rann laughed. "And I'm not worried about the stable."

"Oh dear, I must be slipping." Rita Benson laughed too. "See you in a minute."

Rann was glad for the new dinner jacket when Rita Benson entered the cocktail lounge a few minutes later. Every head in the room turned to her as she came to the table. She looked to be perhaps thirty-five, though Rann suspected she was nearer fifty-five. Her long gown of wine-colored silk clung to her slender frame with the easy grace of a dress made for the one who wears it. Her closely cropped hair fit smoothly to her head, framing her face dramatically and accentuating her long, graceful neck and slender shoulders.

"Rita, you're beautiful." Rann complimented her frankly, rising to hold her chair.

"But of course I am, dear boy. God knows I work hard enough at it. Nice of you to notice, though. But you're the one. How handsome you look. Who cut your hair? Maybe I'll give him a go at mine."

They finished their cocktails quickly and moved to the dining room.

"Rann, I now want to say that your book is absolutely marvelous. I ordered it the moment I got to the hotel and was unable to put it down until I finished it, and I've begun it again. I've toyed all day with the idea of putting it on Broadway but I think perhaps the stage is not right for it. I think maybe film, though I've not done anything with film. We will have to talk about it when we have more time. Right now we are running late."

She rose from the table and Rann helped her with her stole. "Add twenty percent to our check and put it on my bill, Maurice," she said as they passed the headwaiter.

Rann could scarcely keep his mind on the play they were watching. His mind kept drifting to what Rita had said over dinner about his book. He was flattered, of course, but the idea was strange to him. He had never considered the old man's story as anything other than a book and had barely had time to get used to it as a book.

"Did you enjoy the play?" Rita asked as he helped her into her limousine afterward.

"I did very much, though I confess I had difficulty concentrating on it after the remark you made at dinner."

"You mean about your book? I mean it, but I'll have to read it again and then we will talk."

The ride to Sardi's was short. "Mrs. Benson, Mr. Colfax," the headwaiter announced clearly. "We've been expecting you. Your table is right over here. Mr. Caldwell has already arrived."

Emmet Caldwell's column was syndicated in every major newspaper in the world, Rann had long known, but he was not prepared for the man he met when they arrived at the table. He was tall and outgoing, an intelligent look in his wide-set eyes, his brow a little high for him to be considered handsome. He looked like a college professor. He rose.

"Rita, it's always a pleasure." He extended his hand. "And you are Rann Colfax. I must say that yesterday's news photo wouldn't have let me know it."

Rann shook hands. The man's grip was strong and firm and Rann liked him. There was the air of one long accustomed to his profession in all that he did.

They settled comfortably into their chairs at the round corner table and ordered a supper of the well-known Sardi steak sandwich and a tossed green salad.

Emmet Caldwell led the conversation. "Rita, is the rumor I've heard true that you are considering purchasing the dramatic rights to Rann's book?"

Rita looked thoughtful and delayed her answer until the waiter had served their drinks and left the table.

"Yes, I think you can truthfully say I am considering it. I have not decided and I am unable to do so without some very good advice. It is an excellent book, in my opinion, a moving story, beautifully told. Whether or not it will fit on a stage and do justice to the stage and the story, I do not know. Perhaps it needs film. About that I shall have to get advice. I have an appointment with a Hal Grey on Monday morning and I have asked him to read the book before then."

Rann knew of Hal Grey as the head of the most successful

independent production company in the country and winner of many awards for documentary films.

She continued, "I think if Hal is interested then he could do the right job with the book. It is a very historical novel."

Emmet Caldwell unobtrusively made notes in a small pocket-size notebook. "And what do you think of it, Rann?"

"I haven't, frankly, had time to think of it." Rann was quiet for a moment. "Margie Billows of my publisher's office mentioned I should have an agent to handle subsidiary rights, and she has made an appointment with me to introduce me to one. If Rita is interested, however, I am sure she would do well with the material."

Caldwell smiled. "I know Margie well, Rann, and if she is interested in you then you will do well to follow her advice. She is an old hand at this business and there is none better. George Pearce is lucky to have her. She really knows her way around."

The conversation continued through supper and Rann enjoyed the easy exchange between Rita Benson and Emmet Caldwell. Yes, a world within a world, he thought to himself, and its discovery fascinated him.

Sung was waiting for him when he arrived home and brought a drink to him in the library.

"Sung, you must not wait up for me when I am out late," Rann told him. "It seems I shall be late often for a while."

After a hot shower, Rann put on fresh pajamas and lay in the huge old bed in the darkened master bedroom, the night noises of the city beneath him giving a faint background for his thoughts as he remembered the events of the day and reflected on his life that had brought him here. He could almost hear his father's voice speaking to his mother many years ago.

"Give our boy freedom, Susan," his father often said. "Give him freedom and he will find himself."

Had he found himself, he thought? Was this then Rann Colfax? he wondered as sleep came to him.

The room was still darkened when Rann opened his eyes the next morning and he had to think for a moment to recall where he was. His dreams had been a mixture of Lady Mary in England and Stephanie in Paris and his mother in Ohio. How would these women react to the changes taking place in his life? The now familiar surroundings brought him back into the present. He rose and opened the draperies and the French doors leading to the terrace. The warm sunshine fell into the room. Rann put on a pair of shorts and walked out into the sun and glanced at the angle of his shadow. About ten o'clock, he judged, and time for some sun before the afternoon shadows engulfed the terrace. He settled himself comfortably on a long chair, the sun warming his lean frame.

"I got all papers like you say, young sir," Sung told him when he brought Rann's coffee to the terrace. It still amazed and pleased Rann the way his servant watched him and anticipated his wants. "They are on your desk when you ready. Shall I bring here?"

"No, let them wait. I'll enjoy the sun first."

Margie's phone call interrupted his thoughts.

"Rann, have you read the papers yet?"

Rann confessed that he had not.

"Well, I didn't think anyone would make his deadline for today, but one did—Nancy Adams of the *Trib*. I'm afraid she is nasty, Rann. It will sell books, which is good, but her overall tone is nasty. You must pay no attention. What are you doing for luncheon? We have an appointment with the agent at three o'clock and I thought we might have luncheon beforehand."

Rann agreed to meet her at noon, replaced the receiver, and began sorting through the papers for the *Tribune*. The article was on the bottom of the front page. BLACK MARKET BOY HITS BRIGHT LIGHTS. There was a photograph of him and Rita getting out of the limousine in front of the theatre. Rann read the article in which Nancy Adams explained that he, Rann Colfax—who had made a fortune on the black market in Korea, either through personal involvement or by writing about it—had been seen in the right places last night with wealthy widow Rita Benson, living high on his profits. Rann smiled bitterly as he remembered he had been Rita's guest for dinner and his publisher had arranged ahead of time to pay for everything else.

The closing line in the article disturbed Rann deeply: "It would seem that someone should care enough to check with General Appleby in Korea to see exactly how it is that Mr. Colfax was so easily cleared of involvement with the black market. One has only to read his book to see he obviously must have firsthand knowledge of the entire sickening operation."

"But she had no right to say the things she said," Rann protested to Margie as they sat over luncheon later.

"Oh, but yes she has." Margie's voice was gentle but firm. "That is the price we pay for freedom of the press," she went on. "She can write anything she wishes as long as she covers herself, which she did. She said you made a fortune off the black market—either by being involved personally, or by writing about it. That's true. You did write about it in your book, and you are making a fortune. You will make even more after her article. But you can't let it get to you."

They continued the discussion throughout luncheon and later at the office of the agent.

"You are hot, Rann," Ralph Burnett, the head of the agency, said to him. "We have plenty of clients already but we will take you on. Anything anybody wants to discuss with you about your work, refer them to us. That's all there is to it. But you have to stay hot. If you do that, we'll all make a bundle. After today's article, your book will jump to number one within a week, you'll see."

And it did. Rann sat at his desk, the book-review section of the newspaper open before him. A long, thoughtful review of his book was on the page opposite the bestseller list. George Pearce, Margie, and Ralph Burnett should be very pleased, he thought to himself.

This review pleased him also. The reviewer had understood so well everything he had tried to convey that Rann, himself, was surprised. Not all of the articles that had appeared—and there had been many—were as thoughtful or as carefully written. They had all been good and factual, except that Nancy Adams had followed up with two more articles in the *Tribune*, one in which she told of a person-to-person phone call to General Appleby in Korea. General Appleby had not accepted her call, telling the operator merely that he had no comment to make, but reporting the phone call gave her the opportunity to write her nasty insinuations all over again. Two days later she had written of a meeting she had with Sen. John Easton, a young presidential hopeful from a New England state and a member of a committee investigating military affairs, who had promised to read the book and meet with her again. She vowed that her readers would have a full report on what the senator had to say and again used the opportunity to repeat her former remarks.

In the two weeks since Rann came to New York, all that he did was reported. He wondered that the public could actually be interested in his every move. He went to the premiere with Rita on Thursday, and on Saturday they attended a charity ball. On Friday, he had dined with George Pearce and Margie, a busy but simple routine, and all was written in the gossip columns. His mother had dutifully called him several times regarding the articles and he was truly sorry for the way he had affected her life. All he could do was continue to assure her all was well with him. The telephone on his desk interrupted his thought. It was Donald Sharpe.

"Professor Sharpe, you must forgive me for not writing to thank you for introducing me to George Pearce. I've only been back for two weeks and they have been so busy. . . ."

"I know." Donald Sharpe laughed. "I read the papers. You surely do get around. Who is Rita Benson? She must be something to take up so much of your time."

Now Rann laughed. "She is a very nice lady I met on the plane from San Francisco and now she is interested in making a movie of my book. In fact, her attorneys are working to come to terms with my agent now. The newspapers blow everything up."

"I know." Donald Sharpe was silent for a moment. "What are you working on now, Rann?"

"I'm not. In fact, I can't even think of anything I want to write. I'm sure I will but this newspaper business takes all of my energy going from rage to fits of laughter."

"I can tell you how to cope with that, Rann. It may sound strange to you, but just don't read them. There is nothing you can do about anything they say and you can go on with your work if you ignore them. If you pay attention to every thing people say about you, then you will never accomplish all that you could and should accomplish otherwise. I've known people in your position before and, believe me, the only possible way to go on is to ignore all of it."

"I suppose you are right. Everyone who knows anything at all about this business says the same thing. I'm sure you understand, however, that it's a lot easier said than done."

"Of course it is, dear boy, but it's something to work for. Try it this way now and it will work. You will arrive at this position eventually—after much heartbreak and soul-searching—but if you can follow advice and begin now to pay no attention to what other people say, and especially the press, you will save yourself a lot of agony. In my own small way, I have had to learn this for myself."

The reference to him as "dear boy" and the personal overtone to the conversation brought the memory of that night in Donald Sharpe's home vividly into Rann's mind and he felt his face flush as he spoke.

"Professor Sharpe, I—"

Donald Sharpe interrupted. "Wait, Rann. Before we go any further in our relationship there are a couple of things we should clear up, and I think I can do it very quickly. In the first place, call me Don. We are not too far apart in age or station for that now, I think. In the second place, I'm sorry for what happened between us years ago but we must not let that stand in the way of our future friendship if we can help it—and we are both intelligent, so I think we can work it out. I reacted to you as any man in my position would have. Perhaps you can understand that now. You reacted to me as any boy in your position would have. Certainly, I can see that. I won't say I don't wish things could have been different. There is no need for us to lie, but as long as it's this way, then let's be friends on whatever basis we can. I think that's all there is to say on that subject."

Rann was relieved that Donald Sharpe had spoken so frankly.

"I think I'd like that, Don. So long as we can both remember the facts of the situation."

"I shan't ever forget, dear boy. Now, your mother tells me she is coming to New York in a couple of weeks and I think I might fly in with her. Who knows? Maybe now that I've given him you, George Pearce may be willing to publish something of mine. At any rate, hold a little time aside for us and we will see you soon."

Rann promised he would and sat in thought after the conversation had ended. A great deal had taken place in his own life since that night he had spent in Donald Sharpe's home and while his personal feeling of physical revulsion remained strong, he was better able to understand the pity his mother had expressed for the man at that time. It must be difficult, indeed, for a man like him to find any satisfying relationships, caught, as he was, between sexes. With his total recall, Rann could hear his father's voice as it had been during one of their long talks together.

"The world is made up of many different kinds of human beings, son, and while you, yourself, and only you, can be responsible for the kind of person you are to be, you must, however, get to know as many different types as you can, for these are the basic components of life as we know it today. Because there are thieves and because you know does not mean that you must steal. Because there are cannibals and prostitutes does not mean it's all right for you to eat human flesh or sell your own body, but the fact that it is not right for you need not stop you from knowing those who do or from trying to understand why they do so. You will be many times hurt, for you have a deep appreciation of beauty and order in all that you do and people, alas, are not always beautiful or orderly. They will not always be what you would have them be, so be content if at least they can be honest with you and you can learn to understand them as they are. You must hold yourself apart and be the kind of person you want to be. In this way, someone—somewhere—will come along to prove to you that all things of beauty must be good, and when that person does come along you will know him, for you will have known many others before, and you will be ready for the lasting relationship that is, in itself, man's deepest satisfaction."

Rann knew now that he could accept Donald Sharpe as a friend, whatever else he was, and that this friendship need not in any way affect him and what he knew himself to be, except to broaden his own understanding of yet another of the multitude of facets of human nature. Rann's thoughts were interrupted again by the telephone on his desk. It was Rita Benson.

"Rann, if I send my car for you, can you come for cocktails and dinner? I've had Hal Grey here for the weekend and we've talked of nothing but your book and there are a few angles we would like to go over with you. You could stay over and we will ride back to the city together tomorrow."

He said he would go. Sung prepared a light luncheon for him and packed an overnight bag and Rann was ready when the doorman announced that Mrs. Benson's car had arrived. Traffic was light on Sunday afternoon and Rann enjoyed the drive through the suburbs onto the parkway and into Connecticut to Rita Benson's home. It was a large old stone house she had bought and modernized and was well situated on acres of lawns and gardens, all meticulously kept. Cocktails were served to them on the south terrace, and they were enjoying the warmth of the afternoon sun. Hal Grey, seated on a long chair facing Rita and Rann, was talking.

"There are problems with the project, Rann," he was explaining. "It's an excellent story and will lend itself well to the screen, but the trouble is that there is no role important enough for an American star, which we must have to ensure a box office. I had thought the scriptwriters could write in the role of the author as the star so we would be doing the story *of* the book, which would include the story *in* the book and it would give us the role we need."

The conversation continued through dinner and on into the evening and Rann agreed to work with the scriptwriters to create the needed role.

The next day, back in the city, the three of them met with Rann's agent and Rita's and Hal Grey's attorneys, and the necessary papers were signed. George Pearce was delighted and insisted on taking them all to dinner afterward to celebrate. Hal Grey's office arranged a press luncheon for the next day, where the formal announcements were to be made.

Rann was unable to suppress a feeling of hostility for Nancy Adams of the *Tribune,* so, knowing he would see her at luncheon the next day, he expressed his feelings to George Pearce and Rita Benson that evening. Margie and Hal Grey had excused themselves after dinner because of early morning appointments and the three of them had taken Rita's car to Rann's apartment, where Sung had served them drinks in the drawing room.

"Your apartment is charming, Rann. So decidedly masculine and yet I suspect a woman's touch here and there."

Rita sat on the couch facing the fireplace, the fire already crackling though Rann had put a match to it only minutes before when they had entered the room. Something Chinese, Rann supposed, in the way Sung laid a fire always made them catch very quickly.

"It must be Serena, my grandfather's second wife. I've not changed anything since he died and left the place to me."

Rann settled into a comfortable armchair on one side of the fire, and George chose its counterpart on the other side. Rann realized these were the first visitors he had brought here since he returned. It had not occurred to him to change anything in the apartment.

"You really should redo the place to suit your own personality, Rann." Rita sipped her drink and placed the glass on the cocktail table. "It is good for one to express one's self in one's surroundings."

"Perhaps I don't know yet what it is I would express, Rita—but I have time for that. Right now I have a problem I think the two of you can advise me on, which is why I wanted to talk to you this evening. Tomorrow, we will have to talk to Nancy Adams—"

George Pearce interrupted. "I know. I've thought of that. You are understandably upset and angry over all the articles she has written, and now she has that upstart of a senator, what's-his-name, promising a full-scale investigation based on your book. The thing to remember is that she can't really hurt us. Oh, she can irritate and infuriate, but the more she writes the more books we sell and the richer you get in the long run. The worst that can happen is that you will have to answer some questions, but you are innocent so that can't hurt. I say forget about it. Ignore her and go on. She is one of this new breed calling themselves investigative reporters and she is doing her job, which is to sell newspapers. The thing to remember is that she also sells books. Just don't, under any circumstances, lose your temper with her. Then she can say something that is true. She can say you lost your temper when questioned."

"I know how to handle it." Rita looked thoughtful as she spoke. "Let the press conference be mine. That way, the reporters can direct their questions to me and I can ask Rann or Hal for information we want them to give."

George Pearce took a long drink from his glass. "That's a good idea, Rita. It seemed logical to me that you should answer their questions."

"Of course it is. After all, at this point it is I who have spent a million dollars. That, my dears, is still news."

They all laughed.

"There is one other point I'd like your advice on." Rann stirred the fire as he spoke. "I had thought I'd call Senator Easton and offer to answer any questions he might have. I have nothing to hide and this way we might bring things to a head."

"Just let it rest," George said. "Let him call you if he wants to. You haven't done anything—so forget it."

"You are right, George." Rita rose from the couch. "And now I have to get home or I probably won't be there tomorrow."

Rann said good night to them at the door and returned to the fire to finish his own drink.

"THERE IS NOTHING MORE for her to say, Mother."

Rann was sitting in his grandfather's study with his mother and Donald Sharpe. They had arrived on an afternoon flight and his mother was settled in his guest room while Donald Sharpe had chosen a small neighborhood hotel in the next block as his headquarters, and Sung had worked for two days to prepare the first dinner to be served to the mother of his young master. It was already dark in New York at five o'clock and the chill in the air promised that winter was not far away. The fire burned brightly in the grate as Sung refilled their glasses from a pitcher of Bloody Marys he had prepared earlier, and the aroma of hot Chinese hors d'oeuvres roasting in the oven filled the apartment.

Rann continued, "Nancy Adams has said everything she can say. She blew this whole thing up and involved Senator Easton. I went to Washington and answered questions for his committee. General Appleby flew in from Korea and told of all the arrests they had made there and that was all there was to it."

"Well"—his mother frowned—"she could have written an article reporting the outcome. She could have said that you are innocent after all the nasty things she implied."

"Rann is right, Susan. Reporters seldom write articles stating they were mistaken in the first place, and it would certainly be out of character for Nancy Adams. Rann is a public figure now. His book is still number one on all the lists. He simply has to put up with what they say and go on with his work, which brings me around to this." Donald Sharpe pulled a thin black leather attaché case onto his knees and snapped open the latch, removing a large manila envelope. "It's your father's manuscript, Rann. Your mother gave it to me to read some time ago and it's so good I think you should do something with it."

"It doesn't seem to me that I can expand his basic ideas any further than he has already done. I think he has made his point. I am glad to have it, however, and I'll read it again and try to figure some way in which it could be useful in publication. I think it should be published if possible because it is a beautiful piece of work and it represents a great deal of my father's time and study. Also, as you know, I agree so completely with his theories regarding art and science."

"And I too, as you also know." Donald Sharpe rose and placed the manuscript in the center of the large green blotter on the desk under the window, where Rann had moved it so that he could look out when he glanced up from his work. It was among the few changes Rann had made in the apartment since the death of his grandfather.

He enjoyed the visit from his mother and Donald Sharpe. Donald Sharpe returned to Ohio after one week but before he left Rann arranged a dinner party so that his mother could meet George Pearce and Margie and so they could both meet Rita Benson. They were impressed with Rita and George, as everyone was, but both appreciated Margie's down-to-earth approach to Rann and his career. After Donald Sharpe left, Rann and his mother had luncheon with George and Margie, then had dinner and went to the theatre with Rita.

"I like your friends, Rann," his mother said to him. They were in the drawing room, where Sung had served them a late drink when they arrived home after the theatre.

Rann smiled at her. "Even Rita Benson, Mother?"

His mother sensed his teasing. "Yes, perhaps particularly Mrs. Benson, after Margie, of course. She is not at all the way the newspapers make her out to be."

"People are rarely what newspapers make them out to be. I'm glad that you approve of my friends, Mother." Rann spoke the truth. He knew he would continue as he was even if she disapproved, but it was good to have her approval.

"THERE IS NOTHING MORE I can do for you," his mother said.

Her eyes were soft and brown, her smile was wistful. She was still a pretty woman.

"Had you planned to do something for me, Mother?"

He made his voice playful, although he perfectly understood what she meant. Obviously, he knew after a few days that she had come with the vague idea that he might want her to keep house for him. She had not said so, nor had he said he did not, but Sung had made it clear by perfect service, always silent, that he needed no help in the keeping of the house and the tending of its young master, the grandson of the old man who had saved him from the unknown terrors of the American immigration officers. The house for years had been his island of safety. He knew little more of America than if he had stayed in his native village outside Nanking, China. It did not occur to him to seek other Chinese since those outside in this foreign island spoke their own Cantonese dialect, which he did not understand any more than they could understand him. He had never trusted anyone in America except his old master. Especially he did not trust women, not since he had been cheated by his own sister.

Long ago, Sung had bought with his savings a small business in China, a wayside tea shop, and he had put his own older sister in charge while he continued his work as a waiter in a hotel in Shanghai. She told him every month that there were no profits. Then through a neighbor he heard that there were profits but she used them for her husband, an idle opium smoker, and their children. He said nothing to her, since she was his elder, but he decided at that time to leave his country forever and go to America, where he had no relatives. No one had told him about immigration laws. What would have happened to him if he had not found a haven in this house, he could not imagine. But here he was, with a young master to serve forever. He was perfectly courteous to the mother but by his very perfection he conveyed to her exactly what he intended, which was that there was no need for her—indeed, no place for her—in this house.

"No," she was saying, "I hadn't planned my life at all, Rann, until you returned home from Korea. I didn't know how it might change you."

"It was an interruption," he said, reflecting. "It did not change me. Only people can change me, I think, and that takes time. There was no time for anyone—foolish routines, and the official Americans were—"

He shrugged and pushed away the distasteful memory in silence.

"So, what next for you, Rann?" his mother asked.

Rann put down his coffee cup. "I shall sort myself out," he said.

"Shall you go back to college?"

"I can't see any reason for it. I know where to look for the knowledge I need."

"In books?"

"Everywhere."

"Then I'll be going home, I think, Rann."

"Only when you like, Mother."

* * *

SHE LINGERED A FEW DAYS LONGER and he devoted himself to her. She was a dear person but it was true he no longer needed her. Nevertheless, he was not impatient. He took her to museums and theatres and to a symphony concert. These were pleasant hours but noncommunicative. When they came home again, Sung met them at the door and served them their nightcap drink in the library or drawing room. Once, when they were alone, she tried to talk about Lady Mary.

"Is there anything you want to tell me about Lady Mary?"

"Oh—no, that's all over."

"With no regrets?"

"No regrets on either side, Mother."

"An experience for you," she suggested.

"Yes—I learned something about myself, at least."

"No more?"

"No more."

It was impossible, indeed unnecessary, to explain to her. He needed hours alone, hours and days, weeks and months, in which to begin again his work.

She rose. "I think I'll go home tomorrow, darling."

He got to his feet and, putting his arms gently about her, he kissed her cheek. No, he would not tell her any more about Stephanie, either. There was perhaps nothing more to tell. Whatever might be he wanted to keep to himself, to live it before he spoke of it.

"As you wish, Mother. But you'll come whenever you like?"

"Next time you come to me, darling."

"As you wish, Mother," he said again.

The distance between them was composed of time. She belonged to his past and even to his present but his future was as yet his own.

THERE WAS NO NEED to hurry that future—yet the length of his own youth pressed upon him. Whatever he was to do next he wanted to begin now. But how to begin and on what? Sung served him with a silent devotion that provided an environment of ordered peace in his home. His social life had worked into a routine requiring three evenings a week divided between George Pearce, Margie, and Rita Benson. He worked with the scriptwriters to write the role required into his book, and the script, complete and ready for casting, no longer demanded his time and energy. He thought often of Stephanie. They corresponded, useless letters, filled with trivial information, and he had several times considered going to Paris to see her but each time he decided it best to wait until she came to New York. He could not decide how important she was to be in his life, or if, indeed, she was to be very important. He dreamed, he read the leather-bound volumes in the library his grandfather had accumulated over half a century, he walked the streets, he was occupied but preoccupied, not knowing where or how to begin his next work or even what to begin. His brief military experience faded into nothing, a few memories of Korean countryside, of crowded streets and narrow alleys, of barracks and the isolated American compound where officers and their families lived and that so faithfully reproduced the suburb of any small American city.

He was glad that he had not really been a part of that life in Korea. His book was of the life of the Korean people, and while it dealt with American involvement it portrayed it from the Korean viewpoint. Of any experience he had in that small, sad country, one memory emerged cruelly sharp and balefully clear. It was the face of the North Korean Communist soldier marching a few feet from the border, eternally marching, night and day. There, across an invisible line, was the enemy. And yet even he was not so much the enemy as the unknown. Unknown—that was the word and the meaning, even of life itself. He had no hold upon life. He did not know where to begin. Here upon this crowded American island, he, Rann, had no hold, no grip, no niche, no entrance to life.

Crowds moved wherever he went, across the bridge to Manhattan, in New York, wherever he went, life flowed and eddied, but he was not part of it. The newspapers continued to report all that he did in inaccurate detail, but this no longer perturbed him. He did not even read them anymore, for each article was only more nonsense like the one before it. His book remained in the number-one position on the bestseller list, and perhaps after all that was the only important aspect of it all, and the only thing to be considered. He was glad if people read his book, but the money really meant nothing to him, as he did not need it.

George Pearce and his agent and even Rita were inclined to think in terms of money and this was natural to them, he supposed, but in a way this separated him even from them, his closest friends. Only with Margie did he have a feeling that he was always a person and never an object, and they were together often for luncheon or dinner—but even she played a role of minor importance in his real life, his inner life, that part of himself that he had never shared with another person. His friends urged him to redecorate his apartment more to his own taste, but it remained as his grandfather had left it. He took little interest in such things. He could have been lonely except that he was never lonely, since he had always been alone.

Perhaps when Stephanie came—and suddenly one winter's day, she was there. Snow fell thickly that day upon the deserted streets. He sat looking at it from the tall window of the library, watching it festoon roof lines and telegraph wires and doorways, fascinated by its beauty as he could always be fascinated by beauty. The telephone rang on the desk before him, his grandfather's leather-covered desk here in his grandfather's library. He took up the receiver.

"Yes?"

"Yes," Stephanie's voice replied. "Yes, it is I."

"Paris?"

"Not Paris. Here—in New York."

"You didn't tell me you were coming now. I had a letter from you only yesterday. I was planning to write to you today. Why didn't you tell me?"

"I am telling you, am I not?"

"But such a surprise!"

"I am always surprising, is it not so?"

"Then where are you?"

"Fifth Avenue, between Fifty-Sixth and Fifty-Seventh, where my father's new shop is located."

"When did you come?"

"Last night, too late to call. It was a bad flight. There were very rough winds tossing us up and down. It was terrible! I could have been frightened if I had allowed myself to be. But the servants came one week ahead of us, and all was ready for us. We fell asleep. Now my father is already inspecting the shop. I have finished breakfast. Will you come here?"

"Of course. I may be delayed by this snowstorm. But I will leave at once."

"Is it far?"

"Depends—the traffic will be slow."

"Are you not walking?"

"I may have to walk."

"Then I accustom myself here, waiting."

"And I will hurry."

"Only being careful meanwhile."

He laughed. Her English was so perfect, each word perfectly articulated and yet so charmingly imperfect. The idiom was a mixture of Chinese and French expressed in English.

"Why are you now laughing?" she demanded.

"Because now I am happy!"

"You are not happy before?"

"I realize I was not, just as now I realize I am."

"How are you not coming immediately, then?"

"But I am—I am! I leave this instant, not another word!"

He laughed, again, put the receiver in its cradle, dashed to his rooms to get into proper clothes—he'd been lazy when he woke to see the snow flying across the windows and after showering and shaving he had put on one of his grandfather's luxurious brocaded satin dressing gowns, a wine red with a gold silk lining. Shaving! He had been growing a young mustache, but would she like it? It made him look older and that was an advantage. Sung heard him scurrying about and knocked on the door and came in.

"Excusing me, sir, it is too bad snowing. You going some-where?"

"A friend from Paris."

He was knotting his tie—a blue suit, a striped tie of wine and blue, then suddenly he remembered.

"By the way, she's half-Chinese!"

"She? Which half, sir?" Sung smiled a small prim smile, suit-able to his small size. "Father Chinese is good, sir. Never mind Mother."

Rann laughed. "Always a Chinese!"

"Mother dead?" Sung asked hopefully.

"Damned if I know," Rann said, staring at himself in the glass.

Sung was taking an overcoat out of a closet. "Please, you wear this, sir. Inside is very warm fur."

"I don't think I shall be very cold but I'll take it along anyway."

"If no taxi," Sung said, concerned.

"I'll walk!" he retorted.

Rann found a taxi nevertheless, covered with snow but cruis-ing along slowly and he leaped into it.

"Fifth Avenue—between Fifty-Sixth and Fifty-Seventh. I'll tell you where to stop."

The ride would be endless but the snow was magnificent, float-ing down in the clouds of white through which small black fig-ures, bent to the wind, labored their way. He was in haste yet as ever he was diverted by all he saw, his restless mind storing every sight, every sound, against an unknown future. This was his mind, a storehouse, a computer programmed to life, minute by minute, hour by hour, day and night. He forgot nothing, useless and use-ful. Useful! But for what? Never mind the question, never mind the answer. It was enough to be as he was, himself, every instant alive to everyone and everything. Time never crawled, not even now, as the cab lumbered through drifts and lurched over frozen ruts.

Nevertheless, when he reached the house on Fifth Avenue, the great shop, its windows curtained with snow, he made haste to ring the bell on the door of the adjoining house, a red door on which he saw in brass Chinese characters her father's name. He had learned to write that name with a rabbit's-hair brush and dense black Chinese ink—all that in Paris, before ever he went to Asia himself. The door opened immediately and he went in on a gust of snow-laden wind. Rann recognized the manservant, a Chinese, and was recognized by him with a wide and welcoming grin.

"Miss Kung?" he inquired.

"Waiting, sir. I take your hat, coat, sir."

She did not wait. She came downstairs, smiling, graceful in her long Chinese robe of jade-green brocaded satin. The only change was in her hair. She had wound it about her head, a shining black coif. He stood waiting for her. Amazing that he had not realized her beauty! Her cream pale face, the oval of Asian song and poem, the dark Asian eyes—he had seen these in Korea and even in his brief stops in Japan, but the tincture of American blood defined the Asian lines. In Asia she would be called American, though here, in New York, she was Asian.

"Why do you look at me so?"

She paused on a step and waited.

"Have I changed?" she demanded.

"Perhaps it is I who am changed," he said.

"Yes, you have been in Asia," she said.

She moved toward him, put out her hands, and he clasped them in his.

"What luck for me that you are here!" he said.

He looked down into her face, a face radiant and yet with its usual calm. Her control never broke. The surface was smooth, yet she communicated warmth. He hesitated, and decided not to kiss her. Instead, he put her left hand to his cheek and then dropped it gently. She drew him by her right hand toward a closed door.

"My father is waiting for us," she said.

He hesitated, her hand still in his. He searched that lovely face.

"Yes, you have changed!" he accused.

"Of course," she said calmly. "I am no longer a child."

They looked into each other's eyes, deeply. Neither drew back.

"I shall have to know you all over again," he said.

"You—" She hesitated. "You are not a boy anymore either. You are altogether a man. Come! We must go to my father."

MR. KUNG SAT in a huge carved chair to the right of a square table of polished dark wood, which stood against the inner wall. He wore a long, plum-colored Chinese robe and a black satin vest. The large room was an exact replica of his library in Paris. On the table stood a Chinese jar. He was examining the jar through his tortoiseshell Chinese spectacles. When Rann entered, he smiled but did not rise. As though they had met an hour ago, he said in his usual mild voice, a trifle high for a man's voice and gentle, "This is a vase which belongs to a famous American collection. It may be for private sale. Some of the best Chinese collections are here in your country. Extraordinary—I cannot yet understand.

My shop already is busy with American collectors—very rich men! Look at this vase! It is from some ancient Chinese tomb—Han dynasty, more than a thousand years. Probably it had wine in it for the dead. Usually such has an octagonal, faceted base. The material is red clay, but the glaze is this bright green—very beautiful! The sheen—you notice? A silvery iridescence!"

He took the vase in both hands and tenderly smoothed it. Then he set it carefully on the table again.

"Sit down," he commanded. "Let me see you now how you are."

He set his spectacles firmly on his low-bridged nose and, a hand on each outspread knee, he examined Rann carefully across the table. Then he took off his spectacles, folded them, and put them into a velvet case. He turned to Stephanie, who stood waiting.

"Leave us," he commanded. "I have business to talk now."

She smiled at Rann and left the room, her footsteps silent on the heavy Peking carpet.

Mr. Kung cleared his throat loudly and sat back in his chair, his gaze nevertheless fixed upon Rann's face.

"You," he said with emphasis, "you are now a man. You have been in a war."

"Luckily not to kill," Rann said.

Mr. Kung waved this aside with his right hand. "You saw sights, you have learned about life, and so forth. As for me, I have become an old man. I have developed heart disease. Why have I come to a new country at this time? It is because you are here. I have no son. I have only a daughter. She is clever, she understands my business, but she is a woman. Any woman may suddenly marry a fool or a rascal. This is my great fear. I must see her safely married to a man I trust. I prefer Chinese. Alas, what Chinese? We are refugees or—what is a Communist? I do not know. Besides, she is half-American. Perhaps a good Chinese, thinking of his own family line, will wish to keep his blood pure."

"Sir"—Rann could not refrain—"you married an American."

"Who left me for an American," Mr. Kung retorted. "Perhaps similarly, in turn, and so forth, a Chinese might leave my daughter for a Chinese. New Chinese women are very bold. My son-in-law will be rich man."

Mr. Kung looked gloomy. He sighed deeply, coughed, and put his left hand against his left side.

"Pain," he said.

"Shall I call someone, sir?" Rann asked.

"No. I have not finished."

Mr. Kung was silent for one, two, three minutes, his eyes closed, his hand on his heart. Then he opened his eyes, his hand dropped.

"I cannot die," he said slowly. There was indeed a look of suffering on his thin face. "I must not die until my daughter's marriage is arranged—has taken place—until I am assured that her future is safe."

"Have you discussed it with Stephanie?" Rann knew that probably the old man had not. "Perhaps she has some ideas of her own."

"It is not for her to decide." He was as firm as one of the jade figures behind him. "How can a girl so young decide a thing as important as the man to whom she shall entrust her future, the one whose children she will bear? Her own mother decided and see what has happened? No, it is I who must decide and I have decided. I have only now to convince you and we begin today. You will stay and have dinner with us. You are now a famous man, and I have asked my daughter to prepare it with her own hands. What her mother did not do I have had done by faithful servants. She is well trained for your wife. And now in the meantime she must show you around my shop so you can see her brain. She knows my business as well as any man. I have taught her. Then we will have a drink together while she finishes our meal. But you must not take so long to decide. I am already a very old man and I cannot join my honored ancestors until I know this is done."

The old town houses were side by side, one for their residence and one for the shop. The one that the shop occupied had been tastefully decorated with carpets, walls and draperies in neutral tones of beige, and the objects of art stood out in sharp contrast. Soft piano music played through hidden speakers and Rann allowed himself to be led from room to room, where he was shown object after object—each at least as beautiful as the one before it, if not even more beautiful.

"And this is the Quan Yin," Stephanie said when they stood finally in the last room overlooking Fifth Avenue from the fifth floor, the snow still whirling into the streets below. The figure Stephanie indicated was about three feet high, carved in wood and very old, Rann judged, and she stood by herself in an alcove between the two arched windows, the place of most importance in the room. Rann knew the Quan Yin but he allowed Stephanie to continue with her explanation.

"She is my favorite of all. She is the goddess of mercy and she is about five hundred years old. My father found her in a small secondhand shop just outside Paris. There was nothing else of any value in the place and as we were leaving he saw her lying on her side under a table in the back of the room.

"The shopkeeper was very surprised when my father took her up and bought her. And now she is here until someone falls in love with her and she goes to their home for a while, but only for a while, and then she will go on to yet another lover and so on, for goddesses are eternal and can never be possessed by a mere mortal for very long. It is sad in a way to think of her never having an eternal home of her own—but that is the price one must pay for being a goddess of mercy."

Stephanie laughed and slipped her arm through Rann's and tilted her head prettily to look up at him as they stood side-by-side before the goddess.

"She is truly the most beautiful I have ever seen," Rann said, and he made a decision. "I must have her for my own. Her face reminds me of you, somehow, in the expression."

Stephanie smiled. "It is my Chinese half, Rann."

He kissed her then, his kiss long and gentle and full on her soft lips, and she returned his kiss.

"And you must have her," she said when he released her. "You must take her to your home this very night. My father and I present her to you and charge her to look after you."

"But I must pay for her," Rann protested. "I have money, Stephanie, and I can afford her."

Stephanie was firm. "And we too have money and can afford her. There is no need for us to buy and sell goddesses between us. You are to have her as a gift from us. If you must think of money then think of all the money we will make when you have to redecorate your apartment to provide a suitable home for such a goddess."

They laughed then and went arm in arm to the elevator and joined her father in the drawing room of the house next door. The houses had been ingeniously joined by a door in the back of Mr. Kung's office in the shop, which opened onto his study in their home.

"I will bring only my most important and wealthy clients here," Mr. Kung explained to him. "Here we will keep our most treasured and valuable articles and all must be for sale. This is one sad decision which must be made early in this business if one is to be a success. One must either be a collector or a dealer, for one cannot be both. Therefore, if one is to be a dealer, everything must have a sale price. It pleases me to know that I can keep my most treasured things here, however, and if I do not like one who inquires, I do not bring him here and so he does not see my best pieces and so he does not want them. It is a small deception, yes, but it soothes me somehow for buying and selling beautiful things and so it is a harmless deception.

"I am glad you are to have my goddess and Stephanie was right to give her to you. I was making a place for her here, but I like to think of her in your home. She will be happy there and you will be happy with her there and so I shall be happy, also. Ah—it should be so simple for me to place my daughter there as well. It is easier, though, to deal with goddesses than with human beings. Goddesses can be to us only what we need and want them to be while, alas, with humans it is not always so."

Rann laughed and they talked lightly of his business and Rann's writing until the servant appeared to say Stephanie was waiting for them to join her in the dining room. Rann was filled with delicious food and warm wine when he said good night later that evening.

The snow had stopped and he found a taxi easily. He sat in the backseat with the goddess in his arms as indeed Stephanie had been only a few hours earlier. With pleasure he remembered the softness of her supple figure as his arms had enfolded her and the sweet gentleness with which she had pressed her lips to his, returning his kiss. So different from the demanding kisses he had shared with Lady Mary. They had been wild and uncontrolled, each of them demanding satisfaction for himself each from the other, each with no thought of the other beyond that satisfaction. Remembering Stephanie, there was a sweetness that pervaded his entire being with thoughts of her presence, and yet not without passion. Rann felt a familiar warmth rising in his loins as he recalled the shared intimacy with Stephanie.

He ordered the taxi to stop and he walked on the freshly fallen snow for the remaining short blocks to his apartment building.

"That is a very beautiful figure, sir," said the night doorman as he offered to take the goddess from Rann's arms.

"That's all right," Rann told him. "I can make it myself. I'd prefer it. She was a gift from a very dear friend." He could not bear the thought of her in anyone's arms as she had been in his.

He entered his apartment and placed the goddess on the small table in the entrance hall and admired her for a moment, then he went into the study and dialed Stephanie's number.

"She is home," he said when she came on the wire.

"I am glad," Stephanie said.

"She is so beautiful where she stands now that I know I have been saving this space for her. You must come and see her here."

Stephanie agreed. "Yes, I must."

"Will you come here for dinner? Sung can prepare for us and he is very good and perhaps you could bring your father, too."

"I do not think my father will come," Stephanie told him. "He has not been well for some time and rarely goes out anymore. However"—she laughed softly, teasing Rann—"I am a big girl now. I don't need a chaperone. I can come alone if you wish."

"Tomorrow then."

"So soon? Very well, I shall come tomorrow if it pleases you."

"It does. Until tomorrow, then?"

"Until tomorrow, then," she repeated. "Good night, Rann."

He heard the soft click as she broke the connection.

THEY WERE TOGETHER ALMOST EVERY EVENING in the months that followed and Rann's friends eagerly accepted Stephanie into their homes and hearts, especially Rita Benson. They had dinner with her one evening and as Rann fitted the key into the door of his apartment upon returning he heard the telephone begin to ring. He rushed to answer before its ring could wake Sung.

It was Rita. "You had better marry that girl quickly, Rann," she told him. "She is too beautiful to last long and some hot shot will take her away from you if you aren't careful."

Rann laughed. "Rita, we haven't even discussed it."

"So—what's there to talk about?" Rita made her tone indignant. "Men! Always talking. The girl is in love with you. Are you too blind to see the way she looks at you? Besides, I like her and it's a rare thing for me to like a woman, especially one so young and beautiful, but she is just right for you and you are going to lose out if you don't get busy. How did your mother like her?"

Rann had taken Stephanie to Ohio with him to visit with his mother over one weekend.

"She liked her very much," Rann told her. "She even said the same things you have said after our visit."

"That settles it then—get busy or your mother and I will gang up with Stephanie's father and railroad you both into it."

Rita laughed and ended the call, leaving Rann in deep thought. He decided at last that he would discuss his own feelings with Stephanie when next they met.

"Can you not understand, Rann, that is exactly why I cannot marry you?"

They were comfortably settled in the study with coffee and a cordial served to them by Sung after they had completed a delicious seafood dinner he had prepared. It had been Sung's own concoction, consisting of various types of shellfish with bamboo shoots and bean sprouts in a sauce tart but at the same time with the unmistakable pinch of ginger Rann had come to expect of Sung's cooking. It had been a thoroughly successful experiment, and both Rann and Stephanie had complimented him profusely. To show his pleasure, Sung had served them a rare Chinese liqueur from a bottle he had treasured for years and was difficult to locate in New York.

Rann and Stephanie had spent that afternoon walking in the park while Rann explained his feelings to her. She listened to all he had to say and had then said, "Please, do not let us talk more now. Allow me to think while we refresh ourselves at dinner. Then when we have finished we can speak of this again."

Now she shifted her position slightly, leaned forward in her chair, and placed her hand on Rann's arm.

"You must see and respect my feelings also. I do love you. There is no denying that, but even more important to me is that I admire and respect you deeply, at times even more than my own father. I am impressed with your mind and with the wide and varied range of interests you have. I am American enough, perhaps, that I wish to marry you, disregarding all that I am, alas, Chinese enough to know I also must consider."

She again shifted her position, but her eyes met his with her inner conflict evident as she continued.

"We must consider your children, Rann, and you must, of course, have many sons."

Rann lifted his eyebrows, mocking her with amused exaggeration.

"Am I merely to be considered as a stud animal then, and not as a human being?"

Sipping the sweet liquid from the tiny glass, she thought for moments before answering.

"That is my point exactly, my dear. It is as a human being, a brilliant one indeed, that I must now consider you. With your intellect and your genes you will undoubtedly produce beautiful and brilliant children and you must do so. The less intelligent and civilized of the human race continue to reproduce as a matter of course with either no, or at most very little, thought to the future overpopulation and resulting famine or anything else. They go on, generation after generation, reproducing merely because it is their nature to do so. The more intelligent and civilized members of human society, on the other hand, are using birth-control methods in their effort to control population growth and, so, are slowly breeding themselves out of existence or at least into what is already a serious minority. It is this world trend in human development that makes it exceedingly important to me that you do indeed produce many sons."

"But I have no reason to believe that I would produce sons superior in any way to anyone else's." Rann laughed to cover his discomfort. "Besides, can't we go at this another way? I'm beginning to feel as if I were under a microscope."

"To make that statement only shows that you are not viewing the facts in their true light." Stephanie's face took on a look of firmness in decision as she continued. "You know perfectly well that in breeding it is the male who controls the outcome. It has long been known that one can mate a fine bull to a mediocre cow and produce fine offspring. On the other hand, if one mates a fine cow with a poor bull, one produces poor calves."

"But I am not a bull, Stephanie, and you are not a cow, and our children will not be calves romping in a meadow. They will be beautiful and intelligent and with everything at their disposal because we love each other. You do not deny that you love me?"

"No, I do not deny it. But as I have said, you must understand that is exactly why I will not marry you. I decided long ago, Rann, that I would never bear children of my own."

"You cannot be serious, Stephanie," Rann said—though he knew from her expression that she was more serious than ever she had been with him. "You will marry, if not me then someone, and you will have beautiful children who will be very fortunate to have so intelligent a mother."

All appearance of the carefree girl he had grown to love vanished now as she dropped her eyes and spoke to him as a woman speaks to the man she loves out of the anguish in her inner soul.

"No, Rann." There was a slight catch in her voice and she moistened her lips before she continued in her determination. "Perhaps only the racially mixed person can understand the inborn tragedy of so being. I have been raised as a Chinese. Chinese is my native tongue. I am Chinese in my manner and dress and in feeling and yet to the Chinese people I am American because to them I look American and act American. To them, my bone structure and manner of moving lacks the delicacy of the Chinese. They are right. I am never more aware of the difference than when I am with my Chinese friends."

"But in America this makes no difference, Stephanie." Rann's face creased with his sincerity.

"But there you are wrong, my dear." She lifted her face to meet his eyes with her own, moist, as she continued. "You must not be saddened by this, though I know that you are, but you must make it only for a short time. Then you must continue with your own life. This is one of the main reasons I wished to come to America. I wished to see with my own heart if it would be different and it is not. Even here in New York, and I understand it is true of every major city in this vast and beautiful land, there is a Chinatown and a Latin quarter and an Italian section and a Negro neighborhood and blockbusters and riots and all of that as your own fearful civil war continues even one hundred years after it is supposedly over. And look again at the plight of the only real Americans, the American Indians. No, my dear, one cannot really ever know how it is to be anything unless one is indeed that thing."

"Stephanie, please do not refer to yourself as a thing." Rann rose and went to her and kissed her gently. "You are not a thing. You are a human woman, and, moreover, the woman I love."

"And you are wrong again, my dear, for a thing is the tragedy, for to be human is to reason and to understand, and so much understanding makes it pleasant at times to think of simply not being. I do not forget that while I never feel less Chinese than when I am with my Chinese friends, who are always kind, I also never feel less Western than when I'm amongst Westerners, who are not always so kind. No, my dear one, my children would be racially mixed and therefore, more for me than for them—for I could not bear their pain from separation—they must never exist. And now, will you take me home, Rann, for I am tired, and we must not speak of this again."

He pulled her up from her chair and held her firmly in his arms and kissed her.

"Yes, I will take you home, but I will not promise not to speak of this again, for I have made up my mind and I am quite determined!"

"And I, too, have decided, and I, too, Rann, am quite determined. And furthermore, I must ask that you accept my decision and that we not speak of it again, for you must understand the pain to me each time I refuse you, for it is myself I deny also."

"But we don't have to have children, Stephanie," Rann insisted. "There are many children without parents. We can adopt children if we must have a family, but at least we will always have each other."

"What you say is true, Rann, but what I have said is also true. I will never have children of my own and you must do so and, therefore, we must accustom ourselves to the fact that you must love and marry another woman."

Rann sighed deeply as he helped Stephanie into her light spring coat, its soft yellow color becoming to the honey cast of her complexion.

"Never," he said. "Never can I love another."

"Never say never, my dear." Stephanie moved to the door as she spoke and turned to face the goddess in the entrance hall. She looked into the face, itself so impervious to time. "Time has a way of arranging all things, Rann, you shall see."

The goddess remained as she was—silent, unperturbed, understanding carved into every line of her delicately beautiful wooden face, similar to the human face turned toward her.

Rann stood behind Stephanie and put his hands on her shoulders and bent his head to kiss her slender arched neck. "I cannot give up, Stephanie," he whispered.

"But you must, Rann," she said firmly again. She turned from the goddess to face him and pushed him gently away. "And now we must go, please."

"WHAT DO YOU MEAN, you have asked her and she has said no?" Mr. Kung's voice showed disbelief.

They were seated in the old man's study, where Rann had been summoned as soon as he arrived for the dinner party Stephanie had arranged celebrating her father's eightieth birthday. Rann explained what had happened in his apartment two evenings earlier. He had not seen Stephanie since then but he had spoken with her on the telephone and she was adamant in her position.

"You must not persist, Rann," she said. "It is useless to continue to ask when you already know the answer."

Mr. Kung's face grew pale as Rann spoke, and he was silent for a long while after the explanation was finished. When he spoke at last it was slowly and with obvious effort.

"She cannot be so foolish a girl as to speak this way to you. You must leave my daughter to me. I will speak with her and . . ."

His voice trailed away, the remaining blood drained from his face. Rann rose.

"I must call someone—I can't take responsibility—"

To his horror, Mr. Kung rose, and then, wavering, suddenly fell to his knees and clutched Rann's right hand in both his own hands.

"You—," he stammered. "You are the one. I can trust you. You will be—you will . . . you will—"

He crumpled to the floor and Rann caught him in his arms.

"Stephanie!" he shouted. "Stephanie—Stephanie—Stephanie!"

The door opened and she came swiftly in. She knelt beside her father. She supported his head in the crook of her right arm. She felt his heart in the terrible silence. Then she lifted her eyes to Rann's face.

"My father is dead," she said.

AND HOW COULD HE LEAVE HER that night? He had telephoned Sung to come to their aid—Sung, who had been through the ordeal of after-death with Rann's own grandfather. For a few minutes he pondered the possibility of telephoning his mother but refrained. He knew that she would take the jet for New York and he was not ready to explain Stephanie's position to her.

"You asking me come New York side?" Sung inquired in protest.

"Yes," Rann said shortly. "My friend's father has just died. We need help."

"Master Rann, I cannot come Manhattan side. Supposing police catching me. Your grandfather, he never ask me such."

"Sung, Miss Stephanie's father—a Chinese gentleman."

"Chinese man die?"

"Yes."

"I'll come."

Rann heard the receiver replaced. Then he turned again to Stephanie. She was kneeling on the carpet beside her dead father. Under his head she had put a yellow satin cushion. She had straightened his limbs, arms at his sides, and had smoothed his long purple robe to his ankles. He went to her.

"Sung is coming. He will know what to do."

She did not reply or even lift her head. She continued to gaze at her father, but she did not weep. He stooped and lifted her to her feet and she did not resist.

"Come," he said. "We will stay with him until Sung comes. Shall we call your own servants or wait for Sung?"

"Wait," she said. "We must do something about the guests. They are due to arrive soon."

He led her to a yellow satin couch and they sat side by side— he in silence. He reached for her hand, her left hand in his right, and he held it, a soft, narrow hand, a girl's hand.

"I must not be left," she whispered. She turned her eyes from her father to him.

"I shan't leave you," he said.

They did not speak again. The time seemed long, but it was short and the door opened. Sung stood there looking at them.

"Sung, Mr. Kung has—"

"I see for myself, sir," Sung said. "Please, you both go some other room. I will do all."

"There are servants—"

"I find everybody, Miss Kung. Please trust. I do all for your honored father like I do for my old master already. Please go, please rest. I will do."

"He will, Stephanie. So come with me. Shall you go to your own rooms?"

"I can't be alone."

"I will sit in the next room."

"I want to go into the shop."

"The shop, Stephanie?"

"Yes. We worked there together. He placed each piece as he wished. If he is anywhere, he is there. People don't go away at once, you know. They don't know at first that they are dead. They linger in their favorite places, where their treasures are. Come—come quickly!"

She urged him, their hands still clasped, and he kept at her side down the narrow hall and into a vast lighted room filled with art treasures. Room led into room, all lighted.

"He is here, Rann. I can feel his presence."

Rann looked around at the brightly lighted room, half expecting to see Mr. Kung, though he felt no such presence himself. An ancient altar table stood against the far wall, a small golden Quan Yin in the center of the table in front of a rosewood screen, with a bronze incense burner on each side. Stephanie lit incense and the familiar fragrance of sandalwood renewed itself in the air.

"He worked for a long time on this arrangement," she said softly. "It became his favorite and he is here. He is displeased with me. He was unhappy with me when he died. Why was he angry, Rann?"

"He wanted us to marry, Stephanie. You know that. He questioned me about it and I told him the truth. I saw no reason to lie to him. I respected him too much."

"You told him of my refusal and he became so agitated he had a heart attack. Oh, Rann, I have killed my father."

"That is not true, Stephanie." Rann led her to a comfortable love seat placed in the center of one wall so that one seated there could see all of the objects tastefully displayed on the remaining three walls. He sat beside her, his elbow resting on the back of the couch, and he turned to face her, lifting her chin with his forefinger.

"You must not blame yourself. Your father was eighty years old today and he has long had a problem with his heart. It was coincidence that the fatal attack came when it did."

"And is it coincidental also that it came the first time I have ever defied him? My grandfather died of the same problem, but he lived to be ninety-five and my father's life has been shortened. I have always done as he wished but in this one thing I could not, Rann. Marriage and motherhood are very personal to a woman and in these areas I must decide for myself. He made all other decisions and, alas, because he could not make this one he is gone." Tears came to her eyes, spilling onto her cheeks, but in all other ways she maintained her composure.

"Nevertheless, I am right, Rann. Even though he did not agree with me and though he is now dead, I am right in my own decision."

"We must not speak of it further now, Stephanie. Your father's death is not your fault. You must know that."

He took her right hand gently into both of his own and they sat in silence for a long time before Sung appeared.

"All is done, young master," Sung told him. "The servants tell me there are no relatives to notify and so all is done."

"Yes, it is true. There is no one to notify. Everyone we knew in this vast country was coming here tonight and so they must know by now. I wished you also to be surprised, Rann, and so I did not tell you that even your mother was coming. She must be in New York now."

"It is true, young master," Sung told him. "When your honored mother came and found— She is waiting in your apartment."

Rann was pleased now to know his mother was near.

"Call her, Sung," he said. "Ask her to come here."

His mother arrived a short time later. "I am very sorry, Stephanie," she said. "I was looking forward to meeting your father. Now you must rest and you, too, Rann. You go on home, son, and I will remain here with Stephanie."

"I feel I wish to stay with Stephanie," Rann said.

"No, Rann." Stephanie was calm. "Your mother is right. All has been done here. Now you must rest. I will rest also. I have a sedative."

Sung accompanied Rann back to his apartment and drew a bath for him and served a drink to him in the study and excused himself for the night.

Rann fell asleep sitting at his desk and was still there, his head resting on his folded arms, when his mother arrived in the morning. He was aware only that he was very tired as consciousness crept into him. When he opened his eyes to find her seated in the comfortable chair across from him, he was surprised to see her until his memory of the events of the evening before came to him.

"Oh, Mother, is Stephanie? . . ." His voice trailed into silence at the expression on his mother's face.

"Rann, you must be very brave now." His mother's voice was solemn. "You must remember that all that happens has a reason.

You must try to remember the things your father said after he knew he was dying."

His alarm showed in his voice when he spoke. "Mother, what are you saying?"

"Stephanie is dead, son."

For long moments he stared at her in disbelief, collapsing finally, his head on his arms, his body wracked with his own deep sobs as realization came to him.

"YOUR SON WILL BE ALL RIGHT, Mrs. Colfax," the doctor told her.

She had called him when Rann's sobbing seemed endless and uncontrollable. "I have given him a sedative and he must rest now. He will sleep for several hours and then he will be all right. He is young. He will take sorrow in his stride."

"I KNOW WHY Stephanie did what she has done, Mother. There was no accidental overdose of sedative—oh, let it go at that. There was no note—but I know and she knew that I would know. She always felt displaced because of her racial mixture. She even refused to marry me because of it. She did not wish to have children because they, too, would be racially mixed. I'm sure she saw herself in a hopeless situation and simply swallowed a few extra capsules. She was really quite Asian and would attach no particular disgrace to having the courage to do what she considered the only action she could take.

"The point I must reach now is simply that I, alone, can discover for myself a way in which I can go on. My life, as I had seen it before me, has changed irrevocably. It can never be the same again as life is never today as it seemed yesterday. Today there is no future ahead of me as I have seen it, and so I must create one."

Rann sipped coffee from the cup on the desk in front of him.

In the two weeks since Stephanie and her father had died, he and his mother had come to the study each morning after breakfast for another cup of coffee and had talked each day, often for many hours, of events, and how haphazard events and their effects upon one another shaped one's life. Mr. Kung and his beloved Stephanie had both been cremated as they wished, since the Communist regime had not yet ended in China and their bodies could not be returned to their homeland. Rann had inherited the entire Kung fortune from Mr. Kung. It was all entailed, of course, so that Stephanie would need nothing for the rest of her life should her husband not be Rann, but now that Stephanie was also gone, so was the entailment.

"I am glad you have been with me these weeks, Mother. I don't know how I could have gotten through without you. It has helped to have these long talks with you each morning so I could begin to feel my way into the future."

His mother replaced her cup on its saucer on the desk and rose to gaze out the window.

"I am happy if I have helped you, son. I have felt so utterly useless throughout this tragedy. I scarcely knew Stephanie and I did not know her father and I feel almost as if I have never really known you. If I have been of some use to you by listening to you sort out your own thinking, then I find comfort for my own shortcomings by having done so. Your father felt you were a very special person, Rann, and I suppose I have always been in awe of your remarkable abilities while I've waited for you to find yourself. Perhaps, in this sorrow, you have done so."

"I do not know what it is that I shall eventually accomplish in my life, Mother. I have put all of Mr. Kung's fortune into a foundation I have created. Its purposes are broad, but simple. It will work to relieve the hopelessness of the situation in which the racially mixed individual finds himself all over the world. Someday, perhaps, in five or six centuries, the problem will not exist, but now it does.

"The world is growing too small for us to continue to judge persons by race or color. In the past century, we have gone from antiquated modes of travel, taking months to cross our country, and we have pared that time and, as a result, the distance, to weeks, days, and now hours. If we continue to speed up our mode of travel, which I'm sure we will, then soon we won't have to move to get from one place to another. We must give up the luxury of remaining members of small racial groups and all become a part of the whole, the one race, the human race.

"The wars have taken men all over the world and the mixing and molding of this person of the future has already begun. Someone must make the peoples of the Earth ready to accept and even to be grateful for the opportunity to know this person of the future. I have seen them myself in the streets of Korea, and they are in a very pitiful position, indeed. Everyone wishes they did not exist, but nevertheless, they do exist and will continue to do so in ever increasing numbers and we must recognize them for what they are and we must work together for the awesome responsibility they face. I do not yet know what the Kung Foundation can do to help them but we will find out. George Pearce, Rita Benson, and Donald Sharpe have accepted as the beginning board of directors and together we shall find other members equally as important and we shall find this person, wherever he or she may be, and endeavor to help him or her to become a useful citizen in society.

"Perhaps when other peoples see that these important persons all over the world are concerned and interested in the futures of racially mixed persons, they themselves will reconsider and the world will be a better place for it. If so, then we shall have accomplished what I have set out for the foundation to do."

"And what about you, Rann?" His mother continued to stare out the window, her eyes unseeing, and tears glistened on her cheeks as she spoke. So often now she realized she was learning and growing through this child of hers. "What will you do, Rann?"

"You mean personally? To answer truthfully I must say I do not know. I have this enormous work to think of now. I shall continue to write, of course, I am a writer. I cannot think now of anyone I might ever marry—if I do—or of whether else about the future, other than this work to be done. There are so many decisions yet to be made, but each must be made when the need arises and not in advance of the need. I feel as if life has perhaps taught me too much, so far, and has made me wiser than I ought to be or wish to be. I shall not press wisdom on my own children. It is not well to be too wise. Wisdom cuts one off from everyone, even the wise, for then one is afraid of so much wisdom. To take each day as a separate page, to be read carefully, savoring all of the details, this is best for me, I think. My life is yet in spring. I look forward to the summer and I shall enjoy my autumn years and I'm sure I shall approach the finality of life with the same curiosity that has plagued me in everything so far. Perhaps one day I shall look back on this entire life as but a page out of the whole of my existence, and if I do I am sure it will be with the same thirst to know more—the certain knowledge that there are truths, the reasons for which we cannot know. . . . Perhaps that is the whole point of it all—the eternal wonder."